THE INTEGRATION OF
MAYBELLE BROWN

THE INTEGRATION OF MAYBELLE BROWN

BONNIE GOLIGHTLY

CUTTING EDGE

ISBN-13: 978-1-954840-95-9

Published by
Cutting Edge Books
PO Box 8212
Calabasas, CA 91372
www.cuttingedgebooks.com

PART I

CHAPTER ONE

FIRST OF ALL, I'm white. I tell you this because I'm a Southerner, and more or less typical for my time and place. And I don't want anybody to get the idea that I'm trying to crawl into the skin of Maybelle Brown and be her spokesman, or even to empathize with her just because she's a Negro and I now happen to admire her a lot. As I say, I'm a Southerner, and a more or less typical one. All I want to do is put down what happened to Maybelle Brown, a Black Girl most assuredly in search of her God—which, after all, means freedom and security and being loved, just as it always did.

But the first time I saw Maybelle Brown I didn't know any of this; hadn't even thought about it. Instead, I thought what everybody else thought, and knew what everybody else knew: that our school (which shall be nameless, but is a small one for a university in a not very large town) had at last, as so many others throughout the South, been invaded! Tragically, our stronghold was under attack. Everything short of the air-raid sirens were sounded. All out! All out! It was as exciting and dangerous as if Maybelle Brown had come from Mars.

Instead she had come from Pennsylvania, was in her junior year, and was transferring from a teacher's college there. Her credentials were in order, her character untarnished, but her skin was black.

The afternoon the rumor went around, howling through the halls with gale force, that our heretofore sacredly all-white unviolated campus was going to be another one of those "nigger schools," I rushed right home and demanded action. Action was as follows: to send me off to college somewhere right away—to some sound, sane Southern college in one of the few remaining states that had proudly, indomitably resisted the Rising Tide of Color, defied laws, court orders, Yankees, and all other subversives who were trying to ruin America, pollute its pure heritage. And at that moment all the people in our crowd were rushing home, demanding the same thing.

I should say that all this happened during Rush Week, and quite enough had been going on without this. And I also should say that the warpath I was beating at the moment led not so much to my mother as to my father. It wasn't that I felt so much that any change in my college plans was really up to him, as that I felt he was somehow responsible for what had happened. You see, my father is a Yankee. When cornered, I've always admitted it: yes, sure, Daddy's from Chicago and got his master's there. But I always pointed out that my mother's family had been in this country for eleven generations and that six of those generations had been born and reared in this very county, and besides, Daddy had gotten his Ph.D. at L.S.U. and had been in the South for a long, long time. And before the advent of Maybelle Brown, I had always felt there was a certain distinction in having been born part-Yankee, as if by an act of birth I had been bequeathed broader horizons. And I had always been careful that they did not get too broad—no Communist was I.

It was a friend, one of my telephone contacts, who quite bitchily pointed out to me that I, after all, of all the crowd, was morally obligated to make the strongest stand, for *my* father, not hers, or any of the other fathers, for that matter, was actually a faculty member of that once graced and benign school which had deliberately chosen to bastardize itself, the town, and even the entire state. Moreover, she went on to say, my father was a department head and therefore had real influence. So the whole thing was up to me. She didn't exactly say it was a warning, but I knew I would be socially executed as a traitor to the Confederacy if I failed to carry the day.

If the fires of purpose were not extinguished by this, certainly they died down, and the wind took another direction. I was still wrathful, but the nature of my wrath had changed into something bitterly personal: I no longer belonged; indeed I never had. It had slipped my mind that my father's offense was something worse and far greater than being a Yankee—he was an actual real live faculty member—an enemy—of that body of higher education that was prepared to destroy us! How did I know, for instance, that my own father hadn't actually known about the Negro's enrollment all this time, that he hadn't actually approved it? It would not be enough for me to enter my protest by demanding to be sent to another school. That mild course was open only to the non-offenders. It was up to me to be standard bearer, demand that my father use his influence to get rid of the Negro girl, or failing this, resign.

I knew my father well, or thought I did. And as I glumly sat there planning my campaign, I had more or less already accepted defeat. Mild-mannered and adroit as he was as a father (it was not for nothing that he had chosen psychology as his field), he was firm—no, I correct that, he was hardheaded. (My mother's words.) I was fairly certain that he would immediately agree to sending me off to school if I would be happier elsewhere—he might even think it wise—but what did I really know about the other? Was he in favor of desegregation here on his own home ground? Did what I had always thought of as his mild liberality, his sense of justice, mean that he would now turn fighter on behalf of the interloper? Would he stick up with a handful of other conspirators for the so-called rights of Maybelle Brown? Or would he come through for me and turn fighter—firm but kind fighter—to put her down?

I chewed off a considerable amount of nail polish trying to figure that one, hurriedly examining the past. On the plus side was the fact that he was for States' Rights, that he voted pretty much as everybody else we knew did, abstaining only when he thought the conservatives were being too extreme. I had always felt proud of him for being scornful of such far out things as the Klan and White Citizens' Committee, and agreed they were too extreme, as bad in their own way as the NAACP and the other Northern Commy controled organizations. But on the minus side there were these things—though some of them had never seemed at all bad to me before—he was known throughout the state for his interest and work in trying to get better schools for Negroes. At commencement time he had even on occasion addressed the graduating classes of Negro schools. In fact, here in town, he was liked if not loved and respected by the Negroes in appreciation of his efforts. And even more minus than this minus, I knew, despite Mother, and our side of her family, he was suspect among what he called the Radical Rightists for being 1) a Yankee, however tamed 2) an outsider—the only way to be an insider was to be born one—3) a psychologist—a very dirty word.

As for Mother, she had toed the line all the way—no Klan member could accuse *her* of being liberal. Her only sign of the spirit of rebellion had been in marrying my father in the first place. And because he loved her and wanted to protect her, I knew that he had long ago learned to curb his "outspokenness" for her sake. Now what?

I cheered up considerably when I remembered how strongly she would become my ally. Together we would persuade Daddy, should he show signs of needing persuasion, and my brother Bill, too, would be with us all the way.

Bill actually was *too* prejudiced in my opinion: he purported to solemnly believe that Negroes were sub-human, not much better than monkeys. This was the old-fashioned idea, and very tiresome. But maybe he didn't believe it at all. Bill's a great tease.

Anyway, carried aloft again on a great new transport of hope, I at last saw my father, hat in hand, coming along the walk. Guiltily I then remembered that I had promised to pick him up and drive him home from school. It was a terribly hot day, too, and poor Daddy wasn't getting any younger.

CHAPTER TWO

MY FATHER NEVER CURSES, but I hadn't gotten ten words out of my mouth before he became utterly furious and yelled, "God damn it, no!" He became so red in the face that I found myself being simply fascinated by the way he looked—all that rosy skin beneath his white, white hair—and I wasn't even shocked or frightened or anything. After adding that it was absolutely none of my damn business, "young lady," and for me to watch my step, he charged into the house and banged the screen door like somebody else's father—Dot Carter's, for instance—who has a temper like a blast from a furnace.

I got up rather cautiously from the swing and went over to the screen door to look inside and saw him sitting there in the living room absently stroking Psyche, my white Persian cat, and looking over his mail. I stood there a few minutes waiting for reality, or doom, or something, as helpless as a dog in a space-bound missile. Bill broke the spell for me by coming into the dark cool living room and asking Dad if it was hot enough for him. With that I went back to my swing. For now I badly needed Mother to come home. Before that damned phone rang again and Ridey Marshall or Dot or somebody was calling up to see if Dad had come home and how I had made out.

Getting back to serious thinking—and a lot of anxiety—several things came back to me, incidents that I hadn't remembered at first; again, things on the minus side. Like the time a very famous poet I won't mention turned up during the lecture season, having been engaged by a most ignorant, all agreed, committee who were under the erroneous impression that he was white, and all the to-do there was about *that*. I had thought it was extremely amusing at the time, for the whole university was in an absolute snit over this Jaffe. In the first place, the Faculty Wives' Club had scheduled their usual reception for a celebrated lecturer, and in the second place since he was to be in town two days and a night, where was he to put up? The first problem—that of the reception—was finally solved after three emergency meetings of the Faculty Wives' Club. They had all bravely agreed at the first that they had to go through with it somehow—it would be too face-losing to back out; he was internationally known and there wasn't time left to cancel his appearance—but the real snarl came over the matter of how he would be presented in the receiving line. He wasn't just an ordinary darky, so he could not be called by his first name, but, on the other hand, under no circumstances would any white lady stoop to calling him Mister. The solution was at last brought about by the wife of the head of the English department who ingeniously hit upon the fact that he was a Ph.D. and might therefore be presented as Doctor. And the other little matter of his bed and board was solved with the greatest tact and secrecy: Dr. Atwood, who was from New York City, and a new import to the faculty and not expected to know any better, would put him up; he and his brusque, cold Yankee wife (typical of all such) would be entrusted with the task of entertaining him at all meals and at all times save for the reception, his two lectures, and one discreet luncheon to be given by the Atwoods in their home. To this affair would come seven carefully screened guests: two local businessmen—one a blue-blooded but renegade local son turned violently radical, for some reason, but too rich to openly condemn; the other a harmless and rather saintly drunkard, as fond of mankind in general as St. Francis of Assisi was fond of birds—and five Yankee and/or liberal professors from the college.

My father, needless to say, had been one of the seven.

In horror, but my loathing for him grown cold, I remembered my father's defection. It would not have been so bad if he had just kept his mouth shut, but he hadn't. A few weeks after the celebrated gentleman of color had left—in good spirits, I'm sure, feeling rather heartened over the delightfully unexpected graciousness and enlightened attitude he had found—my father forgot and spilled the beans. It happened at the dinner table, and my mother, after she recovered from her horrified shock, decided it was all very funny and began to giggle. My brother had not thought it funny, and had left the table in cold thinlipped disapproval, without asking permission. Daddy cautioned both of us to let this story go no further. I knew what he meant, and my mother should have, but she loves to talk. For that reason the president of the U.D.C. and her husband walked out without saying a word from a Sunday night supper party my parents gave, and they had been on very cool terms since.

That had only been last year, and memories are long—particularly in the South. And, sitting there in the swing, for the life of me I couldn't remember how many people Mommie had had for supper that night, how many she had blurted it to. And of course I couldn't begin to reckon how many people Mrs. ridiculous U.D.C. president had contacted, passing out the tale as if it were a handbill for a new Volstead Act, or something.

Anyway, and in any way, from where I sat it looked damned bad, if not fatal.

And I guess that was the first time I felt a tug, the very tiniest tug, to the other pole.

I won't pretend that reason, humanity, superior intellect or anything else motivated me. No. It was simply that I liked my father as well as loved him, and protecting him and standing by him came first. That afternoon, sticking up for Maybelle Brown and her case or cause was so far out of the question that I would have been rude and hotly angry if anyone had accused me of getting soft. And I wasn't soft, not then. At dinner that night I provoked one of the most anti-Negro three-way testimonials I've ever heard. Only my father remained out of it.

I don't remember the details of my diatribe, my mother's, or Bill's anymore than I remember what we had to eat, but I do remember that it was good and that we all enjoyed it—or three of us did, at any rate. And so did Aunt Stell, our cook, whose family has worked for my mother's family forever, for I remember that everytime she came in to serve she would vigorously nod her head and say, "Y'all's right. If them Up-North coloreds wants to get 'em an education, let 'em stay up North and git it. Just make trouble down here."

After dinner, I went back to the kitchen and asked Aunt Stell if she knew anything about this Maybelle Brown. Was she an NAACP plant? Were all the big Yankee newspapers going to make a big thing out of this? After all, ours was the first university in the state to have a colored person admitted, so they might very well feel like cheering because they had opened up another frontier.

I was being very eloquent that night, and I didn't mind at all—as I never did—that I was mainly talking to hear myself talk, knowing full well that ninety per cent of it was going right over dear old Aunt Stell's ignorant but really quite shrewd head.

"Ya'll got nothing to fret over," she said. "This Maybelle, she's an uppity nigger, a real Yankee just like the white ones, and she won't like being down here with you all. She'll see ain't no room down here for her. Cain't do no good for the Coloreds, if that's what she's after. She say that's what she's going to do, so they tell me. But I don't know her none. You seen her? They say she real pretty, pretty like a white gal with a little bitty thin nose. And light too. Coffee, just like her grandmammy."

I asked who Maybelle's "grandmammy" was.

"Why, she Miss Icie Brown," Aunt Stell said in dignity and astonishment. "And I hear tell she don't want no part of this nohow."

I couldn't wait to get back to Mommie and tell her this suc-culent morsel, for Icie Brown was the pillar of Colored Society. Whites as well as blacks respected her. She was the widow of the best minister the African Methodist Church had ever had, was considered very well educated (self, of course) by everyone in town, had her own business—a secondhand clothing store—and was sufficiently well off to help other members of her race, so it was said, who wanted a stake to go up North, and had put her only son through college.

As I was enthusiastically relating all this to Mom (Dad had gone to bed), it was Bill who raised the pertinent questions which were to prove so pertinent in the immediate future: "Why does Icie Brown object to her own granddaughter trying to break the dry ice around here when she's helped so many of her own kind, not even kin to her? And what's happened to her smart nigger son? Why would he send his daughter back here to school when she's been doing all right up there with all those Yankee nigger lovers?"

"Maybe, son," replied my mother mildly, "she's just a test case, like they say."

"May end up the first black wench ever lynched," my fine brother commented.

"You're a fool," I murmured, knowing, even as I said it, that his head would whip around, like a snake's ready to strike, and he would say, *"What?"* in that darting venomous way he has. And when he did it, I didn't even care. I was too busy feeling something I had felt all along, something I had covered with ela-tion and smart alecky cruel talk: I felt craven. For if Maybelle Brown was a test case, I was a foregone conclusion. I was a weak, limp slob, without will or convictions of my own; even without the ability to aim my loose talk at the proper target. I knew why Daddy had gone off to bed; he was ashamed for me and of me. Aside from those first words I had spoken to him on the porch, I had not once again attempted my mission: I had not stood up and issued my ultimatum about going off to school—the comparatively easy part—much less demanded to know where he stood as a faculty member of a desegregated school. I had even lacked the courage to approach the matter obliquely, to smoke him out. No. All I had been able to do was start a useless barrage of nasty anti-Negro talk, talk that was as low and mean and unthinking as any illiterate White Supremacist rabble rouser's, nine tenths of which I did not mean—all as a dodge to keep from doing what I should have done: examined my conscience, weighed the facts, and then had a quiet private talk with him about it. Yes, no wonder he had gone off to bed.

And the really awful thing about it all was that I knew now what I should have known all along: I didn't want to protest by running away; I didn't want Daddy to get Maybelle Brown ousted. I wanted to stick around, and I wanted her to stick around too. I wanted very much to see what would happen.

CHAPTER THREE

THE MORNING MAYBELLE BROWN walked into "Creative Writing I" we all whipped around, as one, and we turned on the juice. Our victim didn't seem to know she was being brainwashed, much less electrocuted. Maybelle Brown simply chose a chair and sat down. And she stayed calm and unaffected for the whole class period.

True, there were not many notes to take since that was only the second time the class had met, but I didn't take any. When the bell rang, I didn't even have the faintest idea what books, if any, we were supposed to get for the course. Or what Dr. Macon had talked about anyway. Or anything. And even if I had cared, I don't think anyone could have told me. No, sir. The hynotizers had been hynotized by the hypnotizee. For Maybelle Brown was simply incredible looking.

People are always talking about how much really soft, feminine women look like cats: Persian, if they have beautiful, great-eyed tender faces; Siamese, if they are sleek, chic and suave—handsomely good-looking more than anything else; and short-haired (even alley) if they are just alive, graceful, active and rather bright. Well, Maybelle was of that brand-new breed called Colorpoint, a combination of long-haired with Siamese. Her skin was dark gold, and she had sealpoint markings—dark hair and dazzling azure blue eyes—and she was every inch, unmistakably, a thoroughbred, a showpiece. What, all I could ask myself, what was this incredible creature doing in a place like this school, her Grandmammy Icie Brown notwithstanding? She was so overwhelming looking that it was hard to imagine her in any school at all. Atlantic City, Miss America, or Miss Universe was more like it. Why had she come to this pokey little place?

And I should have said, that there had been no publicity about her enrollment, no matter what we all dreaded (half-hoped) and expected: Maybelle Brown was living quietly in town at the home of her grandmother, attending classes as a day student. No dormitory problem, no nothing.

As I was a Freshman, and she a Junior, we had no other courses together: only the off-beat things like Creative Writing were open to all. And I took some other off-beat things, being no Phi Beta Kappa aspirant (in spite of Daddy), but she didn't. Even in those first few weeks of school, everybody pegged her as a serious student. But nobody thought she would last, not even the teachers who admitted that she was a more than adequate student. How could she? they asked, hoping, I think, that sooner or later national attention would be drawn to the fact that she was in school here in the first place.

But nothing happened. Maybelle Brown simply, yet miraculously, continued to come to school. Always wearing very great clothes. From looking at *Vogue* I knew damned well they weren't any cut-rate store things either. Something gave with this Maybelle character.

By October, everybody had, of course, chosen up sides; either you were pledged to a sorority or you weren't; the members of the crowd who had elected to go away to school rather than mingle with Maybelle had gone or were keeping quiet about it, bearing up, like a colony of icicles, and I had, I felt, stolen a march on a couple of very-worthies, and copped the job as feature editor on the school paper. People kept reminding me, after the deed was done, of my great good fortune, as if it had all come about while they were under a magic sleeping spell, or as if I were a four-flushing child prodigy who had talked my way into this exalted post. I won't say I deserved it, but I did know what I was doing. After all,

I had held down the same job for my four high school years. But the crowd had a grudge against me; I knew that, and I knew why. I had slipped my great opportunity for saving us all. I had just let nature take its course, and they thought nature was pretty unnatural. The truth of the matter was so did I. But what harm had been done? Our black fly in the ointment was so well comported she was almost invisible; she had not made any big push, such as we had all hoped for and dreaded, to be singled out as an entity or a nonentity on campus, and she seemed to be completely satisfied just to attend our school for scholastic purposes, nothing else.

I can't say here that if I had left well enough alone nothing would have happened; it's hard to be sure. But I will admit that I was acerbated on many sides: first of all, the quiet, the unnatural quiet of the crowd, waiting for me to be the standard leader I had been elected to be; then Mother, who made her sweet snide cracks occasionally, dulcet, so dulcet about how things were so different from her college days when "Nig-rows" were either janitors or maids, not schoolmates; and the fact that Dad didn't really talk to me anymore, not about anything serious; and Bill, who had become an insurance salesman, complained more and more about the dishonesty, the lying and the difficulties of Negroes and the policies they boastfully promised to take and those they took. The whole thing got to me. I found myself longing to know Maybelle. Which is not to say I longed to know a cause un-*celebre*, but to know one of these people—anybody else would have done as well, even Aunt Stell's son, Cannon, if he had been a similar person—who, for all I could see, really *see*, was simply just a somebody else. That her skin was another hue had ceased to matter, that her background was alien had no bearing. The curiosity I felt about her was no longer South-white, South-black, but rather as if she had been an exchange student from Pakistan. Maybelle Brown, and all she stood for, was clearly someone I did not know, and would never know unless I made the effort. So I did. I did something fairly awful, but the only thing I knew to do:

I called up Icie Brown, and, as feature editor of our school paper, asked for an interview.

At first, over the phone, Icie (as we whites, of course, called her) was, as we say, "just nice." She didn't say, Yes, Miss Hallie, please come by, and she didn't say no. She was just as skillful and gracious in her hedging as her white counterpart would have been. She gave no answer. Instead, she thanked me repeatedly, in a variety of phrasings, for having called, for having remembered her, for having considered her worthy of a write-up in the paper in the first place. And then she asked why.

That was a good question, and one to which I had only the thinnest scrap of an answer: She was considered an unusual personality.

There was a long pause after this, and I was holding my breath for fear she would again ask the dark and inevitable *why*. But she didn't. Apparently, she did not want to turn ugly, use my foolish request as some kind of show-down. Icie Brown was as wise as I was timorously headstrong and foolish. "I don't think so right now," she declined. "I been keeping real busy this fall. Maybe later on." I accepted this as gratefully as a scared neighbor's dog being let out of the gate to scamper home where he belonged.

Again, I felt terribly ashamed of myself, ridden with guilt. Suppose somehow the word got around that I had, on my own, made this overture? There wouldn't be the slightest doubt in anyone's mind that it was a piece of mischief (at best) or proof of my half-Yankee liberalism. The latter would obviously go hard not only with me, but would affect the rest of my family and my relationship with my friends. As for doing such a thing, without the authorization of the editor-in-chief of the paper, need I add, it put me right in the camp with the worst of the White Supremacists, those who were still hopefully eying every movement on campus for a chance to stir things up. In short, I'd be better off keeping my curiosity about Maybelle Brown a private matter, unless I really wanted to create a situation.

CHAPTER FOUR

B Y THE TIME the first snow flew—yes, ours is one of those Southern states that usually has some snow in the cold months—Maybelle Brown was about as remote in my daily thoughts as any other day student around campus who hadn't been asked to join all the right things, and who therefore made herself scarce after her classes were over. And as for the call I'd made to Maybelle's grandmother, well, if anyone had mentioned it I would have innocently said, "Who me?" because that was how buried the whole thing was. Mostly, of course, because I had this thing going with Tom Nesbitt, a junior at Chapel Hill. Tom and I had gone steady his last year in high school, and then we'd just been good friends, but this year something had happened. He came home on weekends, then I'd flown to Chapel Hill for a fraternity dance, then Thanksgiving and lots of letters and all in between. Well, those things just happen.

As for the general attitude toward having a Negro student on campus, again I don't know. I guess the fact that we still had her speaks for itself. Certainly it wasn't that local attitudes had changed, for what with the Louisiana riots, the election and all, the integration and civil rights questions raged all around. But then they say that this is the way big storms work; the direct center, the eye, is always still. Or course I'm sure that Maybelle herself was exercising the utmost tact and perspicacity, but I doubt if this really had much effect on the phenomenal acceptance—if you can call it that—she had been given. Once or twice I talked it over with Tom, and he likened the whole situation to a guy who knows he has cancer but refuses to the end to admit it. However, as he also pointed out, there is an end.

And then about Christmastime, just before the holidays when all the kids off at school would be flooding home, I met this great boy named Pete, so what with him and Tom coming home, I had enough personal complications to keep me stuck close in my spare moments to my diary, trying to work things out. And my mother was her usual no-help; she strongly favored Pete: he came from a very socially prominent family in Memphis, was better looking, was already through college and had excellent prospects, and besides he was very old-world courtly with older women.

But I'll admit it. During the Christmas holidays Maybelle did begin to bug me. Her problem, that is. You see, Phyllis Dolan, who goes to a boarding school outside Washington, asked this girl home for the holidays from South America who was as dark as Maybelle. In fact, the night I saw her at the Mistletoe Ball, just for a second I thought it was Maybelle. If anyone else was taken aback, as I was, I didn't see it. And she was certainly doing all right for herself. I thought Pete was going to rush her right off the floor. And even Tom, who took me, admitted this Latin type was attractive and more than once cast wistful looks in her direction until Phyllis finally introduced them; then he did a lot of cutting in himself. As I say, over the holidays, in this way at least, Maybelle bugged me. Where the real Maybelle was I didn't know.

Then after New Year's everything settled down to, as they say, abnormal, and a new term was coming up.

I breezed through registration and felt the usual student exhilaration for the free time left after; came in the door singing one of my favorite songs, which Mommie had already assured me was simply a revival from the time when she was not-so-old, to be met at the door by Daddy, looking as stern as an American primitive oil painting.

"Come into my study," he said, as if he were my student sponsor, and I followed him back to that sloppy, feckless lumber room sort of chamber in the back of the house where he keeps the rickety bookcases he built himself, his pipes, (most of which seem to get lost, and often while still burning) mounds of papers with scribbles, and an abundance of things which land there because of lack of other storage room. My first tricycle is there, for instance.

I brushed off what I call his uneasy chair and sat down, expecting the worst: three failed subjects; overdrawn checking account; being irritable with Mommie.

Instead, he said, "You might as well know that the Negro girl, Maybelle Brown, has me as sponsor this term, that I've already seen her, and that the first thing she has requested is that you do a profile—an interview, or whatever—of her grandmother for the paper, as apparently you requested early this year. Did you approach Icie Brown for a story?"

"Yes, Daddy, but—" I answered in confusion.

"Then you did? Then I'm glad. I don't know why you did, but it's a good sign." He paused and strode around as he does, thinking, as if the thought process were merely pulling at one's mouth. "It's good for everyone. Did you do this on your own, for whatever reason?"

"I had no reason," I said, feeling as small as my tricycle in the corner. "Joyce Mainard didn't tell me to; no one did."

"Joyce Mainard? Is she the editor?"

I nodded.

"Why did you then?"

And of course I took the easy way out by saying, "I don't know."

Usually this aggravates Daddy. This time he simply looked at me thoughtfully. Then he said, "No. I suppose you don't."

End of interview. But an assignment had been made. I was to call Icie Brown again—she wasn't so busy now, it seemed—and make an appointment to go by and see her.

Naturally, I postponed doing this as long as I could, using getting the new term underway as an excuse, for I knew this time I would not, could not, be so reckless as I had been in the fall: this time I *had* to get an editorial okay or the story might not be the only thing thrown out of the paper. Before, you see, I guess I had never had any real intention of actually writing up Icie Brown; all I had thought was that it was a good wily way to get the lowdown on Maybelle and what she was and what she was up to.

So, knocking at least ten years off my sense of independence, on the morning of the day I planned to call I approached Daddy for advice. He frowned slightly when I told him my problem, then drew me out of earshot of Mommie and Bill who were lingering over breakfast in the dining rom, having one of those interminable discussions she likes to make over concern for his well-being.

Daddy and I set up our conference room on the front porch, cold as it was, for he was hurrying off to class, as usual. As we stood there breathing out air, like two smoking dragons, we both stared at the ice palace of the outside world. There had been a sleet and rain storm the night before, and now, on top of the snow, everything was frozen solid. It was strange standing there in this fairyland of such beauty for the purpose of discussing something so warm, so dark, and so quite ugly as how to handle, or get around, race prejudice—which is what it really was—as if the subject were as delicate and brittle and icy as a branch of the forsythia bush.

"Well, how do I ask Joyce Mainard?" I said.

"Don't ask her," he said. "Just do it on your own. Then submit the story."

I felt my eyes widen in astonishment, and met his gaze which was alive, grave, and clear. We continued to stare at each other unblinkingly.

Then Daddy simply walked off and left me. I felt surprised, frightened and yet excited.

Icie Brown said not to come until Thursday because her furnace would be out of fix until then and her house might be too
cold for me. I demurred, but she was politely insistent. Then she
said, "What are you going to do your write-up on me about, Miss
Hallie?"

"I don't quite know, Icie," I told her. "I thought we'd just talk
and see."

"Um-hm," she replied, and that was the end of the conversation except for fixing the time I would come. I tried not to think
about it, but I knew four things: she had sounded dignified and
guarded and I had sounded nervous and too friendly. Hardly a
good start for an objective reporter and a sympathetic subject,
but, as I say, I tried not to think of it.

Icie, unlike most coloreds in our town, lives right among the
white people. True, that part of University Avenue is hardly the
best part, but some very nice, though not very well-off people,
live practically next door to her. But she owns her own house,
has always lived there, and besides, it is next door to their church.
I used to think it was the manse she lived in, but then I heard
that it wasn't; as a matter of fact, if that branch of the African
Methodist Church has a manse, I don't know where it is. In fact,
I know very little about the whole subject, and what I know, I am
not sure I know, not so sure as I once was.

Anyway, Icie Brown lives in this one-story frame house
alongside the African Methodist Church, which is a very, very
old brick building, and has shutters on the windows, like in the
last century, which was when it was built. Her house is built close
to the street, as are most of the houses along in there, and looks
pretty much like the others, which are also frame and one story,
only hers doesn't need paint. And it doesn't have a front porch
swing tied up by its chains close to the porch ceiling, like others
you see in such dwellings in the winter. In her yard, which is
quite small, of course, she has a magnolia and a maple tree. And

her magnolia and maple trees help make University Avenue in that section still a pretty street in spite of the drab houses, for in summer it is very shady, as are most of the streets we have; all like long, cool, green caverns, very high arched, very stately.

But as I got out of the car, taking the ignition keys for once, University Avenue, and all those little frame houses didn't look so stately, or even so homey. They looked pinched and poor and cold. Even hers, and it looked the best, considering. I walked up to the door in a sort of trance, or a swoon is more like it, for never in my life had I paid such an almost social call upon a member of the Negro race: it had either been to collect the washing, or to Aunt Stell's to find out if she was feeling any better, or to Lettie's to see if she could come help serve, or something like that. And this call I was making wasn't anything like the others: it was, you might say, an official call. I think I would have died on the spot if Maybelle Brown had answered the door.

CHAPTER FIVE

WHEN ICIE OPENED the door, I knew I never would have recognized her; I hadn't seen her that often, for one thing. She was more of a hearsay personage among the whites than anything else. For while we knew her worth to the Colored community—and to the white, too, since she ruled their world with a benign but firm totality that ultimately affected ours—she was not an everyday sight on the courthouse square. I knew her second-hand store, but only by hearsay; Aunt Stell, for instance, often took my old things and Mother's to her to sell, if she or her family didn't want them as hand-me-downs, and many was the time Mother had said, "Guess what, Icie Brown gave Stell four dollars for your old evening dress," or coat, or whatever, and I was a few bucks richer. So now I faced what amounted to my black benefactress, and she wasn't so black either.

"Miss Hallie," she said rather breathlessly, as soon as I stepped inside, "will you pardon me for just a second? I've got the TV on in the bedroom and the volume won't turn down. It's something's wrong with it, and I think it's fixing to blow a fuse."

As she hurried off, as impromptu as anybody else would have been in such a circumstance, my one thought was to follow and be of help. Of course I didn't, but my concern certainly registered in an anxious frown, and for a few minutes I didn't—truly, I didn't—think where I was. Simply, a friend was in need—there was no doubt of that. I guess you could have heard that TV blaring for blocks, or so it seemed. Then it died, all of a sudden, and

I recollected myself, and felt very cold, far more than the chilly day warranted.

I heard her coming back to the living room, coming down a hall, and quickly, surreptitious as a private eye, a sneaky reporter, or just an over-curious spy I took in the room. Small. Lots of antiques. Covered with tacky slipcovers—splashy orangey flowered material—cretonne? An ottoman matching a Barca Lounger-type chair. Upright piano. Fresh flowers, iris, narcissus (wasn't it awfully early in the season? where had they come from?) in a big vase on a candlestand. And on the mantel pictures in gold frames: Icie and a Colored man; undoubtedly a wedding picture. And a photograph, of less remote vintage. A colored Colored photograph so to speak. Handsome, light-skinned darky, thin mustache. And last, but very recent, a colored photograph of her granddaughter, Maybelle, in a white dress, holding a large bouquet of red roses. High school graduation? I cut my eyes around to meet Icie's, my face creasing into prearranged folds for smiles, like a letter that has been carefully prepared—no, precisely, painstakingly—for an envelope. Then I saw that the light on her glasses, coming from the dying sun through the side window, completely hid from me all I had hoped in that first look to know. The windows of her soul had, ironically, had their shades automatically lowered. I blinked. And then *she* smiled, and her smile was as generous and spontaneous—as unselfconscious—as mine was not. "Well, I'll declare" she said beaming, very pleasant looking, but still disturbingly sightless as she put her hands on her hips. "Lettie told me you looked like the Craddock's side, but I never would have known you were going to be the image of Miss Mamie."

"Why, thank you, Icie," I breathed, startled and quite pleased to hear I looked like my grandmother who was supposed to have been a real something in her day.

"Sit down, child," she said, and waved me to the Barca Lounger thing right beside me. And she sat too.

Now with the light off her spectacles I could see she was rather as I had expected, but somehow much more. The look from her eyes was amiable, wise, and confident. It gave to her stocky, quite Negroid appearance something important that would have otherwise been lacking. And in that moment of realization, Icie Brown, Negress, ceased to be; instead there was just Icie Brown, a nice woman who had let herself get a little dowdy from being a little overweight, and she wasn't all that old; I longed to tell her. Instead I smiled—I don't know what kind of smile—but if inner thoughts dictate expression, it was wistful like a dog wagging its tail, hoping to be friends.

But she didn't notice; she was busy fumbling around with something on the coffee table: a cigarette box. "Here," she said, getting the top open. "My granddaughter tells me everybody these days smokes and I ought to offer cigarettes."

I tittered as politely, as gauchely, as I would have in any hospitable company where such a simple but somehow suspect gesture had been made. "No, thanks," I said, even though I do, it's true, smoke some.

She sort of wagged her head, as if to say, 'I knew that girl was wrong,' and replaced the top. "Tea, then?" she asked. "Or maybe you'd like a Coke?"

I hesitated a moment too long, and she decided for me. "You're scared you'll spoil your supper," she said.

"Not really," I gulped and half laughed, an awkward fool again. "And I'm terribly late. School kept me."

To this Icie Brown answered with the friendliest most natural laugh in the world, and before I had a chance to go on with my lame-footedness, breathing through my fins—all scales— why, Icie Brown had carried the whole thing right off, and we were suddenly talking about Lettie, who was her sister, a fact I had forgotten, and how well Lettie was, and how much she liked St. Louis, to which place I'd also forgotten she'd gone. Then Icie confessed:

"I've been up there, but those winters they have—umh umh," she gave an emphatic shake of her head. "This 'un's been enough for me right here. Too much, to tell the truth. Florida's going to get me just as soon as I retire."

"Retire?" I said in the polite anxiety I would have affected for any of our leading citizenry who proposed to leave our midst, and then we got down to the Whole Story, as it were.

In here somewhere I got out my notebook and pencil and jotted. Icie Brown, nee Collins, had inherited the row of office buildings on West Harding Street (the Negro section, of course) from her father who had been one of the bestloved Negroes in town; my own father, Henry Hamilton, had known him well. He had been a leading Colored doctor—everybody had known and respected Doctor Collins—and he had died fifteen years before at the age of ninety-three. Born a slave as the son of a slave, he had been freed, of course after the war, but his master, old Mr. Lawyer Collins—the family had died out before I was born—had given her father an education. "In the medicinery," as Icie Brown quite confidently called it, and her father had not only come back here to practice, but to prosper, and when he died he had left her and the Reverend Brown, her husband, quite well-to-do.

"We owns our own home, you see," she said proudly, then frowned a little, as if she realized her grammatical slip, or maybe it was grief over the "we" as she was now widowed. "And I still got quite a bit of property on Harding Street, including my store building. And I was a school teacher once. Before I met my husband."

Carefully, I noted these things; so far I had nothing else. What did I want? Sitting there, listening, absorbed, even a little heady, as if this new experience were as strong as wine, only dimly did I have Maybelle, the granddaughter, in mind. But Icie Brown was wound up, she was enjoying talking about herself; her eyes twinkled, her expression was indulgent, happy, and she was expansive and relaxed as a fat woman released from a girdle. She told me about her store: how whites as well as blacks patronized it; oh, she wouldn't name names, but some big well-to-dos had been known to buy second-hand tuxedos for their sons from her, only from known origins, of course, and some very rich "high yallers" from the city came to her regularly for their furs and evening clothes. I longed to ask if any of mine had ever been selected, but hadn't the nerve. And in the end she inveighed against those charitable societies—the Junior League, the Woman's Club, the Spend-the-Days (all the others too, I could name, which either my mother, I, or my cousins not only belonged to but were officers of)—which thoughtlessly competed with her by having rummage sales. Why, on occasion, "we" even withdrew articles we had put up for sale in her store and then donated to our rummage sale, where they were subsequently sold for as little as a tenth of what they were supposed to bring. I agreed it was awful. I personally promised never again to let such a thing happen, in my family, at least; assured her that it would be a great loss to all of us if she retired to Florida, promised to bring her the Dior suit (copy) I'd bought last spring, just as soon as Mother thought less of it, thanked her for the interview, said I'd send her my article as soon as I wrote it, told her how very much I'd enjoyed talking to her and departed.

Outside, it was quite dark. And inside it was too, for I realized that the only real mention we had made of Maybelle—the object of all this—had been the most indirect reference early in the meeting when Icie Brown had offered me a cigarette, on the advice of her granddaughter who thought everybody smoked.

Well, she was right. I smoked; I certainly did. I was smoking, smoking mad, as frustrated as any would-be journalist ever was who has been waylaid by a private secretary, or a diverting in-law, or anything but the real thing.

CHAPTER SIX

WHEN I TOLD DADDY about this, after supper, back in his lumber room-study, he didn't interrupt me, or put anything in during my long, painful pauses. He just kept nodding and drawing strongly at his pipe, his eyes directed at mine—in other words, he was cool, calm, collected, observant and listening. A real psychologist.

"What am I going to do?" I ended on a plaintive note.

He looked reflective for a moment, still drawing away at his pipe, then, knocking the ashes out of the blamed thing (on the bare desk top, of course,) he said: "Icie Brown is a clever woman, hon. A very clever woman. And she's also a very self-centered one. I don't know what she was trying to accomplish through you, but I'm sure it was something. What did you tell her about yourself?"

"Why, nothing," I said sort of surprised. "She wouldn't let me get a word in edgewise, not even to ask any lead questions, the kind a reporter is supposed to do."

He gave me his magnetic blotting-paper look again (Mother says one of the things she married him for was his "piercing blue eyes"), and said "—and you're sure she didn't talk at all about her granddaughter? Say how proud she was of her, or about her son?"

I shook my head.

"How about Stell—or what's that other Colored woman's name your mother gets sometimes, the one who is her sister? Lettie? Yes, Lettie."

"Sure, she talked about Lettie. She talked about lots of things I suppose she thought we had in common. She was real nice, Daddy. Pleasant and poised—more like one of Mommy's friends—"

He laughed softly and refilled his pipe. "She talked about her second-hand clothing business, and how the caprices of the white folks affected her business, you say?"

I nodded.

He stood up, a faint secretlike grown-up smile still on his face, and his eyes weren't with me anymore. "Then tear up your story, hon, if you actually started writing one."

"I haven't started," I protested, following him, and wondering why he was breaking up our session so soon. I wasn't near satisfied. "How could I start? I just got home in time for supper. And why shouldn't I write the story anyway? It's harmless enough—it would make a good feature. After all, she's considered a colorful personality, a success—"

"That's just it," he said with a grin. "The story is harmless—at least harmless to her. And ten years ago it would have been, as you say, a good feature, about an interesting local Negro personality, and everyone would have complimented you on your ingenuity and individuality for thinking of it in the first place. In fact, it would have been generally well accepted, would have fitted in with the patronizing attitude so much in style then."

"I guess you're right," I conceded, only half understanding why, and I lingered in his room after he left.

What had he been trying to tell me? Certainly something more than that my subject and the material I had gotten was no longer timely, or that patronage of the Negro race now drew scorn from them and hostility and suspicion from our side. I knew well enough that this sort of thing no longer satisfied anybody. But why had he encouraged me to go after the story? What had he thought I'd find out? I felt as if I were being used as bait or as a pawn in a dangerous game. But what game? And after all, I had thought up the idea of the interview myself.

Upon reflection, of course, the danger part of what I had done, even though I did not know its nature, was the aspect that lodged uppermost in my mind, and I determined at all costs—all over again—to tell my suspicious friend Dot a good lie so she would never find out where I had been, and to deny, hotly and coldly, as the occasion might demand, that I had ever stepped foot in Icie Brown's house. Somehow, though, I came out of his study that night feeling more like a fool than ever—ever so innocent, ignorant and ungainly; a young cow crunching through the remains of the China shop, though, fortunately, the Haviland had not been left in my path. Had it been sensibly put away beforehand, or had I, cowlike, missed it because I didn't care and didn't know the difference?

Whatever, I was dulled and be-dociled by my failure and mistake. All too shy-making. I felt like taking off my lipstick, mascara and eyeliner and going back to the nursery.

Meanwhile, naturally, I avoided anything alluding to Maybelle Brown, including Maybelle Brown, for though Daddy had drawn her as a student to serve in an advisory capacity, that had nothing to do with me, and furthermore, she had not signed up again this term for the writing course, so we had no classes together.

However, this was by no means the end of it.

Did I say somewhere in here that thanks to Daddy and a few other enlightened citizens, a brand new Negro elementary and high school was built a few years ago? Well, I should have. And, ironically enough, the name of this combination grade and high school was named Collins School, after Icie Brown's father, I suppose. Anyway, it is a terrific school, or so Daddy said at the time, absolutely the most modern equipment, etc., good teachers at comparatively good salaries and so forth. And this, of course, is why none of our local Negro population had seen fit to try to enter their children in white schools—everybody said, and there's something to it, that their school was probably superior to any of ours. As a matter of fact, I can remember that when integration became a Federal law, some of the grown-up local wags said their educations were half-baked due to the inferior white school conditions they'd grown up under, and they thought they might go enroll in Collins, since integration was legal, and get full-baked in the head. At the time, I remember Daddy's rejoinder had been: "That's an excellent idea," and everybody thought he was pretty witty, as usual. Maybe it's too bad this wasn't a serious idea, as well. But, at any rate, for whatever reason—whether their school system was now as good as ours, or whether they were, like the radical rightists said, "good niggers in this town who knew their place," the old order in the secondary school line had remained undisturbed. So you see why Maybelle Brown's education here at the university hit us like a brown bombshell, unexploded or not. Until she came, seemingly, sleepy life, old customs, old established amenities and truces in this place stood as firm, respected, and honorable as the statue of the Confederate soldier in the courthouse square—if as out of date with national sympathies, actions and ideas.

They say that change is usually imperceptible, and especially if it is gradual and one's own personal change. So probably that's why I didn't think of it as "change" when the following occurred:

Not too long after my abortive attempt to get Icie Brown's name and mine into print, I went, as I frequently do, on a shopping trip with Mother to C———boro, which is a real city, though nothing so big as. those you have in the East, and is conveniently only forty miles away. Nearly everybody goes there for any serious shopping—furniture, a thorough wardrobe replenishing, fur coats, wedding presents; anything that requires an ample selection of goods to choose from. Everybody here has charge accounts at all the large stores there, and, really, these days, since the population explosion has filled up all the hamlets and small villages in between, we are sort of that city's most outlying suburb. And, too, because the traffic problem there has grown into something like the most monstrous knitting yarn snarl you ever saw, more and more people leave their cars at home and simply rely on the bus.

So Mommie and I took the bus. We sat in the front middle, as usual, where we always try to sit as Mommie doesn't like to sit over the wheel, and, as usual, the Negroes who were going to the city too took their seats in the back. After the bus was loaded—and it was certainly loaded—I remember the driver kept looking around in apprehension before he started, and finally got up and walked to the back and spoke to some of the Colored people back there. There was no fuss, and I didn't hear what he said, but, like practically everyone else, I turned around and stared, curious to know what was up. It was then I noticed how many Negroes had gotten on the bus, which no one had noticed before, and they were standing up in the back, all the way to the white section. The white section itself was full, so I don't know what was worrying the bus driver—maybe he was counting heads to be sure he wasn't over the legal capacity, if there is one. Anyway, we were a few minutes late in getting started.

The trip itself was like many another: same old scenery—our section of the state looks particularly barren and poor in the winter—same old outcroppings of rock from our red clay earth, same lingering snow patches under the stands of cedar trees, same old ramshackle farmhouses amidst the new split-level traps no one knows who built or where-they-got-the-money-to-build-them-with, they-just-sprung-up-overnight, same stone fences and split rail fences enclosing the same scrawny fields and pastures—or, as my Mother says, just looking at this winter landscape always makes her blue. It is indeed depressing, and it seems no amount of new housing or farm improvement or whatever, brought in in the last fifteen years, can alleviate the over-all aspect of poverty, neglect, and disharmony. In summer the leaves and grass help, but it's still there, like a thin gnarled elbow sticking through a colorful sweater.

Mommie and I got into a fuss, before we were three miles out—also par for the course—so we didn't do much talking. I was sitting next to the window and I gazed out of it instead—seeing and unseeing, thinking blue, mean thoughts, such as how stingy she was sometimes with me—like now when she'd told me I could *not* get the red suit and a skirt as well—and how sweet and loving and generous she always seemed to be with Bill. Consequently, we were almost there before I realized it, and I might not have emerged from my dismal reclusion then had it not been for the bus driver.

Dimly, I was aware we had stopped again, as we had done a dozen times along the line to pick up or put off passengers, and also I was half aware that a couple of Negores had boarded the bus. When I saw them take the seats, now empty, in front of us, it scarcely registered. What did register was my mother's elbow in my ribs.

"What?" I muttered, still feeling sour at her, and so annoyed at her for poking me—a habit she knows I despise—that I didn't turn to face her.

"Look in front of you," she whispered.

I looked, was astounded, but my astonishment was quickly masked after a glance at her expression. What was it? Not the cat who swallowed the canary, though smug and almost smiling it was; not that of a maniacal incendiary who has just fired a building, though her eyes were unusually bright; nor was it the excited disapproval, the look of pleased outrage, that comes on the face of an irate parent given just cause for punishing an unfavored child. Her look was of all these things, plus pure simple wonder. I must say here, quite candidly, that I instantly hated her expression, and would have taken an opposite point of view, regardless of the issue, so I said in a most bored voice, "What is it you want me to look at?"

She made a quick gesture with her head.

"So what?" I said in my original bored rather insolent tone, added a yawn for good measure, and turned back to the window.

That drew her out. "Well! The idea!" she said huffily. "What do those darkies think they're doing?"

"Sitting," I said tightly, sounding on purpose more angry than it was conceivable for me to have been, and still refusing to offer her more of my sympathy and face than my profile.

"I think it's awful!" she declared, her voice rising. "What a nerve they've got!"

"Jim Crow was originally just a minstrel song," I told her, speaking out of my voluminous erudition, but in the same tired voice. "It's a pity people like you forgot the music instead of the words."

"What?" she asked icily. "What words are you talking about?"

" 'Jump, Jim Crow,' " I quoted. "Isn't that what you want those passengers to do? Jump up and go land in the back? Why are you so bugged about all this?"

"Bugged. I don't know what you mean by that. I never do."

"You're flipping," I said, now genuinely quite furious, having worked my way up to it. "You've flipped your wig."

At that she got to her feet. "I'm going up and tell that driver to stop this bus and let me out," she said. "I refuse to ride with those darkies sitting in front of me."

I pulled at her, but she was already making her way up the aisle in a striding lurch of somewhat ludicrous dignity; as a matter of fact, she nearly landed in the laps of the darkies in question on her first zigzag. But of course, she did gain her objective, and the fat was in the fire. She came back, her face as stern and triumphant as *The Battle Hymn of the Republic*, followed at a less brisk pace by the driver.

He flicked the briefest glance at Mommie and me and then leaned over the seat in front, his fat hands clutching the seat back.

"You all better get on back where you belong now," he said quietly to the Negro couple.

There was no answer. Instead, they stared straight ahead of them, as if he had not addressed them in the first place. He waited a rather embarrassed second, then tried again. "Ya'll hear? You better get on there in the back where you're supposed to sit."

Still no reply of any sort, and, of course, the bus had become completely still, all eyes and ears upon the scene. "I don't want to have to get rough with you all," the driver said, rather more firmly, but dispassionately. "Either get back there or I'll have to put you off the bus."

"You can't put us off. We paid our fares," said the Negro woman. Her voice was a little breathless, and if she had not been controlling it, you could tell she would have sounded strident.

That, however, was enough to bring out the driver's belligerence which was, I must say, whether due to his slow-moving nature or his sympathies, of a mild variety. "Now, look here. I don't want to have to get rough with no Colored woman. But I can. You try me. So go on, now, and get back where you belong."

"We belong right here and right here is where we are staying," the Negro man said flatly.

The driver, for some reason, seemed totally unprepared for this rejoinder; he looked literally amazed. So he changed his tack; it became a combination of grumbling, persuasion, and thinking out loud. "I'll bet y'all aren't from around here, are you? You'd know better. Where'd I pick you up? That's right, back there at Kitrell. Bet you've come down here from up North to work in the new plant there. I hear they're paying big wages—going to hire people away from all the plants around here. Well, that's all right. I don't begrudge anybody anything, black or white. But ya'll got to move. That's the way it is around here. We don't let niggers sit with white folks. I know some drivers on this line lets you sit up front when it's crowded in the back, but this lady here behind you, she don't like it. And I don't neither. So move!" This last with some force.

Neither the man nor the woman responded in any way; they sat still as effigies, staring straight ahead.

"Now I'm getting tired of this!" the driver blared, his face now working with angry exasperation. "You got no right to sit here!"

"The law says we have!" the Negro woman cried in defiance. And that's when the driver's arm shot out, grabbed the man by the shoulder and started tugging, nudging and pushing him forward.

Like a robot, he sprang to his feet, as did his companion, and without another word, they filed toward the front of the bus, stood at the door, and, when the driver in dazed disbelief finally caught on, followed, and released the pneumatic device that provided the exit, the Negro couple promptly stepped off onto the highway.

Within seconds, and without a word, a glance to anybody, the driver had the bus again in motion, on its destined way.

CHAPTER SEVEN

T HAT INCIDENT, I suppose, was really the moment of my re-
birth; the moment of conception, and the germinating time,
had all gone long before. I emerged from that bus that day in the
city with a heart of rage and violence. I coldly hated my mother
for what she had done, or for inciting what had happened, but I
knew my hatred for her personally would pass; for my re-birth
had put a calm and somewhat analytical head upon my shoulders, replacing that blind butterfly brain that I had fluttered
around with before. And so, when my mother, as contrite as I've
ever seen her in such circumstances, and as contrite as I'm ever
apt to see her about such subjects, asked, "Are you mad at me?
Have I done something awful?" I simply nodded.

"I feel simply terrible about it," she said unhappily.

The old me said in unspoken sarcasm, "Terrible is not bad
enough," but the new person I had become said really nothing;
I just made soft murmurs, hoping both to assuage her and shut
her up. I certainly knew I would not ever, ever discuss it; not with
her—her opinions and her reclamation, if possible, were of relative unimportance. I had much bigger fish to fry.

Taking my stance, my bland expression, and my lack of harsh
protest as forgiveness, she immediately relaxed into her old way,
promptly putting this disquieting thing from her mind. And she
set up a chirping, cheery conversation, as senseless, faultless, and
as blithe as a bird's.

"You're going to kill me, but the first thing we've got to do is
take a bus out to Mrs. Strozier's and get that bedspread."

"Why out to West End?" I said. She was right: I was of course, displeased, but this was now a time for mildness. "Why can't she mail it?"

"The poor old thing can't get to the post office. And," she added significantly, "after all, it is to be *your* bedspread."

This was true. Mother had ordered a bedspread for my hope chest—yes, we still have them in the South—many months before by one of the few really fine crocheters anybody knew these days. And the woman was old, much in demand, and it was true that she might sell it to someone else, ordered or not, if we didn't pick it up soon. It had been ready for some time.

"All right," I agreed, "but only if we take a taxi."

"All the way out there?" my thrifty mother exclaimed.

But I was firm, so we walked to the taxi-loading part of the bus station. There was quite a collection of people waiting, and no taxis in sight.

"Why can't we take a bus?" my mother fumed upon seeing this. "Look at all those people. Wonder why there are so many today?"

I did look at all those people, and it suddenly struck me that only a small percentage of them were whites. And I wondered why, but having no answer, I simply stood beside Mommie in the line to wait our turn.

Her restiveness seemed to make me calmer, as usual. But at last the line did start to move. Two taxis came up and were filled. Then another and another.

All this time I couldn't get out of my mind the moment of my re-birth, so to speak, what had happened back there on the bus. Particularly, I couldn't stay away from the image of those two, that Negro couple, climbing down from the bus, he helping her, just as a white man would have helped his female companion, looking as unruffled, as unscarred by the ignominy they had suffered as though they had gotten off at their prearranged stop. I wondered what had happened to them. Had they walked on into the city? It would have been a good five mile hike. Or maybe, as the driver had said, they were Kitrell plant employees and could afford a taxi. Or maybe city buses ran out that far. Or maybe they wanted to get out near there anyway. Or maybe anything. The point was I had seen with my own eyes what they called "passive resistance" and with my eyes, my convictions, and any sense of balance I had I knew what I had seen was as strong and as lasting and as necessary as the earth itself. These people had had the power of steel, and the reason and right of the whole human race. It was as simple and final as that.

The very thought filled me with such purpose that I cast a glance at Mommie; she's always saying to me, "Don't look so grim. Don't take things so hard," even when she hasn't the faintest idea what is going on in my mind. I might have a toothache for all she knows. I noticed that she was looking a little frayed and quite put out; she hates to wait. Then she said, "Thank heavens. Here's a taxi now," and I moved forward with her. Then I held back. "What's wrong?" she wanted to know.

"They're first," I said, inclining my head toward a Negro woman and two small children who stood slightly to the side but in front of us.

She gave a long, stagey sigh of impatience, but I knew she wouldn't try anything; her bus defection was still too new in her memory, and sometimes, too, Mommie is afraid of me and my wrath. She knew I'd had enough for one day. So when the Negro woman opened the taxi door and started lifting in one of her children, we simply watched, as we had been watching for the last fifteen minutes, as the lucky ones boarded their taxis. Therefore, both of us were quite startled when we heard the taxi driver say, "Get back there, nigger. Them white ladies is ahead of you."

Just for a moment the Negro woman suspended the child in midair, and then she promptly withdrew him, put him on the ground beside his older sister. And she didn't even turn to look at us.

Blood began to pound at my brain, like heat coming into a radiator, and my breath simply stuck. I looked at my mother. She didn't move.

"Go ahead, take them first!" I cried out to him. Now my blood stung me, and the breath rushed from me in exhilaration. "They were before us," I added in reasonable explanation and smiled broadly toward the Negress, but her back was toward me, her head bowed, her expression subdued. The only sign that she felt insulted was the protective hand she kept on the head of the child she had taken back from the cab.

The taxi driver exploded back at me, "You want a taxi, lady, or not?"

"Of course I do," I said authoritatively, "but that woman and her children were first."

"Not with me, they weren't," he answered in loud anger. "I don't take no niggers before whites. If you don't want the cab, git out of the way so someone else who does can pass."

That was when my mother whispered, "Get in, Hallie. Go on."

"I will not!" I said in a vehement voice. "And don't you either!"

"But he won't take them before us," she argued, as if that made sense. "And there are lots of people left. Look behind you."

"I still won't go!" I repeated stubbornly, fighting hysterical anger.

And with that, she shrugged and got in the taxi. As he pulled off, she leaned out of the window and said, "I'll meet you in a hour at Judson's," naming the department store where I'd seen the red suit, and sounding as calm and unmoved as though what she had just done was not only the most natural thing in the world, but the only sensible thing to do.

After she was gone, I can't tell you how I felt. Glued to the spot was just the first thing. It was the Negro mother's, "Thank you, miss, for trying, but all of 'em's like that," was the spell-breaker. I tried to smile back at her, but stopped because my lip was quivering, so I slunk off from that black sea of Negro onlookers, who felt—pity? Scorn? Gratitude? Suspicion for me and my motives? Who could tell? But I felt shame. Shame for myself, for my mother, for the taxi driver and for the whole of mankind, and for this rotten black world we had created for ourselves.

Like an almost drowned swimmer, I came up into the bus station depot, exhausted, and hit the waiting room bench as if it were a beach. After a while, I regained my composure and started off toward Judson's, only a few blocks from the bus station. I went to look at my suit, which had been in the debutante shop on the fourth floor, and I wasn't even very disappointed when I heard they didn't have any more size nines. And I told the saleswoman, no, I wasn't interested in anything else right then, and that was the truth. Not even food, though I realized I was hungry. Eating would, at any rate, help pass the hour until I met mother back in the suits on the fourth floor.

The elevator I took upstairs to the Plantation Room was as hot as the summertime, and jammed. And when I saw the line waiting to get into that phony, tea-roomy place, I wilted. All I could possibly manage was a sandwich, anyway, so I got back on the elevator and took it down to the basement, to the lunch counter there, trying to decide what kind of sandwich I might manage without gagging—I have one of those nervous epiglotises, if that's how you spell it.

I'd decided on chicken salad.

Looking at that, now, what I've just written, I'm tempted to cross it out and write "mincemeat," for once I hit the lunch counter I knew a great many things:

1) Why the bus had been so crowded with Negro passengers.
2) Where Maybelle Brown was.
3) The meaning of a sit-in strike in public eating places in the South.

CHAPTER EIGHT

I T'S FUNNY HOW you always think you don't notice individual faces in a crowd, yet when I inadvertently walked in on that sit-in strike, I knew at once that Maybelle's wasn't the only familiar face; first of all, there was the Pickard's cook, as big as life (and that she is), then lots of colored people who had been on that same bus Mommie and I took to the city, including the one the driver had spoken to before we pulled out of town, and, of course, the couple who had been put off, because of my own mother.

Yet familiar or not, somehow this didn't make it any better. The whole scene was alarming, and I'll tell you why. To begin with, by white standards, Negroes as a racial group are not pretty. More often than not, there's too much mouth—and teeth—too little chin, non-upright foreheads, noses unbearably different from ours, and hair so curly that it is undesirable. All this before taking into account the color of their skins, running from purple black to muddy white. And this aesthetic prejudice is by no means confined to the South.

Therefore, when I, Hallie Hamilton, girl reporter, eighteen years old, and a champion as much as I was a victim of style, habit and caprice, looked at that black lunch counter gathering in Judson's Department hitherto Pure White Store, I just turned plain sick; my new-found togetherness wafted out like a fragile cloud and *apartheid* moved in on an icy blast and lodged there, firm and solid as an iceberg.

All those Negroes clustered there together, their heads round, dark as poisoned fruit, were so ugly, so solemn, so intrusive. It was as if ugliness were a sin, their coloration some awful disease, and their solemnity a judgement—a vicious unfair one. Even beautiful Maybelle had melded into this, her individuality lost, and I stared in utter revulsion at the few Negroes who had somehow managed to be served, watching as they gnawed upon sandwiches—made of brilliantly white bread, so it seemed— with their purple-pink mouths, the bread clutched in their black hands. The sight could not have been more repellent if a colony of monster roaches had been sitting there feeding upon good clean food. "Good night!" was what I exclaimed, and immediately tried to make my way out of the crowd.

But a sit-in strike is no more a casual gathering than any strike, and once having crossed the picket line, so to speak, even innocently, you are more or less in for it. And I certainly was in for it. Right behind me I heard: "That's right, sister! Go up and tell them waitresses you don't want to eat with no niggers or *after* no niggers. Tell 'em to clear this place out, stop serving 'em!"

Even before I turned around, and I did so instantly, I knew these words had come from the mouth of an agitator, out of his milieu, specifically put there for his job. And sure enough, there he was, a towering burly man, so big that his paunch was practically at my eye level. "How dare you call me sister!" I piped in an extra high voice, thus ruining my outrage.

His grin at me was as offensive as his illiterate speech and his large smelly person, and the thick red hand he placed on my arm to restrain me was as odious as his next advice, delivered in his fresh if not lewd suggestive manner: "That's all right, blondie. We both come here to get shed of them niggers, didn't we. Come on. Push 'em off the seats!"

"How dare you!" I said again, this time rather more forcefully, and adding the most scathing insult of all "—you filthy ole piece of po' white trash!"

At this his hand fell from my arm, but only to be lifted toward my face.

"You'd better not!" I muttered breathlessly and tried to scoot away from him, but no luck. The crowd in this once dainty-genteel, unhurried lunch room was like a cattle stampede, all pressed together, all rather wild, all intent upon creating a roughhouse or escaping one. My friend in the overalls—a man of maybe forty, and what was generally known as a country hick, had he been in a gentler state—firmly replaced his paw on my arm and held tight while he urged me forward.

"Get your white stuck-up ass on one of them stools and stick up for our rights. Tell 'em you don't want to eat with no niggers, or *after* no niggers!"

"I will not, I will not!" I gasped, struggling against him. "Besides, I've eaten with Negroes all my life. I had a black mammy—something scum like you never had!"

"You better shut your little ole face, blondie," he warned me, and I gave him a triumphant look, glad for his anger. Glad I'd gotten through to him, though I was still afraid he might hit me at any moment.

"How'd they let a common piece of trash like you in here anyway?" I panted as he shoved me, and gave his ugly red face an insolent reckless look, trying to convey all I felt.

But he'd decided to ignore my words; my stubbornness requiring both his strength and attention to get me forward to do my duty, as he saw it.

Frantically, I looked around that turbulent, tossing mob and it was like a bobbing sea of blackness, flecked now and then with white faces, frightened, pale punctuations, of others, like myself, mostly elderly, frail ladies, however, caught in this maelstrom unwittingly. The exceptions, of course, were the brawny, vulgarly dressed strikebreakers, representing God knows what fanatic, senseless organization, who did all the pushing and shoving. Mostly, I must say, they concentrated on shoving the white women, getting them to do their riotous work for them, not bothering to try to put the Negroes out. Even at this high moment, busy as I was, I thought how cleverly all this had been worked out beforehand by these personally nasty, strong, ignorant creatures. And it was working, too. Many ladies, the umbrella-brandishing kind, had allowed themselves to be thrust forward, or had willingly gone, to oust some Negro from his or her seat at the counter, then proudly settling her posterior upon the counter stool, clawing with be-diamonded fingers, as antique as the settings of her rings, at the counter to maintain her imperious balance. Everyone seemed quite mad, both in the colloquial Southern sense, and the real one.

But my eloquence—and almost my protest—had run dry. My keeper was as strong as dirt, as determined as nature. "Please," I murmured, more wistful than plaintive, so tired had I become, as he moved me ahead—quite skillfully now, since I couldn't continue my initial resistance—and I felt as herded as I was. And doomed. Martyred. Finished. We were now at the counter, where no seat was to be had; it was up to me to make one.

A quite old woman was seated in the spot he had chosen for me to usurp—older than Aunt Stell—and full of the dignity and refinement of appearance that colored people somehow express so well. I would have sooner died. "No!" I said suddenly. "What kind of fiend are you? Let me go, I want my mother!" and I began to cry.

And he began to laugh.

But the colored woman, in boundless compassion said, "That's all right, Missie. I was just fixing to leave."

"No!" I protested, my heart pounding as if I were having a heart attack. "I won't take your seat! I won't take anybody's seat!" But she got down anyway, and my co-member of the white race who was being so helpful, pushed me rudely, rather cunningly so that I jostled the poor old woman, who was really feeble, I saw, as she moved away.

"Now you jest set your little ole ass up there," he said, ignoring the old Negress, ignoring my attempts to apologize for having bumped her. She gave me one of the sweetest smiles I ever saw, and a very grave look at my tormentor, an unspoken rebuke to him for manhandling me and saying words that no lady should hear.

My face flamed, and I knew that in a moment or two I would start to cry. My heart still pounded as if I'd been running for miles and I had that funny metal taste in my mouth, acrid and like hot iron, which I've always gotten the few times in my life when I've been so angry I can't see. Being told to "set my ass down" on the seat was horrid enough, but to have been made to do it was unbearable. The word still stung my ears and the act filled me with such fury and mortification that my tears, when they came, were accompanied by loud sobs I simply couldn't stifle. I felt as if that horrible creature had put me up on the auction block, and when I heard someone say, "There, there. Don't cry. Crying won't help," I instinctively reached out my hand to clutch another hand which sympathetically hovered nearby.

The hand I clutched was Maybelle Brown's.

As soon as I realized this, I immediately stopped—the shock of it did it. I looked into the cool, unsmiling face of this girl who sat beside me, and just as the shock of her had stopped me so it started me again. And I just bawled. But I didn't let her hand go; no, rather I clutched it desperately. And in silence she let me have my cry out, and when I lifted my head again, sniffling, of course, she was still gazing at me in her calm way, not smiling at all, but not grave either. "Thanks," I managed to murmur and our hands fell apart.

Then I felt too embarrassed to look at her, felt my blush spreading again, and almost involuntarily, and certainly sheepishly, I looked around me to see if anybody from home had noticed. And indeed someone had: Miss Sally Sue Sutherland. And she looked as disapproving as my own mother might have. Miss Sally was a very rich old woman who had never married, who was very active in local politics, and an ardent supporter of States' Rights, and once upon a time she had been a Republican delegate to a national convention. She didn't look like any Republican now, though her eccentricity was so well known that she could have been anything. I ducked my head once more, flaming all over now, and just felt miserable.

Terribly conscious of Maybelle at my elbow, I don't know what might have happened if Maybelle had not suggested in a quiet voice that it might make me feel better if I had something to eat.

"I couldn't," I gulped, instinct—or habit—answering for me because having been reminded that the purpose for sitting at this counter was to get food, I had instantly recalled my condition: I sat now among a bunch of Negroes and that was all wrong. Thank God Maybelle made no reply, for if she had I would not have been able to add, however lamely, "Maybe in a few minutes. Right now, I don't think I could get anything down." And thank God I had the presence of mind to add this, for had she liked, she could have asked me why I had come to the lunch counter in the first place if I hadn't intended to eat, and I would have had to remain silent because I could not say—not any more—that I had intended to eat, but that it was wrong to eat with Negroes. Because a few moment's reflection had brought back the light: I did *not* think it was wrong to eat with Negroes or for Negroes to eat with me.

My new untried and recently switched loyalties made me sound awkward I knew, and rather stark when I tried to ask Maybelle casually, "What are you having to eat?"

"A ham sandwich," she said.

"I think I'll have a chicken salad," I replied, as doleful as a death knell, for it saddened me as much as it heartened me, this whole thing.

But as it turned out neither of us got anything to eat, for it was then that the police entered.

"Break it up, break it up!" We heard from the rear of the crowd, and we all turned around to see the officers of the law press forward, armed with police sticks and wearing holsters from which, wickedly and grimly, the butts of pistols could be seen. My mouth literally hung open: I had never seen unfriendly policemen before, and had never seen official police weapons at such close range, or thought of them in relation to myself. "Clear out!" was the order these men gave, and slowly, those of us at the counter, the few whites blinking in disbelief, climbed off our stools.

CHAPTER NINE

WELL, THE UPSHOT of all this was that all of the Negroes, three other whites and I were herded together into the patrol wagon ("Run, Nigger, Run, the pattyrole's a-comin' " ran through my mind the whole trip) and were taken to the city jail. That obscene beast who had pushed me up on the stool in the first place was the direct cause of my being included.

"Take that 'un!" he had shouted in the midst of all the hubhub that ensued as soon as the lunchers had gotten off their seats, and to make sure "that 'un" was me, he pointed at me, and squirmed and pushed his way over to touch me, I guess, and make sure the identification was complete. When he had nabbed me, he cried, "Officer, officer. This 'un's one!" and cleared his throat; he had a great deal to say.

The officer, looking quite bored, looked me over like a man who is tired of catching runaway slaves. I spoke right up, but again in an uncertain rather than an authoritative voice. "Officer, this man's been bothering me ever since I came in here."

"That's right!" my hillbilly captor answered. "Just like I aim to bother any nigger lovers!"

The officer gave him the faintest of smiles, but asked him if he'd been bothering me.

"Yeah, I been bothering her! I said so and she said so!" he exclaimed manfully. "She's one of 'em. She and that light nigger over there was even holdin' hands!" Naturally he meant Maybelle.

The officer now gave me a very official frown. It was quite frightening. "Did you come here to disrupt the peace? Are you a CORE?"

"A core?" I repeated, immediately thinking of apples, but there was no time for mind-wandering, frivolous puns, or even conjecture. And when he sternly told me what CORE was and added that what I was doing was against the law, I stared at him wide-eyed and as serious as he. "I came in here to eat," I said emphatically. "And now since it's pretty obvious I won't be able to, I'll thank you just to step aside and let me pass. I don't even know what you're talking about, you and your CORE."

He put out his arm, just like they do in the movies, and, so help me, I saw his hand settle on me in a steady restraining grip. "I think you'd better come along with us and answer a few questions," he said.

"But I've got to meet my mother!" I told him frantically.

"That's what all you nigger lovin' stuck-up white kids say when you get pinched for being members of the NAACP!" My bully cried triumphantly.

"How dare you!" I exclaimed, and breathing fire I turned to the officer and demanded that he arrest the man.

The officer was as cool as I was hot and simply said, "Now simmer down, Wilfred," to the odious creature. Then he repeated to me that he was sorry, but he was going to have to take me in to answer some questions.

Either the officer's relative politeness to me or the mild chastisement filled Wilfred with rage, for he now glared at me and snarled, "What are you, some kind of mulatto like your hand-holding friend?"

This, once again, brought down the house, and Wilfred beamed thinking the laughter was due to his cleverness. But the laughter was due to the fact that I am as blonde as a Nordic; my hair is almost as white as the sun at midday, and I am blue-eyed and fair complected. I couldn't possibly have been a mulatto, and the crowd realized this and also realized that poor Wilfred couldn't possibly have known the meaning of the word. Even the cop smiled.

But above the dying laughter one steady undiminished—and rather strange—sound of mirth continued. It was Miss Sally Sue, and she was, as we say, whooping and hollering—a thing she's famous for, especially in church. They say once she gets started she can't stop. So everybody grinned at Miss Sally Sue, and I mean everybody. For a minute there you would have thought that integration had really taken place and that we could all go home and forget about it. Then people began to look tired and their grins either turned all small and sour, or remained on their mouths like funny faces that had been pinned there and forgotten, or else they looked sober and stern, like the cop.

Miss Sally straightened her hat, which was a very fussy little velvet thing, fallen over to one side of her head, and though she still hadn't stopped laughing, she had passed her peak and the volume seemed to be going. But just as the policeman was turning back to me, she started up again, louder than ever, this time punctuating her laughs with "Whoeeee!" even as she gasped for breath.

The officer, one could see, had had enough of this, "Ma'am!" he cried, polite but exasperated, "will you shut that off?" We all agreed with him. It was as irritating as a stuck automobile horn. We all agreed, that is, but Miss Sally.

"Well! I never!" she exclaimed and advanced upon us, talking as she came, rather breathless from the exertion as she is said to suffer from heart trouble, paying about as much attention to the people who watched her, rather fascinated, as they cleared a path for her, as if those people were flowers in her garden, and she were coming down the walk speaking rather amiably yet firmly to her gardener who is about to do something wrong. "When people can't laugh in this country, I think things have gone pretty bad, young man," she informed the police officer. "And if I were you,

I'd be a little bit more picky and choosy about the *way* I requested that someone stop a distraction. You can't tell me your mother would care for you taking that harsh tone with a gentlewoman. Even though she may not be one herself, I'm sure she knows how to behave, and must have taught you to mind your manners—" and much, much more of the same.

The policeman looked first just flabbergasted, then quite angry, then uneasy, then just frustrated, for though Miss Sally Sue might have been of the opinion that she and the officer were having a private conversation, and that the rest of the company counted as much as flowers lining her garden path, the officer knew better, and he didn't care for her dressing down the least little bit; but on the other hand, he didn't seem to know what to do about it, and he personally could not wipe the grins off all the assorted faces.

"—Now I'm an old maiden lady, I'm aware of that," she was saying, her face stuck right into his for she was almost as tall as he was, "—and I may be peculiar, but I'm also particular, and I *am* a lady. Now here's my calling card." She took it from her purse, along with some other papers with such swift skill that one knew she was the kind of woman who would rather die than have a messy handbag. "—And here's my driver's license, and my charge-a-plate which, as you can see, is notched for every store in town so that proves my credit is good—"

"Look, Ma'am," the policeman finally managed to interject, but what he wanted her to look at she didn't wait to see.

"—And you can ask that nice young lady, Miss Hallie Bean Hamilton that you're holding there, and half of the darkies in here, just who I am. I come from a long, long line of—if I may say so—very distinguished Southern ladies and gentlemen, some of whose names you would recognize at once if I told you—I'm the last of my line, I regret to say—and I've never known anything all my life but the deepest respect and courtesy from a guardian of the law—

"That's all you'd get from me if you'd just—" the much rattled present guardian of the law succeeded in saying, and looked intent upon adding more, but this time it was Wilfred who snatched the microphone. "Yeah, just shut your trap!" he bellowed at Miss Sally Sue.

And then Miss Sally Sue slammed her pocketbook into his face, and all hell broke loose.

CHAPTER TEN

A s I say, all of the Negroes, three other whites and I were put in pattyrole wagons and taken down to the jail—Miss Sally Sue, Wilfred Lumpkin (Miss Sally Sue and I both giggled with pleasure over his name when he was being booked), and a Mr. Klipstein, an out-of-state department store buyer, who was detained not so much because he was the one who stepped in and kept Wilfred from hitting Miss Sally Sue back, as that he "sounded like a Yankee," had a name like a Jew, and what was he snooping around in Judson's Department store for anyhow? He was not booked on disorderly conduct, but upon suspicion.

Because the whole affair, grim as it was, had comic overtones—or maybe just because we were slightly hysterical, like people often are in crises (it's better to laugh than to cry)—Miss Sally Sue, Mr. Klipstein and I were having a rather good time. Miss Sally Sue whispered to me that she was "hugely enjoying" herself, and Mr. Klipstein, one could see, was quite amused. Wilfred, of course, was as sour as hell, and I, as I say, was hysterical. Not very, but some. But everytime I giggled I was aware of the lump in my throat, for I was really very frightened. Moreover, though I could see in a way why Miss Sally Sue found being in jail such a lark—after all, she was a *really* grown person, had lots of influence and things—but there was something about it for me that just made me feel plain dirty and exactly like a criminal. I kept telling myself I hadn't done anything, but guilt was as thick on me as a fur coat.

As for the Negroes, Maybelle included, naturally they didn't think it was very funny, and by the time we finally got to the judge, who didn't think it was at *all* funny, even Miss Sally Sue wasn't smiling anymore or craning her neck around, viewing her surroundings with that look of superior interest. The jail had everything that one thinks of a jail having—smelly bare walls, grimy with years of tobacco smoke, filthy old spittoons full of something ghastly, lots of cigarette and cigar butts around, wooden benches along the wall for the prisoners to sit on while waiting to be booked, and a desk and a few straight office-type chairs for the desk sergeant and other cops on duty. That was the jail lobby, or office, or whatever you call such a place where you are signed in. I was rather surprised that they didn't have a separate entrance for the Negroes, but they didn't seem to. I started to ask the policeman who had arrested us if Negroes and whites were kept in different parts of the jail, but then I didn't—he'd probably just think I was being sarcastic and use it as further evidence that I was a CORE or some other kind of subversive. But I did whisper to Miss Sally Sue to find out whether it was against the law to be a member of the NAACP, and she whispered back "Of course not," and then the desk sergeant told us to be quiet. We never did get to any cells though; the judge came in right away and we got taken into what I guess was a courtroom. In there the Negroes were kept on one side and the whites on the other. It rather tickled me because they made Wilfred sit right beside me; naturally he wouldn't look at me.

After the judge came in and gave us all a good scowl, sat down, and we could sit down again, he read through some papers—the charges against us, I guess—and then he and the arresting officer held a whispered conference and the judge started frowning at me. As the arresting officer went on the judge's frown got deeper and deeper. Then my name was called.

"You're in mighty serious trouble," was the first thing he said after the formal complaint was read. "How well do you know this colored girl, this Maybelle Brown?"

Why I didn't phrase it some other way, I don't know, but I said, "We're schoolmates," and he didn't like this a bit.

"You pal around together, is that it?"

This made me so damned mad I thought I would die; but instead of dying I just got defiant. I've got my daddy's stubborn streak, you know. "No!" I said quite loudly, for me that is. "We don't pal around together, but if we did it wouldn't be a crime."

"You think not?" he said.

"I most certainly do think not," I said with a catch in my voice for now I was starting to cry. "Furthermore, you make me wish I *did* pal around with Maybelle Brown! If it's not against the law for her to go to the same school, I don't know why it would be against the law for her to know me socially."

Then he started asking me a lot of questions, about what my daddy did, where he was from, and had I ever known any Negroes when I visited my Chicago relatives—a lot of questions I already knew I didn't have to answer because Miss Sally Sue, whose lawyer was already on the way and who had promised to get in touch with Daddy and also pick up Mommie if he could find her in Judson's—Miss Sally Sue had told me I didn't have to answer a thing until her lawyer got there. But I answered anyway. I wanted to. And after I told the judge I'd never been in Chicago, that all my daddy's close relatives were dead, the judge told me I was being sassy. I guess maybe I was, but I didn't care. Then he asked me a whole bunch of questions, half of which I couldn't even understand, much less repeat, about this organization and that, and warned me against mixing into things where I didn't belong and a whole lot of other rigmarole that absolutely mystified me. I kept staring at him, wondering which one was out of their mind, him or me. Couldn't he see what I was, just a nice, well-brought up Southern girl who had led a life as sheltered as his own daughter's—a person he kept hauling into the picture for comparison?

At one point, over something or other, I started vigorously shaking my head, and finally said, "It's as farfetched for you to think all these advanced, complicated ideas about me as it would probably be to have them about the daughter you're talking about."

This made him very annoyed—probably because I had said "probably," or maybe he didn't think I had any right to talk about his daughter—but anyway, after that, he didn't sound nearly so convinced. And when it was Wilfred's turn, he seemed less convinced than ever, for he shut off Wilfred's harangue about me before it even got started good, told him he hadn't been brought there as a witness, but was under arrest for disorderly conduct. While the evidence against him, or whatever you call it, was being given, Wilfred looked awfully hurt, and kept staring at his betrayer, the arresting officer. Maybe he was a betrayer too, because certainly he was on friendly terms with Wilfred. That's how we had found out his name.

Anyway, by that time Mr. Stickney, Miss Sally Sue's lawyer, had come, and after that things were wound up in a quick though a rather impressive hurry. Mr. Klipstein was let go, the charges against me and of course Miss Sally Sue were dismissed, and Wilfred got fined $50 and a terrific tongue-lashing by the judge who was obviously taking out on him the embarrassment and anger he felt over the whole thing. For Mr. Stickney did not mince words; in fact what he said was so strong that I'm surprised the judge stood for it. He kept throwing out things like "you should be disbarred for this outrage," told him precisely whom he was dealing with—meaning Miss Sally Sue, "a woman of culture, great wealth and influence" whose grandfather had been a governor of the state, and her own father a judge and couldn't he see how absurd, if not presumptuous it was to have arrested her in the first place, and then not to have had the sense to dismiss the charges as soon as he took a look at them? After all, Miss Sally Sue was doing what any Southern lady would have done to defend herself against her inferior, "this odious buffoon." And further, he went on, even the charges were wrong—it wasn't disorderly conduct at all; if anything it was assault and battery, and would have had to have been preferred by that "ignoble brute." Some of it was pretty flowery; me, for instance, he called "this lovely young debutante; one of the most popular members of society." Miss Sally Sue just smiled and smiled.

But when the judge told us all we could go, Miss Sally Sue said no, she wanted to stay and see what the judge was going to do about all those Negroes. Then the judge told her she had to go, that this was not a public hearing. And you know what she did? Nobody had had any idea what she was up to. But when the judge told her she had to leave, Miss Sally Sue Hamilton stood right up and said, speaking to Mr. Stickney, "Billy, pay that nice young colored girl's bail—Hallie's friend over there. No, on second thought, pay all their bails, the whole lot of 'em."

CHAPTER ELEVEN

OR THE FIRST TWENTY of those forty miles on the way back home Maybelle didn't say a word except "Yes'm," or "No'm," to Miss Sally Sue, who was talking a mile a minute, until Miss Sally Sue said, "Now don't tell me a smart pretty girl like you grew up in the north saying 'No'm' to people, now did you?"

Maybelle laughed and it was one of the prettiest sounds you ever heard—soft as a kitten's voice, chimey and very warm. As Miss Sally Sue said later, "It was enchanting."

Anyway, after Maybelle laughed, she said, "No, Miss Sally Sue—may I call you Miss Sally Sue?—I never said it until I came down here."

"I bet you your grandmother thought it was a good idea, hmm?"

Maybelle nodded, and smiled. "Yes, she did."

"Why, child!" Miss Sally Sue exclaimed, "if you're going to integrate, *integrate*!"

"*I* say 'no'm, Miss Sally Sue," I put in mischeviously.

"Well, you should," she said, killing my sport. "You grew up in the South, not the North. But no'm certainly is ugly. I bet you Harriet Hamilton didn't teach you that."

"She says, 'say no ma'am,'" I confessed, because Mother does object to it. "I just picked up no'm."

"Uh, huh, I can believe that," she said drily, then focused her attention once more upon Maybelle. I thought to myself: won't Mommie die when I tell her that Miss Sally Sue insisted on Maybelle's joining us to ride home?

Miss Sally Sue, as often as not, takes the bus to the city like anybody else, but since she's got this big car—a very old old-fashioned thing, a Packard—and Jimmy to drive for her (Jimmy is her cook's son and works as Miss Sally Sue's houseboy-chauffeur) she's not so concerned with the traffic problem. As long as I'm on the subject of Miss Sally Sue and her possessions, I might as well go on. First of all, she lives about halfway from town in a great big old-fashioned home on East Main Street—the kind of house that Mommie says was stylish in the last century. It's got a big verandah that runs all across the front and down both sides, is red brick with white trim, and when I say trim I mean "like man real decorated," as they say in beat talk. She lives there all by herself. I don't guess I've been in the place more than twice in my life for she and Mommie aren't close—Miss Sally Sue's way up in years—so I can't tell you how many rooms it has. But plenty. Or, as everybody says, she has too much of everything for her own good. Maybe that's why she turned eccentric.

Here's how she looks: like an effeminate warrior, and I don't mean an Amazon, but something more on the Indian side. She has coal black eyes that glitter with keen intelligence and awareness, and coal black hair that would look more real on a doll. She must dye it herself because she's never been known to go to the hairdresser's. And she gets herself up like she had not just a split personality to express but a shattered one. For instance, today she had on that tiny scrap of a velvet hat, a suit that looked like a horse blanket, and what my brother calls whore shoes: terribly high-heeled sandals with straps that tie around the ankles. She must be very vain about her tiny feet, and I guess this is the way she tries to show them off. She's a tall woman, but not a big woman, except for her stomach; this makes her look large framed. (Daddy says she is a closet drinker; that women middle aged and past swell up in the middle if they don't have a man and do have a lot to drink.) But, withal, Miss Sally Sue is not really unattractive; her features, except for those snapping eyes, are delicate and rather sweet. And I was certainly finding out that sweet was hardly the word for it; she was simply grand, amazing.

I listened to what she was telling Maybelle about her own school days. "Papa wanted me to be broad in my views, so he took me out of Ward-Belmont and sent me up North to Wellesley to finish my education. And then when he thought he had it finished, I decided it hadn't really started and I made him send me off to Europe. I went to the University of London and the University of Heidelberg, and then I said to myself: 'What is all this durn fool-ishness? You're just going to educate yourself out of existence'— because I knew Papa would never put up with my being anything more than a lady—not a lady scientist, or a lady professor, or a lady doctor, and a lady lawyer, God forbid. Broad as he was in some ways, he never could get used to the idea of ladies being anything but ladies. He wanted me to be accomplished and know something about the world, but he wanted that accomplishment not to be shown off beyond the limits of the parlor. Poor Papa. If he had lived I believe he would have realized that you can't be broad when you're narrow, but there were mighty few men of his time who didn't think the world would settle right back to what it was after the war—that's the first one I'm talking about, of course. Papa never lived to see the end of it; he died during the flu epi-demic, like so many other fine people. That was the winter of '18." She paused and looked very stern. "I guess I had what they now call an Electra complex about Papa, but that isn't why I never mar-ried. There were a half a dozen men I would have gladly married, but I guess I scared 'em off. I was too independent, and too smart. One of my beaux told me I argued just like a man." She laughed to herself. "—And *I* thought he was paying me a compliment. No siree, even now brains for women aren't really in fashion—never mind all the lip-service they get paid—when you get right down to rock bottom most men want what they call a 'womanly woman' and that means a woman who thinks—if she does—and acts like the traditional woman. So Papa's notions aren't really obsolete, they've just gone underground. And that day when I realized I was smartening myself up too much, it was already too late. Yes, girls," she ended with a sigh, "I'd have much rather had a husband—I think, though I don't know that I would have kept him long." Her eyes twinkled at the thought. "—I really don't. I don't know that I could have put up with him bossing me around and telling me not to argue with him. It was one thing with Papa—after all, he was my father and it was right that I listen to him; he was older, had more experience. But to kowtow to my own contemporary just because he was a man? Whoeee!" She gave her long whistling noise, this time denoting disgust rather than surprise.

The three of us exchanged big smiles, for we all concurred in her opinion. At least to a certain extent.

"My father was a little like that," Maybelle said, so at her ease that it didn't strike her as inappropriate to compare a black man with a white man. "He was very progressive in some ways, like wanting me to have a good education and to know all sides to a question, but he never really got over thinking of himself as a Southern Negro, and he would have been horrified at my decision to come down here and go to college."

"Would he indeed?" Miss Sally Sue returned. "Well, I needn't tell you, young woman, that a great many members of his race, as well as white people, have been and are no less so. And I'll confess that until today I went right along with them. But I've lived long enough to know that this is exactly the way prejudice and bad habits—the same thing, of course—are broken: by getting down to the individual. If every white in town could get to know you and talk to you like this—the way Hallie and I are doing this evening—segregation in one Southern town, at least, would have been struck a serious blow. You know," she cocked her head speculatively at Maybelle, "I don't know that I ought not to sponsor you. Have a big party, say."

Smiling, Maybelle began to shake her head. "No, Miss Sally Sue. First of all, nobody would come if word got around that I was to be there, no matter how prominent you are. And even if they did, they'd know you were stuffing me down their throats and resent you for it. Even if I were taken up, they wouldn't take me up for myself. I'd be some kind of freak to them—a one-of-a-kind deal. It wouldn't strike any blows for integration; it might set it back a whole lot. No, whatever is done I have to do for myself in that town. Otherwise, it wouldn't be lasting, wouldn't mean a thing."

Miss Sally Sue patted one of Maybelle's golden hands. "You're very wise, my dear. You've got a good head as well as a mighty pretty one on your shoulders, but—" and she gave Maybelle a broad grin "—take care that the pretty one is more visible to the boyfriends than the wise one, or you may end up without a husband too."

Maybelle shook her head again, looking serious. "I don't think so, Miss Sally Sue. Young white men may not be interested in having their girls as smart as they should be, but the young men of my race can't afford—yet—" (and here she smiled) "the luxury of wasting brains and talent. We need all we can get. And I don't have to tell you there's little enough as it is—anywhere in the world, but especially in the black world. The black man let himself be used and intimidated too long—and it's not altogether the fault of the whites either. People who allow themselves to be exploited for as long as we have are more than just ignorant and naive; something in them wants it that way. My race suffers from mass masochism which has been aided and abetted by ignorance, simple-mindedness, and downright laziness and stupidity—a condition of being that the majority of any race has to combat. I can't think that any intelligent Negro, not riddled with prejudice himself, can blame our lot entirely on the white race, or even really fail to understand, if not actually cease to blame the white race for exploiting us. It's true that slavery was evil, but the whites were by no means the only ones who practised slavery—it still goes on elsewhere today, and more often than not the slavers are blacks enslaving blacks, or at least what the world has come to think of as 'coloreds.' In any primitive yet arrogant and materialistic society, slavery is a natural phenomena, and, because selfishness is the hardest human trait to control, slavery can even exist in cultures that are relatively advanced."

"Yes, the Greeks, of course," Miss Sally Sue murmured, quite impressed.

"If I were ignorant, poor and stupid and was married to a man who beat me, I would stay with him, let him beat me to his heart's desire, and even, perhaps, enjoy it whether I was a masochist by nature or not; I'd think it an expression of his love—unfortunately, it's true that people can get used to anything and read love into something that is really hate or a number of other negative things. Then again, if I were poor, ignorant but smart and not at all masochistic by nature, I might stay married to the same man, but not for the same reasons. I wouldn't lack the imagination or intelligence to leave him, but I would lack the means; my ignorance would render me a cripple. If I left him, where would I go? Certainly not to something better. So the whole thing is a matter, in the end, of education—seeing to it that those who are capable of being educated are educated. That's why I have yet to meet a serious intelligent boy of my own race who doesn't believe women shouldn't pitch in and help. It's going to be. slow enough at best for intelligence is not only a rarity among races, but intelligence capable of sloughing off prejudices is, well—" She made an empty gesture, giving us a charming smile.

"You're a most remarkable girl. Where did you get all that?" Miss Sally Sue asked.

"Well, lately," Maybelle said looking at me in a sly but friendly way, "I've been getting a lot of it in Dr. Hamilton's psychology class."

"Maybe I'd better sign up for his course," I said, rather awestruck.

"Maybe I'd better too," Miss Sally Sue said, smirking at her own humor, and now patted both of our hands. We all smiled at each other in satisfaction again.

"This may sound funny," I said, feeling my way along, "but what I want to know is, what can we do to help? Back there with that judge, when he asked me if we 'paled around together'—" I paused, my frankness making me feel flustered "—what I mean is, when I told him I sort of wished we did, well, I sort of meant it, Maybelle."

She gave me a benign smile, good humor crinkling her startling blue eyes. "Same thing goes for you as for Miss Sally Sue's party. If you and I openly became friends, there would be no end to it. No, the two of you have done enough; you've given me something that every person needs—especially in a strange town—the knowledge that I am liked and that you have an understanding of me."

"But the better one knows a person, the better the understanding," I said, feeling rather intelligent.

"Not necessarily," Miss Sally Sue remarked crisply. "There are too many other elements involved—where's your Shakespeare, child? Don't you know that familiarity breeds contempt?"

"Not always," I countered.

"Of course not," Maybelle hastened to say. "But I think Miss Sally Sue's right; that understanding of a person, or an idea either, for that matter, doesn't necessarily grow through proximity."

"Education again," I commented.

"Yes, that and good old down-to-earth brains and initiative—or being educatable, as Maybelle put it," Miss Sally Sue said with not unkind asperity. "Just use what sense you have, child, and you'll help Maybelle Brown a lot more than you would trying to get her a bid to your sorority on the grounds that she's your friend. But there're some questions I want to ask you, Maybelle," she said turning to her. "Just where did you get so smart? I know all your family, have all my life, and I knew your father when he was a little boy, and they were all enterprising members of their race up to a certain point, but except for your father—and some of your kin were by no means uneducated—not one of them had the slightest desire to go up North or somewhere where they really had a chance. Not that I could see," she added just to be on the safe side, for she was a reasonable woman with a respect for accuracy, and she couldn't know too much about the inner desires, slight or great, of Maybelle's people.

"You said 'up North or somewhere,' " Maybelle answered genially. "But up until quite recent times much of the North was as badly prejudiced against the Negro in its own way as the Southerners. Yes, Colored people could move among whites, eat in the same places, ride the same bus and all that, but that was the nearest thing I can think of as a literal example of what Booker T. Washington believed the solution: equal but separate. The Northern Negro was shunned—still is widely—he had equal rights but he was socially separate. He was treated by the white people the same way they treat their own outcasts—the hopelessly deformed, the public drunkard, the village idiot, the man with an awful disease visibly consuming him, the bums on the Bowery—"

"Yes," Miss Sally Sue put in reflectively. "I've seen 'em—I get up to New York once in a while and kick up my heels. But it's long been my contention, child—stop me if I'm wrong—that the Southern opinion that the Negroes *want,* indeed crave, intermarriage and socializing is just not so. I was of the opinion that the Negro preferred his own people."

"You're absolutely right," Maybelle told her. "And the day will come when being as light as I am is no longer a status symbol. People my color will simply be light people and accepted as such, in the same way that blondes, brunettes and redheads among the white people are simply accepted as variations on the theme. But that day, no matter what happens, won't be tomorrow. It takes a long time for an ugly duckling to get used to the fact that he's no longer ugly and undesirable. Negroes don't want to fraternize in the headlong fashion that most people imagine, just as you say. But they do want the right of refusal. After they got used to the fact that they were no longer social poison, they'd have no desire to gate-crash the white world. No secure person, for instance, goes to every party he's invited to simply because he's invited. That's why I think assimilation, if it ever really happened, would take thousands of years.

"But you asked me about Daddy and his family. He always used to say—he's dead now, you know—"

"I *didn't* know," Miss Sally Sue put in. "I'm sorry to hear it. When did he pass away?"

"This last August," Maybelle replied. "That's why I came down here. There was no where else to go. Like you, I was an only child, and my mother died when I was thirteen—"

"You poor child," Miss Sally Sue said in genuine sympathy. "No wonder! But what was wrong with your daddy? As a child he was such a healthy little fellow."

"Cancer," Maybelle said. "But I was going to tell you what Daddy used to say on the subject of Negroes running away from the South: The lucky ones, according to him, are better off up North—the lucky, smart and educated ones—but the unlucky, even smart and educated, and naturally the unlucky are the majority, are sometimes worse off, and if they're lazy as well, they're usually much, much worse off and, being natively intelligent and having other qualifications, inclined to become rabidly embittered. They, often, are the ones the whites call 'mean niggers' and uppity ones. And as for going somewhere else, there are not many somewhere elses to go to. The Negro is accepted in Europe—or was before the Second World War—with something like normality, though the acceptance there also leaves a lot to be desired. But how many people, black or white, can afford to go to Europe? No, the only answer, up until 1954, was to be bright, well-bred, educated and lucky—and to live up North. Daddy was one of the lucky ones—at least I always thought he was until after he died and I found there was practically no money after all—he was a doctor, and a good one. He had a good private practice and was connected with a large hospital in Philadelphia. But you know, as I said, for all his learning and common sense, he was still a Southern Negro at heart. I went to a very good boarding school, for instance, but it was a Negro boarding school, and we were taught to be little snobs, but little Negro snobs, and most of us were violently anti-white. If I didn't have a block against it, I might remember the words to one of the songs we used to sing in chapel—the song was so strongly tinged with black arrogance that it was almost a war cry against the white race."

"I wish you could remember it," Miss Sally Sue said. "I'd be interested in hearing it."

"Maybe I'll be able to think of it," Maybelle said, then paused a moment before getting back on the subject of her father.

"He even wanted me to go to a Negro university," she said thoughtfully. "But I refused to. We had an awful fight about it. That's why I went to a teacher's college, instead of a school with really high scholastic standards. I knew I would have to work my way through and the tuition was smaller, and being an in-state resident—the college I went to was in central Pennsylvania—it was less expensive than a teacher's college in New York or some-where else."

"But why did you refuse to go to a Negro school?" Miss Sally Sue asked curiously.

Maybelle sighed. "All my life, because of Daddy, I never saw anything but Negroes, Negroes, and more Negroes. My mother, who was half white, couldn't even go to see her own father in New York. That's how emphatic he was. And we never had Negroes as servants—always Irish women, or Poles. But they were the only whites who ever came to the house. And, as I began to grow up, I got curious about white people—after all, they were all around me—and the only ones I knew were, as Daddy said, 'below my station.' And also I was curious about my grandparents—on both sides. I wanted to know what they were like. I wanted to know my white grandfather, even if he was, as Daddy said, 'just a Greenwich Village bum.' I guess the Greenwich Village aspect made him more exciting and romantic to me than even the fact that he was different from us, lived, at least partially in the white world. But I never saw him," she said wistful with regret. "He died not long before Mother did. I think the fact that Daddy wouldn't let her go to the funeral helped kill her as much as anything else."

"There are hard men everywhere," Miss Sally Sue told her with sympathetic tact, "and pigmentation doesn't seem to have much to do with it. But I hope you and your father got to be friends again. No?"

Maybelle was shaking her head. "No. Because I added insult to injury by sneaking off the summer of my freshman year and coming down here to see my grandmother—you see, he wouldn't let me have anything to do with his people either; said they would either turn me into a handkerchief head like themselves, or else—and to him equally degrading—turn me into a sort of Negro Emma Goldman, make me so fighting mad that I'd forget my station—that word again—and betray my class."

"Just what is your class?" Miss Sally Sue asked her with unmasked interest.

"At school? Or do you mean socially? But I'll answer both: I'm in my junior year of college now, and socially—well, I was brought up as a sort of Main Liner, Negro variety, of course."

"My heavens!" Miss Sally Sue exclaimed.

"Yes, it's so. There is such a thing. And in Philadelphia it was on quite an elaborate scale. And, as a matter of fact, this is true in all large cities. Even Southern ones. Don't imagine," she said looking from Miss Sally Sue to me, "that this is my first trip South. I have boarding school friends all over, and I used to visit them. You'd be really quite surprised at the elegance and the affluence in which they are able to live, even down South. Up North, naturally, it's much easier. But there are still plenty of Negroes who own simply huge estates in the South that may have once belonged, who knows? to people who had their ancestors for slaves." She laughed aloud thinking about it, and it was the first sign I had seen of anything like jeering at us, or hostility. But she quickly went on. "But of course to buy such a place takes a lot of doing, and I'm not sure it's worth it. In a way, I envy my grandmother's kind of upper class—I mean my grandmother Brown—it's small, it's provincial, but she is the unquestioned ruler of Negro society and she doesn't have to compete or play any tricks."

And just then Miss Sally Sue yawned. Sensitive Maybelle noticed it at once. "I'm talking my head off," she said apologetically. "Neither of you has been able to say a word."

"Neither of us has wanted to," Miss Sally Sue said, patting her mouth apologetically. "You forget—or maybe you don't—that I'm an old woman, and old people tire easily. But that's my body I'm speaking for, not my mind or my heart. Both of them are with you. And utterly fascinated. Just to prove it, here we are passing Perkins' Filling Station, see? almost home. But before we get there, I want you to tell me how I can help—you in particular, but also all other young people like you. Would you advise me to give a larger contribution to the NAACP? I've been sending them a check for years, you know."

"You have?" I asked incredulously, and blurted before I could stop myself, "I thought you were a Republican and for States' Rights."

Well, she just nearly died laughing at me. "I am, child," she said. "But that doesn't mean that I never vote for a Democrat when he's the right man, and it doesn't mean, just because I'm generally a States' Righter, that I think they're always *right!* It's just that until I met Maybelle here I was convinced that our states should be allowed to make their own mistakes in their own way. I've been for integration for years—oh, any fool could see it was coming, it had to because justice, being really common sense, in the end usually prevails. But it made me mad as a wet hen the way that Supreme Court was so highhanded. Why didn't they take a national vote on it first? And, as so many people, I don't like to talk politics with, say: if they can take away our rights on this issue, what's to stop them from taking away all others? This issue I've never quarreled with; you must know me well enough by now to realize I believe it is morally wrong to deprive any people whatsoever of their human rights and dignities, their rights to thrive as their individual talents allow them. Oh, no. I've always been a great supporter of the NAACP, and firmly intend to continue to be until the day I die. Does that please you, Maybelle?" she asked, turning from me.

Maybelle smiled a cryptic little smile. "Money won't do everything," she said, "but it always helps."

With Miss Sally Sue promising to send the NAACP a big fat check, we dropped Maybelle at home and drove on, for the most part semi-silent. But there was one thing bothering me about this whole astonishing afternoon, and I decided to just out with it. "Miss Sally Sue, I don't know how to ask you, but I just have to ask you—and it doesn't make sense now after all that has happened—you see, I just didn't know the first thing about the kind of person you really are—I thought you were as desegregation as anybody else around here and would rather die than sit in the back seat of an automobile with a Negro, socially that is, and—"

"Well that's not your question, surely, child," she put in rather forbearingly, but sounding quite tired.

"No, it isn't," I confessed. "My question is, why back there at Judson's lunch counter did you give me such a stern disapproving look when I was crying and Maybelle let me hang onto her hand?"

"Why, baby," she said with compassion that was nearly pity. "Don't you know I'm blind as a bat without my spectacles except when I get up close? I didn't even recognize you as Harriet's daughter until I came up to where you were standing with that policeman and gave him a piece of my mind."

CHAPTER TWELVE

WHEN WE STOPPED in front of my house and Jimmy got out and held the door open for me, I nervously saw that not only was the front porch light on, but the whole place was blazing with lights—which meant great excitement inside, and probably trouble. "Now call me up real soon," Miss Sally Sue said again, putting her small beringed hand out the window for me to squeeze again. "And I'll telephone Harriet tomorrow morning." And once more I thanked her and then watched them drive off, feeling reluctant for some reason to go inside and face whatever there was to face, and feeling lonely like a hitch-hiker put out on a deserted highway to wait in the blue twilight, all by himself, for some unknown salvation to help him toward his destiny. What was my destiny, I wondered as I went slowly up the sidewalk? And what, tomorrow, could Miss Sally Sue say to Mommie that would soften what I knew with dread would be her bitter rage? I was in for it. Mommie would somehow blame me for everything just to keep the stain of guilt from her own hands; that was the way she was.

And I wasn't wrong. In the living room Daddy was pacing up and down, looking worried; Bill and Aunt Sophie Craddock and my Uncle Percy Bean were talking in lowered tones over near the dining room French doors, and Aunt Stell was hurrying toward the back part of the house. It was exactly as if they were all waiting for my mother to produce a baby, or to die. The whole scene, from which my mother was conspicuously absent, spelled sickness, and even before they saw me or said anything I knew the doctor had been or was still in with my mother; that she had taken to her bed. If I had expected—or yearned for—a pair of comforting maternal arms in my hour of need, I would have had to be another kind of me. I knew—yes, I absolutely knew—that she would walk off with the show and turn the whole thing to her advantage. She had to. As I say, that was the way she was. That's why I had entered the house softly, since I had to enter it at all. For a second there, it actually occurred me to tiptoe out, rush to the highway and hitch-hike my way in the blue twilight to a new destiny; damnation or salvation, what did it matter?

But, instead, I said in a small voice, "Hello."

Bill whipped around, my aunt and uncle stiffened their postures, and my sweet Daddy took me in his arms and kissed me lightly on my forehead. "Oh, Daddy!" I cried out, and Aunt Sophie immediately shushed me.

"Your mother's finally gotten quiet," she advised me with a look that was three parts suspicion to two parts sympathy.

"She's resting in the downstairs guestroom," Daddy said in a hushed voice. And indicated that we should go into the dining room where we could talk without being overheard. The three of them rather led me along, keeping an eye on me, as if I were too backward to proceed without their guidance, or else they saw the need to protect me from my own fear and my desire to escape. But who wouldn't have felt shy and scared? For I knew well enough what was coming; the pressure of my father's arms had somehow conveyed the pressure that had come before: I knew that my mother had made a violent and loud scene from the time she had hit the house until the migraine headache and Dr. Spears had consigned her to her bed. Her version of the day and what had happened—not so much to me as to her—had been all my fault; the result of my wilful and bad behavior.

So I listened to what they said: Uncle Percy, wearing his hurt dignity like war decorations to the court martial of a kinsman turned traitor; my Aunt Sophie, who is a great talker anyway, twittering and chattering like a nervous bird, alternatingly scolding me and telling me that I was a "poor little ole mess, too young to know what I'd gotten into;" and Bill saying, with biting contempt, that I made him "sick." Only Daddy seemed willing to postpone judgment until I had my say, and of course I couldn't even do this while they were so busy telling me what had happened; what they were so *certain* had happened, because Mommie had said so. At last, when they'd quieted down, Daddy stepped in to present in coherence the case against me. I felt that he was putting it rather more strongly than he actually felt in order to satisfy the others.

"Hallie, your mother reached home in a state of hysteria, and I can't say that I blame her. Now, I know that you must have some explanation for having taken part in that sit-in strike—and, wait a minute, don't interrupt—I believed, as I'm sure your mother would have if she hadn't seen better with her own eyes, that you were the innocent victim Mr. Stickney said you were when he telephoned me—"

"What did she see?" I interrupted all the same. But he continued in his own slow way.

"We'll get to that," he told me. "But before we do, I want to say this: if you are, as your mother now believes, part of an organized group of misguided young whites prepared to fight with passive resistance, or any other kind, side by side with the Negroes in this state, I think you have 'been had,' as Bill put it when we were discussing it earlier. I agree with your Aunt Sophie that you don't know—can't know—what you've gotten yourself into, or what you are letting the rest of us in for—and the worst of it is that you will end up by hurting the very people you have now so rashly decided to save when, with equal rashness, early this fall you were all for having me resign from the university unless our Negro student could be barred from the school. I am to blame if you interpreted my behavior as an encouragement to go to such lengths. Above all, you must remember who you are and what you are, and that your first duties belong to your own kind. I disagree with your mother about your behavior earlier in the day—on the bus, and then again with that Negress and her children who were turned away by the taxi driver; I don't think she was right in what she did, and I certainly don't think she was right in saying that your attitude was 'proof' that you had 'lured' her to the city on a shopping spree simply as a guise to attend a sit-in strike that had been planned well in advance. I think her mortification made her jump to conclusions. But she did see you, Hallie, with her own eyes; sitting there with the Negroes, eating a sandwich."

"Eating a sandwich," I murmured, overwhelmed by the picture that formed in my mind of the whole scene . . . how it must have really been, had I at the time had the eyes to see it: those poor Negroes! so solemn, so full of fearful calm, the bravery that is the aura fashioned by cowardice when cowardice has been overcome by purpose and conviction. I saw how their purple-black, their brown-black, their sand-black hands must have trembled as they lifted their few trophies to their mouths—the few cups of coffee and sandwiches initially served by the confused waitresses before the organized Wilfred types had come in. Yes, that was the picture, the early picture, the one before I had participated in the group shot. And if my mother *had* actually seen me, then whatever she had felt at the time, whatever heady poisonous outrage had raced in to blind her, had rendered her incapable of seeing me, for I hadn't been eating a sandwich. I was never served. I said this to my father.

"Are you telling the truth, Hallie, or just being evasive?"

"What difference does it make?" I asked harshly. "But for the record I was not eating a sandwich. I wasn't even sitting there because I wanted to. I didn't—I tried to get away. I don't know who—who you'd believe—I could get to back me up, but as soon as I saw all those poor Negroes and what they were doing, I tried to get out—"

Daddy shook his head at me. "Now be careful what you say, Hallie. There's no use to lie. If you've joined up in some kind of pro-Negro sit-in group, you can simply back out. I *know* how young people are, and you should know that—but don't forget, there are healthier and happier ways to find excitement, and you'd better leave justice to more mature minds than your own—"

"Daddy, Daddy, Daddy!" I pleaded and sobbed. "Why won't you listen to me, why won't you believe me?"

"I'll listen to you, Hallie; that's what we're here for," he said quietly. "But you must remember your mother saw you sitting there."

"But why did she jump to the conclusion that I *wanted* to be there? Why did you?"

Aunt Sophie looked away, Uncle Percy looked at Aunt Sophie, Bill looked straight at me, his eyes blazing away like space guns, and Daddy shrugged and wet his lips uncertainly. "Wouldn't you have been tempted to conclude much the same thing, if it had been a friend of yours, say, who had been displaying pro-Negro sympathies?"

"Pro-Negro sympathies!" I cried. "Simple human decency!"

"That may be," Daddy said with a nod. "But I think your mother had a point. But tell us what happened—how it all came about."

"Why don't you call Mr. Stickney? Or, better still, Miss Sally Sue? Maybe you'll feel better relying on them?"

"I did call Mr. Stickney," Daddy admitted coolly. "He told me all he knew. But of course he was not at the lunch counter himself, so he simply took Miss Sutherland's word that you were not involved. And of course he assured me that even if you were, he and Miss Sutherland would have done exactly as they did on your behalf. He has children of his own, and has some under-standing—Now, Hallie, don't start crying again," Daddy said. But I had started to cry again.

"Go call Miss Sally Sue right now," I sobbed. "I don't care if it is late, and—"

"No, hon. In the morning will be soon enough. You're not on trial here. We simply want to know what happened. We are all prepared to accept your explanation if you're going to be the honest girl I know you to be—"

"Shut up!" I bawled, and then I said to him—to all of them—insulting things I never thought I could say. I'd never been disrespectful to a grown person before in my life, I tried to shame them for trying to shame me, for having so little consideration as to add this inquisition to the ordeal that had gone before, for their prejudice against me for no reason—all based on that one fleeting glimpse my mother had taken of me, before she walked out on me, virtually throwing me to the dogs.

Then as Aunt Sophie, having risen from her seat, her eyes glittering with anger, began to babble about how my poor stricken mother had fainted in the restroom at Judson's, and how Aunt Sophie would never know how "Poor Harriet ever had the courage to get herself on that bus and start home" my poor sick frightened humiliated disgraced put-upon mother made her appearance. In her dressing gown, but still wearing her make-up, her long ash-blonde hair unleashed for the night, but flatteringly hanging like a young girl's about her face. She made an entrance from the back hallway, serene as an angel, if not exactly as free from worldly care. "I know you didn't mean to disturb me, but I'm rather glad you did," she said in her natural speaking voice. Then she came over and put her arm around me and her face next to mine. "Poor little Hallie," she said. "What a terrible time! What a day we've had! Daddy, you are being hard on her," she straightened up and said to my father. "Maybe she wasn't actually eating a sandwich. Maybe I was just so upset I thought she was."

And she took a seat at the dining room table to listen to my testimony.

My testimony seemed to have the effect of boring everybody, except Daddy who looked at me with sad troubled eyes. Mommie,

I could tell, wasn't even bothering to pretend to follow my story; she just kept nodding with a soft dazed look that said, "I forgive you." Apparently she had heard all she needed to hear from the hallway. Bill I was boring for reasons of his own, dark and possibly resentful ones, but his face registered the same degree of disinterest as my aunt's and uncle's, if not the same kind, and once he solicitously leaned over to Mommie and asked her if she was sure she felt well enough to sit with us, and Aunt Sophie, glad for a chance to speak, asked Mommie if Dr. Spears had left her enough sleeping tablets for the night, for wouldn't it be better if she went to bed again? Daddy and Uncle Percy refrained from taking advantage of this impromptu intermission—why, I don't know; but had all of my audience turned away from me in side conversations I know I would have gone on anyway. I have never felt such a compulison to get something off my chest, and to be painstakingly precise about it. At least this was true for the first quarter of my narrative, which carried me over the ground Mother had already covered—the bus incident and the taxi incident (and what care I took to be thorough and objective!) Then I reported my steps from the bus station to the lunchroom, described my repugnance for what I found, which brought me to Wilfred.

This was the second quarter and my listeners, one and all sat up and took notice. It's amazing what a spell, what nasty magic can be evoked, by the recreation of violence—and that pun is intended. When I told them how this uncouth, stout stranger laid hands upon me, bullied me, used me to help him in his horrid work, they all began to murmur and cluck. "Po' little innocent thing" "The dirty son-of-a-bitch—excuse me, Mother" (this from Bill) "My precious lamb!" "Why, hon, why didn't you say so in the first place?" So there was no longer any question of my guilt; no longer the least trace of antagonism. I was loved; I was a member of the family once more. And I continued my story to its superb end (deleting Maybelle now, where I had been so diligently honest before) and my loved ones sat stunned, awed. And I, too, sat stunned, but not by my heroism but because I felt slightly sick; rather much as I had early in the day over Mother's actions, only more so, for now the defection was compounded.

Nor was I proud of myself. While they cooed and clucked over me, while my mother (sick as she was) went herself to ask Aunt Stell to bring a supper tray to my room, for she was putting me to bed right away, I couldn't get over my self-accusation for pruning my story. Why shouldn't I have included the part about having groped for Maybelle Brown's hand, and admitted I held onto it for strength once I found it? It was a natural enough mistake, if mistake it was. Why hadn't I told them exactly how I had sassed the judge who had accused me of "paling around" with Maybelle Brown? Instead, I had cravenly led them to believe I'd almost denied knowing her. And, of course, I had left out the fact that Miss Sally Sue had given Maybelle a lift—along with me—back to town, and this was the only piece of editorial wisdom I could honestly claim. Already, I was doubtful of my decision to include the fact that Miss Sally Sue had stood bail for all those Negroes. Eccentric though she was, and privileged, I wondered how long it would be before some one of them commented upon her capriciousness. And, sure enough, it wasn't two seconds before Aunt Sophie left off her laying on of hands, so to speak, and, fondling her own untidy coiffeur instead, said musingly, "Wonder what possessed Sally Sue Sutherland to pay all those Nigras' bail? Must have cost her a lot of money for that little joke." (My Aunt Sophie is old enough to be allowed to drop the "Miss" from in front of Sally Sue.)

"She's a headstrong woman," Uncle Percy said. "One of these days she's going too far."

"Maybe she's already gone," said my brother and looked to my father to corroborate. But Daddy was restored to his accustomed equanimity.

He was relaxing with his pipe now, the court being adjourned, and he shook his head thoughtfully and said, "No, son. I don't agree. Why shouldn't she have helped them out? She can afford to, and eventually they would have been released anyway."

"Yeah, to stage some more sit-in strikes," my brother said in disgust. "She was just helping 'em. Dumb old thing."

"Well, she is getting on," my father agreed. "But she's not dumb."

"Why, Henry, she must be senile to have done a thing like that!" Aunt Sophie sided with Bill.

"Maybe so," my father agreed. "But I'm sure she didn't mean any harm." And then Uncle Percy, who can never pass up the opportunity for using a platitude, sententiously gave us the one about hell being paved with good intentions, looking as pleased with himself as if he had made an epigram, and my mother returned on the tail end of it; naturally, he had to repeat it for her benefit, and all of them wagged their heads at him to indicate that truer words had never been spoken.

CHAPTER THIRTEEN

ODDLY ENOUGH, it was Mommie who put in a clemency plea for Miss Sally Sue; one that seemed to do the trick. "Now, don't you all go spreading it all over town that Miss Sally Sue did this. I expect she just got carried away with herself—you know how she is; she always wants to be the center of the stage—and after that good blessing out Mr. Stickney gave the judge, I expect she just wanted to show everybody that she could go him or anyone one better."

"You may be right," Aunt Sophie conceded. "But I still think Sally Sue should exercise more judgement. Wonder if it will be in the papers?"

"Mr. Stickney said not," I informed them.

"You mean the whole thing's going to be hushed up? How can that ber?" Bill demanded. "I think the public should know the Nigras have started their sit-in strikes in this part of the state."

"If you'd read the papers more carefully, son," my father said mildly, "you'd see that there have been two previous sit-in incidents—one before at Judson's and one at a ten-cent store."

"Wonder if there haven't been a lot more hushed up like this one's going to be," Bill grumbled.

"Probably," Daddy said.

"Well, I think it ought to be in the papers," said Bill, rather fierce again. "Why don't you call Mr. Stickney, Dad?"

"Part of it may be in the papers," Dad replied. "What I expect will happen is that they will withhold the names of the white people involved. What did Mr. Stickney say, exactly, Hallie?"

"I'm not sure," I said. "I'm just repeating what Miss Sally Sue said he said just before we left—there was lots of confusion; everybody was leaving at once, and he had to stay behind and arrange about the bails—"

"You mean they let all those Nigras go before the money was actually put up?" Bill asked indignantly. "Just on that old lady's word? If she's all that influential, my Lord!"

"I don't know," I said dimly. "I wasn't paying too much attention to anything except leaving and getting home—"

"My, think of all those happy darkies!" it suddenly occured to Aunt Sophie to remark. She's fond of sentiment in any form.

"Yeah, laughing to themselves about what a fool that old woman was to get 'em off scot free," Bill said, looking at me as if it were all my doing somehow. Then he asked craftily, "How come if you left first you didn't beat Mr. Stickney home? Dad talked to him a good half hour before you came in."

For a moment I went blind with terrified guilt. Had he somehow divined that Miss Sally Sue's generosity had been more extensive than I had indicated? Did he suspect that we had carried Maybelle Brown home?

"Now, stop taking that tone with her, brother," my father saw fit to say in my defense. "Mr. Stickney warned me they wouldn't make as good time as he did. Miss Sutherland doesn't like to drive fast."

"Like hell she doesn't!" my brother snorted. "Ever jumped up on the curb to save your skin when she's driving that Triumph sports car of hers?"

This broke the tension, and everybody had a good laugh about that, because Miss Sally Sue, driving her sports car much too fast, was one of the town's dangerous curiosities. But all agreed that she probably felt differently about speed when she herself was not at the wheel. And on this note, Mommie rose and said she was going to trundle me off to bed, tuck me in, see that I ate my supper, then lights out. "No TV for you tonight, dear, and no reading in bed either; not even homework." She patted my cheek almost playfully, her eyes shining with affection. She looked very young and happy, and the last glimpse I caught of Daddy as, arms about each other's waists, we mounted the stairs, was a long look of love—not for both of us, but for her—and if I'd ever doubted before that they still went to bed together, I did not now. But it didn't make me feel funny, not as it might have if I'd seen such a sign of naked desire on his face even hours before. It just made me feel more outcast and, yes, sick at my stomach.

But I'd had enough self-expression for one day, so I did something I'm rarely able to do: when Mommie urged and coaxed me to eat a good supper, I forced myself to eat a good supper. After all, I could always throw up later.

And when, just before she snapped the lights off, she made her first reference to her part of the blame in all this whoop-de-do—"I realized when I overheard Daddy and the others getting after you, thinking you could be in on that Nigra plan, I immediately thought to myself, 'Why, the very ideal My little Hallie?' and hon, I was so ashamed of myself. I should have come right in the lunchroom and taken you right home—" I let her stumble along unhelped, feeling as unmoved as a stone. She paused, of course, expecting me to say something, and I don't think she expected anything nice, for her voice was heavy with shame. When I didn't answer, she switched off the lights; it was obvious to me that she preferred the dark for the rest of her speech. "You know how upset I can get," she continued sadly. "And everything was so upsetting today, and I was so exasperated with you for not meeting me up in the suits like we'd planned—Well, good night, Hallie. Never think that Mommie doesn't love you." I heard her sigh.

Then on sudden inspiration I called out, "Mommie, did anybody in that crowd tell you I was one of the sit-inners?"

There was a long silence. "Yes," she said at last. "Some great big vulgar man—I—I'm afraid it might have been the same one who—." She had definitely broken off her confession; she had gone as far as she could go.

"I thought so," I said evenly. "Well, good night, Mother."

"Hallie?"

"Yes?"

"You're sure you're all right?"

What was I to say? especially with a big lump of self-pitying tears suddenly clogging my throat. So I didn't answer. I gulped to myself in the dark, feeling my cheeks streaming with tears, feeling them run down my neck onto the pillow, knowing that even now she was rushing toward me to embrace me, to comfort me, and the tears would tell her how hurt I was. I tensed myself for it, trying to dry my face with my hands, trying not to sob out loud.

I don't know how long I stayed in my brace of self-control, but it was long enough to make my muscles ache. And then I realized that she wasn't coming, that somewhere in my moment of agony she had quietly gone away. "Mommie, Mommie!" I cried aloud. But when you're downstairs you can't hear upstairs.

I cried for hours; sometimes because she had gone off and left me and sometimes because I couldn't make myself leap out of bed and hurtle off to find her—in the guestroom asleep by herself? in their room in bed together, perhaps even making love? Or were they all in the living room talking me over together? I knew Bill had not come upstairs—he never went to bed early. Had he gone out? I hadn't heard his car, but then I'd been too busy crying to have heard it. At each of these ponderings, which diverted my mind for a few frantic seconds, my tears would magically stop only to start afresh as soon as the impact of emotional meaning hit me. Examine it how I may—and I kept trying to sensibly remind myself that it would all appear differently in the morning's light—I knew a whole host of dirty, unspeakable things about me and about those people downstairs who said—who probably even believed—they loved me. Loved me! What a laugh. And my father a psychology professor! That was the funniest thing of all. And to think Maybelle Brown had been heartened, had learned, had trusted in what he said! It made me choke with laughter even though I was crying harder than ever. Then I would grow still again, filled with philosophical conjectures about how everybody has to grow up, and eighteen wasn't too tender an age for learning not only that that stout silver cord is not silver, but is as intangible as ectoplasm, and about as necessary. Who wanted to be forever a lamb in its mother's bosom? Who wanted to worship one's father like an idol? After all, they were just people—weak, mixed-up, feckless people. Couldn't I accept that? No! And I would break out in deep terrible sobs all over again.

I go into my travail in all its nuances for reasons which I hope are obvious. If my mother had not been quite such a hysterical coward, so eager to maintain her shining faultless surface, so little caring or so gauche in hiding her true indifference to me; if my father had not been the pussy-footing, small-minded mock liberal he had showed himself, had not so willingly himself lifted the ax to the image he had deliberately caused me, encouraged me to create of him; had not so easily yet profoundly failed to see the wisdom of sticking by me at this crucial time, even though it might mean a temporary disloyalty, a seeming disloyalty to his wife—the obvious queen of his heart—if, if and if. In other words, this had been the night of the parade of the clay feet, a triumphal march. That I had lain in their path simply had not mattered to anyone. I wasn't even sure anyone had noticed it. I had always known that my brother was grossly insensitive—even my scarcely less sensitive mother mildly rebuked him sometimes for this; but I had thought Daddy valued me, and that he would tenderly, sensitively protect me always. Upon consideration, I decided that all in all my brother was the best of the three: at least he was honest; his only use for me was to tease me, love me he did not, had never pretended to. He was too spoiled, too selfish, too certain of his position as son and first born to need to participate in a mock sibling affection, and he intended to guard and defend that position with all his power.

What beasts they all were!

And I went to sleep crying softly to myself over this, desolate at being unloved, yet soul-sick that I had ever wanted to be.

CHAPTER FOURTEEN

I F THE NEXT DAY had been dreary, threatening rain or pouring with it, perhaps my springs of suffering would have continued to overflow. But when I saw how the sun was shining, not in its usual bleak wintry way, but as if a new season had come, I got out of bed hardly conscious of the bad night I had had with myself. For a moment before I went in to run my bath, I paused, smitten with black sorrow, but the turgid springs refused to flow. "Oh, well," I said aloud and shrugged my shoulders, thinking it was nice to feel so rested for a change, wishing I had thought the night before to ask someone during a lull in all that theatrical hubbub if Pete had called. I was getting fonder and fonder of Pete. Then I saw the time by my electric clock on the bedside table and knew I'd have to make a dash for it. And as I rushed through my bath I worried more because I hadn't studied for my geology test than I did about anything that had happened the day before.

I got dressed, went leaping down the stairs, and halfway down called, "Mommie, Mommie!" remembering in a great frenzy that she'd have to write me an excuse for cutting ole fool Dr. King's class—he'd threatened at the beginning of the semester to flunk anybody with more than three unexcused cuts and I had two already.

"My, doesn't my daughter look pretty this morning?" my mother said to me at the bottom of the stairs.

"You look pretty great yourself, kid!" I joked hurriedly. "Not a day over forty."

She made a swipe at me, as she always did for this standing family jest, putting her usual good face on it, though I know she hadn't found it was so funny when the joke had been established two years before—I had innocently sent her a card on her thirty-ninth birthday, one of those nasty comic ones, which had a picture of a flapper-type girl and said underneath, "When I grow up I want to be..." and continued inside the cover where "40!" was written in big bold numerals. But today she looked full of high spirits, and, as I say, pretty great. Her eyes twinkled at me as we frisked around, and I was the one who turned serious first. "Mommie, you've got to write me an excuse to Dr. King, and then I have to go. Right now!"

"You're not going off again without some breakfast," she said firmly.

I whined and wheedled for a few precious seconds, then she went over to the desk to write the note, calling to Aunt Stell to bring me a cup of coffee at least.

Then I was off. And when I got to school I was so full of elation that we weren't going to have a geology test after all, but were going on a field trip instead, that I was set up for the rest of the morning. I was in such good form that I actually supplemented Mommie's excuse to Dr. King with such success that I persuaded a grin out of the poor decrepit old monster, and he said, displaying far more of a sense of humor than anybody knew he had, "that he had never seen anybody look so charming and happy over having spent all afternoon at the dentist's, but there was a first time for everything."

At lunchtime I didn't go home because June Miller (nicknamed Bug, naturally) asked me and Ridey Marshall to eat at the sorority house. Then afterwards, Ridey and I decided to cut class and go to town as she had seen a cute red suit in the French Shoppe since I hadn't been able to get the one I'd gone shopping for the day before. "Where all did you and your mother look for one?" she asked me as we drove through the campus. "I know

Pearce & Avery had some cute suits last week, though I don't remember specifically if there were any red. Did you look?"

"Uh, uh," I said, giving my head a shake, but keeping my eyes on the road.

"You mean you didn't look anywhere but Judson's?" she wanted to know.

"That's right," I admitted.

"Then you just came home?" her astonishment grew.

"That's right," I said again. I knew she was looking at me curiously. And I wasn't surprised when I heard her ask:

"Why?"

I shrugged. "I don't know. Mother and I had a sort of a falling out—you know the bit."

She nodded. We discussed our mutual parents' failings often; she too had a maternal cross to bear. "What did you do, leave her and go off to a show?"

"No. We got separated," I said in complete truth. "And we came home separately." I felt quite pleased at my own adroitness and just hoped she wouldn't ask any more questions that might spoil it. But she didn't. It was time for her to get off on her own problems, of which she has many.

Ridey isn't the least bit pretty, and she's got this figure problem of having no hips and no breasts. Also, she keeps her hair cut so short and yet so shaggy that she looks like a boy in the face too; a sort of slovenly, naughty boy, but you can't help liking ole Ridey, she's so good-natured. Then, too, there's something downright appealing about that impish face of hers, especially when she grins. However, she wasn't grinning now. She was telling me about being stood up by this boy she's been trying for sometime to make the scene with, and, poor thing, she doesn't know why. I was thinking, what can I tell her, and wishing in annoyance that she wasn't, as Mommie calls it, "so rough in her talk," meaning she uses more beat expressions than anyone else in our crowd; especially when she feels threatened, and I wasn't paying much attention to where I was going. Then I heard this piercing horn and moved out of the middle of the street, and who do you think roared by? Miss Sally Sue, hellbent for leather. And I thought at first, thank God she didn't recognize me because she was just the kind who would come to a screeching halt, back up to exchange pleasantries with her new friend.

Well, that was exactly what she did. I nearly rammed into her.

"I called your mama this morning!" she hollered at me.

"Good, Miss Sally Sue, thanks." I beamed at her falsely, waved and started to pull out from behind her and pass on, but she flagged me.

"Wait a minute, wait a minute!" she cried and jumped out of her car, leaving it right in the middle of the street, of course, and came around and stooped into my window, towering over my small car before she did so like a giant bent on investigating a doll's house. "Oh, hello. There's the Marshall child. How's your mother?" she asked Ridey, then ignored her and said into my face, her thick-lensed spectacles giving her the appearance of not just a giant, but a giant bird of prey, "All's forgiven, huh? Harriet said she was afraid all of them had been a little hard on you, but you seemed all right this morning."

I bobbed my head up and down, feeling as if it belonged not to me but an automaton which Miss Sally Sue had set in motion.

Then she said, "You girls on your way to town? Follow me and let me treat you to a soda at the drugstore."

In something akin to horror, I said, "Oh, no, Miss Sally Sue. We'd love to but we can't. We're just running up for a second then we've got to go back to school."

"All right," she said in genial regret. "But I'll hold you to your promise to come see me soon. You don't know how stimulated I was by our talk, and I've made up my mind that no matter what she said that I'm not going to just sit still and do nothing."

"Oh, Miss Sally Sue," I murmured in profound alarm.

"Well, you'll see," she wagged her head brightly before withdrawing it from the window, and hollering "Bye!" gay and spirited as the superannuated teenager she apparently fancied herself to be, she tore off to her car, possessed it, and slammed the door, as if bagging the game she'd stalked.

"That tacky old thing," Ridley muttered, obviously put out because she had been virtually ignored. "She's out of her head. What on earth was she yammering about? I didn't hardly think you knew her."

I grimaced, pretending to be offended at her grammar—anything to change the subject. "Ridey, how can you make straight A's in English and talk like that?"

"Like what?" Ridey asked, but being far more interested in getting her curiosity satisfied, she continued, "And why did you turn down the soda? It might have been sort of a fun bit. You know we're not in any hurry to get back. What's the matter with you? You look like you're mad or something."

"I'm not mad," I said.

"Well, what's the matter then? And who was this mystery— she who said whatever she said? What's up, doc?"

"Nothing, nothing," I said crossly. "It was just that she did me a favor sort of."

"I dig," Ridey said, looking arch. "You met her on the bus coming home yesterday and she offered you her shoulder to cry on about your fuss with your mommie. And like a fool you took it."

"Something like that," I said sourly, and couldn't help adding, "She's very nice."

"That's good to know," Ridey purred, rolling her eyes suggestively, "in case I ever decide to take up being a lesbian."

"Ha, ha, ha," I said, not laughed, in sarcasm. "And even if she was one, isn't eighty a little old for you?"

We drove the rest of the way in a pregnant silence that I was determined would be stillborn. Ridey Marshall is about as trustworthy as a wire-tapping device, and pretty much as personally innocent too; what she reveals is done mechanically.

However, I did wonder how soon it would take the news to leak out; inevitably, I knew at least some of it would, even if the newspapers suppressed all or part of the story. There had been a lot of local Negroes in on it, some of them servants of families of my friends or friends of my family. But I thought to myself that this was one time when they'd keep gossiping at a minimum; not just out of gratitude to Miss Sally Sue either, but because silence was to their serious advantage. So where would the leak start? My nosy relatives? Or would Miss Sally Sue herself be the one to poke the finger through the dyke? It might all come in a rush—any day—or drop by drop. When it did come, I certainly hoped I would have my canoe handy.

Daddy, who was trying very hard to make friends with me when I got home late in the afternoon, eagerly met me at the door, holding the newspaper, as if he'd been watching for me to come. The article was in the city newspaper (the local one never published it) and though it was on the front page, it was brief and quite vague. "Names of the participants, several of whom were white," it read, "were undisclosed."

"It doesn't even mention that some of the whites were women," I murmured to myself in surprise.

"Look at it again, hon," Daddy advised. I could tell he was looking forward to my over-all comment and some kind of discussion of the whole thing—it would serve as a perfect vehicle for working in a deftly casual apology to me and a reinstatement of himself to his former high paternal position.

"Oh, yes, I see," I murmured as I gave the write-up a less hurried reading. The very first paragraph, in which the what-where-when-how-who's, or whatever, of journalism are supposed to be put, said, "At the basement lunch counter in Judson's Department Store just after noon yesterday, a sit-in demonstration was staged by a large group of Negroes and a number of whites…. Among the 26 persons arrested were several whites, including women. All the strikers were released on bail except three white persons whose cases were dismissed." The news story ended with the information that one Wilfred Bumpkin, (the spelling was their happy error) white, had been fined $50 for disorderly conduct occurring simultaneously on the scene of the arrest.

There was no mention of who had put up the bail. Silently, I handed Daddy his paper.

"Well?" he asked me with a grin, then added, "Now, that didn't hurt a bit, did it?"

I shook my head.

"—So there's nothing to worry about from the press, now is there, hon?"

"Nope," I said. "Guess not."

"—And you can be sure none of our local Negroes are going to be tattling about who put up their bail. People will assume that CORE was responsible for that."

I longed to ask him what CORE was, but I just decided I wouldn't. I didn't want him to get his foot in the door.

But that some kind of thought process was going on in me evidently showed, for he said, "So stop worrying, hon. You know what your mommie said about that little frown in your forehead getting to be a big frown before you know it."

I didn't smile; I didn't even look at him.

"Well, anyway, sweetie," he said with a sigh. "I think this news is good news, considering. Maybe they'll even think that the white women referred to were some gal friends of your boy Lumpkin-Bumpkin." He winked into my cold unsmiling stare. Then, pretending not to notice anything, he stood up, yawned, and asked me if I wanted the funnies and left them for me anyway when I didn't answer. I knew He was sufficiently confident of my dependence on him to think I'd come around in time. I wondered if I ever would, or if I'd just seem to.

Now, it seems logical that Mommie would be the last one I'd forgive because her denial of me was the most absolute, but even if I had planned to show her what I thought of her, I'd missed my chance that morning by waking in such good spirits and being taken unawares. But grudges anyway have always been hard for me to hold—I keep having to restimulate myself in order to do it—and after Daddy left me in the living room with the funnies that night, instead of looking at them, I thought about her, about him, about the whole thing. I thought seriously, rather sadly, but not in the acute misery of the night before. Meeting Miss Sally Sue and having to answer Ridey's questions had put me in the mood for it anyway. Then the thing in the paper and just seeing Daddy in his display of easy cheer had sobered me to the proper reflective point.

And as I lay on the floor, propped up on my elbows staring into space, it came to me that I didn't have, and never had had the least little respect for my mother. Not where it counted. There were things about her I admired, but they were all outside things. The truth of the matter was that I knew she had no character, that with a little effort of will I could completely overpower her, expose her for what she was through the strength of my despising; if I handled it cleverly, dispassionately, even Daddy would be forced to see what I was certain he had always seen, and that could ruin their marriage. But I knew I didn't want to—not from any regard for either of them—but because it wasn't to my own interests. Besides, she simply wasn't worth it, miniature adder that she was with her tiny sting. And for the first non-daydreaming time, I began to think of who I'd like to marry because I knew I had to get out of here—the sooner the better—now that I had been kicked out of the cradle. But until I found a way to survive comfortably outside it, I would crawl back in, pretend I'd never been away.

I rolled over on my back, put my hands behind my head and speculated as to just how dumb, how unconscious Daddy really was. And I concluded that he was pretty dumb. That fine ego of his was responsible; he really thought of himself as such a good man, such a just man, such an honest man. So he, even more than Mommie, could inevitably forgive himself anything. Oh, I knew eventually he would apologize, but he would do it in such a way that it would cost him nothing—he'd either spring it on me casually when he thought he'd caught me in a receptive mood, or he'd compose a flowery speech, so touching, so impressive in splendid, yet simple sincerity that I'd be captivated and at the same time gratefully released. I even tried to think of the words he might use. It would be amusing if I guessed right, and I wondered if he would be surprised—and what would happen then— if I said, "I'm on to you, boy. Take your apology and stuff it." But this was something as rough as Ridey might say, besides being too revealingly bitter. And I must not let him have the satisfaction of my bitterness.

Then I got up and walked around and wondered if I were really being childish rather than perceptive, deep. I went over to Psyche sleeping like a mound of white froth in the corner of the sofa, and I buried my nose in her fur and whispered, "You I love," and then started to cry again in instant sorrow for myself because I didn't have anything else to love, and after all, she was just a cat and couldn't care less. I heard someone come into the room and jumped up from poor astonished Psyche in guilty haste, as if I were about to be caught necking. It was only Aunt Stell.

"Go wash your face," she said gruffly, and I knew from that one swift look that my face needed the tears washed off. How I wished I thought she meant it was dirty!

But on the way to get rid of my dirty tears, I thought of an ingenious way to get even with all of them. And how easy it would all be! How marvelously simple.

As soon as I had my face cleared of all signs of weakness and irresolution, I went to the phone and made my call.

CHAPTER FIFTEEN

M ISS SALLY SUE said she thought it was a capital idea that we get together, after expressing pleased surprise at hearing from me so soon. Yes, indeed, she would think of some inducement to snare "our rare bird" into our "net of friendship," and she would let me know if this could be done on Saturday night.

After I hung up, feeling frightened, daring, and surreptitious, I remembered that Pete had said something about maybe making it into town for the weekend, and wouldn't that be a mess. "Fool, fool," I cursed myself, and Daddy's voice behind me said:

"What's that? Are you talking to me or my little daughter?"

"To your idiot, not mine," I returned, feeling suddenly quite lightheaded and in the mood to be silly.

"Now what does that mean?" he pretended to ask seriously, but his tone was one of relieved delight; he thought he was forgiven.

I threw back my head, as they say in the books, and laughed. "Oh, Daddy, oh my own Daddy-O!"

His face lighted with glee, and feeling a burst of delicious pride at how easy it all was, I did a pert little dance around him, almost a shameless little dance. I knew I was being just this side of seductive, and I didn't care, I didn't care!

Rather awkwardly, his face still wide in a smile, he tried to catch me. "Why are you so happy, hon?" he asked, following me around.

"Because I'm free, I'm free!" I sang senselessly, and continued to whirl in ecstacy over my own discovery. But I stopped just as he was beginning to find my behavior no longer refreshing, but strange, and let him plant his loving kiss on my forehead.

"You and your mother—both such light gay creatures, full of unpredictable heights, yet full of moods too," he murmured endearingly, then patted my arm and released me.

The comparison made me feel quite sullen, but I smiled at him prettily for what he considered his compliment and didn't let the pose drop until I turned my back and went back into the living room.

"Were the funnies funny tonight?" he asked following after me.

"I didn't read them," I replied airily. "I thought thoughts instead."

"Did you now?" he asked, his eyes crinkled in amusement. "And what kind of thoughts did you think?"

"Oh, cruel thoughts, of course," I babbled coquettishly. "Horrid mean thoughts of dire deeds." I watched his reaction with crafty intentness, smiling all the time, wondering when my pixyness would begin to puzzle him. And I caught the cue in the split instant when seriousness was about to darken his eyes, and said in an entirely new voice, "Say, I meant to ask you last night. Did I get a long distance call from Memphis?"

"No, hon, not that I know of," he said in his normal fatherly tone, and before he could gaze at me and measure the degree of my concern over Pete—for he knew I was referring to Pete, of course—I hopped out of the room. "Where are you off to now?" he called fondly. "Dinner will be ready soon."

"I know. I'm just going to stir Aunt Stell a little," I replied, and saw from where I stood the air of peace and confidence that manifested itself in so simple a thing as the way he turned his head back to his newspaper which he held lazily propped against his knee; I saw his right hand tamp the tobacco in the pipe which hung at a relaxed angle from his mouth. How full of well-being, loving kindness and contentment! The king in his kingdom. And oh, when I took it from him, how he was going to miss it!

Pretending I was going upstairs to study after dinner, I excused myself, leaving my incomparable parents in the living room to soak in the bath of their fatuous contentment; so relieved that harmony was restored, their minds cleared of the binding discomforts of unspoken self-doubt rumbling deep inside their consciences like an upset stomach. And so too was gone that tainted victual, always sure to cause distress if not ptomaine, the wounded child—as if I had been eaten, and well-digested after all. How I loathed them as they sat in their self-satisfaction! And grown-ups talked about how quickly children recovered from things! My mother, who likes to "scribble," as she calls it, and occasionally has sold a "tiny verse" to come obscure magazine or other which pays her by giving her a subscription, once showed me in shy pride such a verse, one which she had written about me. "To Hallie," it said under the title. And it was all about how parents inadvertently wound their children, "bruise their cloud-soft skins and tear their tender minds," was one line I remember. But the one that really got me was one that is now badly frag-mented: "the little thing's heart-shaped worries and woes" and something about they blew away, or something. I know it ended "where nobody knows."

I hadn't thought of that creation for years. Probably she had written it when I was ten. I remembered how proud I had been of it. I carried it around in my schoolbag—in that little pocket on top meant for pencils—until it fell to pieces. And when it was all crumbled and I could barely make out the words, I buried it in the garden and solemnly managed to wring out a tear over its grave. What sentimental, simple-hearted little jerks kids are! But all are little apes or parrots; pirouetting, fluttering, bound-ing, chattering, depending on the models, in hopeful replica of their parents. My cynicism suddenly struck me a blinding blow, and I felt like kneeling in awe at the shrine of my own brilliance.

Quickly, I leapt to me feet and rushed this insight to the type-writer before it got away.

I got my quivering butterfly off the pin and properly pre-served in good time, and then I looked around for something to do, rather surprised, (now that my muse, elusive as usual, had fled, leaving my net empty,) that I couldn't face the very diver-sion that had excited me so all through our quiet and seemingly placid dinner (Bill was out tonight, so no fights). Yes, I had been so keyed up with thoughts about Maybelle Brown and our com-ing friendship and the effect this would have on the world, that I had rushed right upstairs with them, clutching them mentally as if they were a good book. My mistake had been to stop on the landing and view my parents; this had side-tracked me, and now worn out with peevish thoughts of them, I found the vitality completely gone from the rich and voluminous Maybelle mate-rial. I threw myself into an armchair in front of my fireplace that held no fire. The lifelessness of it depressed me, so I got up again and stretched out on the bed.

Why didn't Pete call? I wondered. Why not study? I'd lied to them, but it was a good idea. But what did I care now any-way what kind of grades I made? Were most people's parents so awful? But I was worn out with thinking about their awfulness; there was a limit to the subject's interest. But there was none to the subject of Maybelle. Why couldn't I concentrate on that? The word concentrate reminded me of a book—a dirty book—Ridey had lent me, all a-giggle, and I hadn't had a chance to read it. Surely I could concentrate on that. Anyway, I had promised to bring it back.

But the book, once I'd taken it from its secret hiding place, proved a dud, and my thoughts immediately began to toss and turn again. I skipped through the long scientific-sounding pas-sage at the front, sifting through for the good parts. But again and again I struck fool's gold; either it proved not so dirty after all, or else too boring to go after. There were so many words I didn't know. Who had ever thought pornography could be hard? Was Ridey smarter than I? Yes, I admitted in secret shame, she probably was; she'd had to tell me what pornography was, and that was pretty ignorant. Then to my utter amazement my eyes fell upon a paragraph of such awful filth that I slammed the book shut, and sat there in shock and loathing, trying to eject the terrible images from my relatively unsullied mind. But despite all I could do, I could not coax it away from sex. It clung desperately to the rock-hard subject, as if my brain were equipped with claws. At last I lured it off, promising to compromise by thinking of romantic marriage. May I think of Pete then? it asked brightly, and, with a wicked little giggle, I told it no, you just think of Tom Nesbitt, for I didn't care much about Tom anymore. I hadn't even bothered to answer his last letter. Cheated, it paid me back by going to sleep and dreaming of a black Persian named Peter Tom-Cat who ran after Psyche and jumped her, and she had millions of grinning black babies.

I guess I must have slept for about an hour or so, for it was nearly ten when the phone woke me, I saw by the clock. Already, as I said, "hello," my heart beating faster, I had decided to hell with Maybelle Brown on Saturday night, this was the man I loved.

"Sweetheart," he said as soon as the operator had ascertained that yes, this was Miss Hallie Hamilton speaking, "Darn. I can't make it."

"Oh, Pete," I wailed, loving him for the way he had called me "sweetheart." (Tom Bubber Nesbitt always called me "doll," which I detested, and always made it sound slouchy when the word was careless enough in itself.)

"The family's moving to Louisville, and Mother says as soon as we get settled to please ask you up for the weekend. Think you can stand it till then?"

"I'll have to," I said with a genuine sigh. The news was depressing me far more than I would have thought.

"But it won't be long," he said. "Promise to be a good girl?"

"Oh, Pete!" I quickly turned the mouthpiece up in the air so he wouldn't hear me sob.

"Are you crying, honey?"

"No," I lied with a faint sniffle, and hoping to undo the damage, added, "why? Are you?"

He laughed, relief in his voice. "Okay, charmer. See you soon."

And then he hung up as soon as he'd said good-bye, a thing he always does, without waiting for mine, and I thought to myself, as usual, that it was too bad there was always something wrong with everybody, but there you are. Then I stretched out on the bed again, feeling only the remotest kind of displeasure, wondering idly if I was sleepy still, and you wouldn't believe it, but the next thing I knew I was crying like my heart would break. I pounded the bed again and again. When I couldn't stand it any longer—the loneliness, the frustration, the guilt, the hurt, the anger—I jumped up and raced out of my room, screaming "Mommie, Mommie!" and if she hadn't been in the living room still reading with Daddy, I think I would have died.

PART II

CHAPTER SIXTEEN

L OOKING BACK UPON that strange season, that was no proper season at all, it having really begun in early spring with that trip to the city when everything was deceptively wintry, I feel as if Nature or some ancient god tied me by white ribbons to the moon, and had me hauled around until it drove me mad, just for kicks. Only naturally I wasn't aware of it.

Spring is the time of madness anyway, so maybe I was just an ordinary victim of the vernal equinox, if a premature one. For mad I certainly was, though always having been a little hare-brained—"lighthearted," Mommie calls it, "and happy-go-lucky," or "a chronic moronic and a cry-baby," according to my brother's lights—it's not surprising that I didn't notice the stepped up pace of my ups and downs until I practically hummed with perpetual emotion.

Maybe I had enough to get me in this state. I'll agree that some of it was pretty traumatic, starting of course with that shopping trip to the city; ten separate but related traumatic experiences all in one day—not bad for a beginner. And I reckon that was the biggest day, all told. That day I was born the most and died the most, and for sometime after I zigzagged and ricocheted between these two states with something like the speed of sound. Reading over my diary for the period is a real kooky experience. For example, deciding that the way to wreak supreme vengeance on my poor mother and father was to get Miss Sally Sue to arrange an evening with Maybelle Brown is one of the funniest things. Evidently, I thought the evening would close, settling everything, in the following manner:

1) Maybelle would buy me a ticket on the underground rail-way to the North where I would eventually kill myself from hard work for the NAACP. Or:
2) I'd run away from home and go live with Miss Sally Sue, my only white friend (with the exception of Psyche, my cat). Or:
3) I'd triumphantly bring Maybelle home to live with me. Or:
4) I'd simply go up in smoke.

I must have frightened myself pretty badly because the night I made all these plans for wringing blood out of stones (my parents), I turned all pink baby fat again, worked myself into what some people call a crying fit, but known in our house as a "state," wouldn't let my mother leave me all night, and cried myself to sleep in her arms.

Big, independent me. And the sole entry in my diary for the day after is, "I LOVE MUMMIE!!!" printed out in big uneven block letters, as though I had retrogressed to the age of ten. Which I probably had. I hadn't called Mommie that earlier form of address in years.

The next entry is some three days later, the other days being strangely blank, so I don't know what filled the interim exactly, though I do know, tempted as I was to ask Miss Sally Sue to call the whole thing off, I didn't. And now, without any diary entries for that period as guideposts, it's hard for me to remember just what I *did* think of Maybelle, and seeing Maybelle in such a preposterously daring and unlikely setting as proposed. I had liked her enormously, had been enormously impressed with her, of course; but, after all, she was a Negro and I was a white. It had been one thing for Miss Sally Sue, acting on the spur of the moment and her own whimsy, to install the girl in the back of her car with us to drive back from the city, but it was quite another to actually *entertain* her by plan, to put her on a white social level, and a very high unblemished one at that. I guess I felt pretty chicken-hearted, despite all my new convictions about integration and my sympathy for the Negro people, for sympathy is not empathy.

Anyway, the day I took up diary-keeping again was THE day, or night rather, and here was my heading for the account of it: "*Self Meets with Maybelle Brown* (Negress) *and Miss S.S. 2nd Session.*" The very wording would indicate not only top secrecy but subversion, as if Miss Sally Sue and I were forming some kind of club, and my parenthetical use of the word Negress gives away what I thought of Maybelle and her part in it when I left the house that evening. I know I wrote the heading portion before I left for I remember doing so—another indication that I was expecting anything to happen.

In any event, it was not just an evening out with the girls that I prepared myself for, but that it was an evening of social significance in the broadest sense, as well as one of initiation, is proved by the fact that I wore my most expensive costume, suitable for the occasion, and put on just pounds of makeup. And there were other elaborate preparations too, all of which Miss Sally Sue must have enjoyed though they filled my chicken heart with terror. First of all, the hour was set for 8:30 and it was decided that it would look better if I walked, as who knew who might pass Miss Sally Sue's and recognize my car in her drive? This, in itself, mind you, we even discussed from the point of view of "others." I think everybody in town takes some kind of oblique pride in the reputation we have of being "the nosiest town in the state," or we wouldn't keep it up—if we didn't actually start it ourselves, that is. But, this being the case, it's true that the most curiosity ridden, who make nightly patrols of East Main Street just to see who is visiting who, would be sure to remark upon the fact that *my* car—not my family's—was seen in Miss Sally Sue's driveway and what was I doing there?

"But suppose I'm seen walking?" I whispered to Miss Sally Sue during the guarded telephone conversation we held to set the thing up. And she came up with the solution, still on the spy-story precautionary level, of course, of letting the air out of one of my tires, thereby achieving a flat one. This explanation for my ambulation, in place of my nearparaplegic dependence on my car, had the advantage of serving for both public and parents. The arrangements for whisking Maybelle out of her grandmother's and getting her back in, Miss Sally Sue said she would handle though trustworthy Jimmy, who was, already, perforce, a sort of accessory to our league. But in any case, both of us agreed, all this was necessary, silly or not, for which of the three wanted to be jeopardized? "We're just getting together for a little harmless fun," was the way Miss Sally Sue put it. "And I'll be damned if this town is going to criticize me, or be given the chance to, for my way of getting some innocent pleasure out of life." I didn't tell her that what for her was "harmless fun" represented for me something as soul-gripping as a mystic rite.

As I dressed that night, I wondered if Miss Sally Sue, admitted NAACP card holder, had known Negroes socially before, or if she could be a lesbian, aged or not, as Ridey had said? If she were a pervert, that could explain her enthusiasm; for perversion, so Daddy had told me in one of our talks about "physical fundamentals," as we call them, recognizes neither age nor class barriers when it is avid. These thoughts only added to my grief, guilt and excitement over what I was about to do. But I went downstairs persuaded that Miss Sally Sue was just Miss Sally Sue: a bright capable woman who had lived too long without proper expression of her personality; in other words, a bored woman— one who had been forced into the moral periphery in order to get her kicks. If she had had the husband she wanted, I decided, there would have been no Miss Sally Sue, just Mrs. somebody.

Naturally, when I appeared at the foot of the stairs, my parents had no idea where I was going. But then they seldom do. Customarily, when my dates call for me, Mommie and Daddy don't even know I'm going out until they open the door. But sometimes, when I'm dressed up, and go out after dinner alone, they stop me. I prayed, as I told them a genial good night and made for the door, that this would not be one of the times. But I guess I had fussed over my toilette so long upstairs that they had thought I had gone to bed early, for they both looked surprised to see me all dressed up, obviously going out.

"Got a date, hon?" Daddy asked.

If I knew then what I know now, I would have simply answered yes; a hen party, but at that time I wasn't so quick or so devious. "Not exactly," I hedged, smiling uncertainly, not meeting his eye.

"Well you're mighty dressed up to be going out with Mister Not-Exactly," my mother said, taking an ancestral pleasure in her own sense of humor.

I tried to giggle too, but it didn't come out that way. Icy fear had me by the throat. Suppose they ever found out I was bound on this wickedness?

"Well, just who are you going out with?" Daddy persisted gently, smiling at me, trying to catch my eye. "What time is he supposed to pick you up?"

"Nobody's picking me up," I said, raising my voice to hide my guilt. Which was a mistake. And I knew it. Daddy took it as a sign of defiance.

"Now, look here, Hallie, when we bought you that car you gave us your solemn promise that you would not take it out on dates. You know that if some young man was driving it and had an accident we could be sued for—"

"I know, I know," I interrupted impatiently. "Don't worry. I'm going to do the driving."

"But dear," Mommie put in. "It's not just that—" she bit her lip. "It's that it doesn't *look* right for a young girl your age to be squiring young men around in your automobile—"

"I don't have a date, I told you. I'm going somewhere by myself!"

"Don't yell at your mother, Hallie."

"I'm not yelling."

"Well, dear, if you'll just tell us where you're going—"

"That's okay! I'll walk. And here're the Goddam keys! Keep 'em for all I care!"

"Hallie, you're not yourself." My mother stood up, looking very worried. "What's the matter with you lately? You must get that awful sit-in experience out of your mind."

"It isn't that at all," I said, feeling as faint as I sounded. I knew my mouth was trembling.

"No, Harriet," my father corrected her mildly for her tactic. Then he addressed me. "Hallie, come on and tell your old pop your troubles. How about it?"

"I don't have any," I muttered from out of my evil humor.

"Lucky you," he said airily, and picked up his book which had been lying spread-eagled on his lap.

"Henry Hamilton!" my mother rang her voice out imperiously. "Are you going to let that child go out in the dead of night all by herself?"

"Be sensible, Hat," he murmured abstractedly. "It isn't the dead of night. It's just a little after eight."

"I'll be sitting up waiting for you, remember!" she warned me in her best fishwife voice as I scuttled to the door, and, as I slammed it, she hurled after me, "I know what's wrong with you! That nice young Pete has found you out. He knows all about how you treat your mother—"

And with the slamming of the door, I burst into my seemingly endless supply of tears. It was the rainy season for me, all right. I cried every day now, at least once, and often as much as five or six times. My face got washed more often than the rest of me did. This struck me as quite a droll interior comment, and thinking I would now simply laugh myself dry, as if humor were a sort of mental terrycloth, the opposite effect took place and I boohooed all the way down Main Street, making my mission about as secret as an alarm clock, had there been anyone to alarm, and completely hosing down all my very careful, glamorous makeup. I'm having a nervous breakdown, I told myself with a shiver, and even then, having said it, I guessed that I was. Why didn't Daddy notice and get me a trained nurse? Dumb Daddy; psycho psychologist. Both of them cubes from Cubesville.

So, after ten blocks, I arrived at Miss Sally Sue's, as prompt as I was nervous. I rang the old-fashioned bell and saw her, through the frosted glass, cautiously come down the hall toward the door. "What's the password?" she asked with a furtive giggle as she let me in.

But I didn't even smile. I was afraid it might make me cry again. I just stepped inside.

"Come on in here, Missie," she said clawing at a huge white folding door. "It's chilly tonight and I had Jimmy lay us a fire. Ain't it cheerful?" she asked, cocking her head at me, as the door slid back and the inviting room came into view.

I nodded glumly and took the seat she waved me to—one of two loveseats upholstered in blue velvet, facing each other, by the fire. She took the other, then noticed I was slumped down, still wearing my coat.

First, she demanded that I stand up, remove the garment, give it to her, then sit down properly. These things being accomplished, she took her seat again and said conspiratorily that she hoped nothing untoward had happened to Maybelle; Jimmy had gone for her in his car, as planned, but they should have been back by now. "Hark, is that they?" she put a hand to her ear, her lips ajar, immobile as a statue's.

"You're a perfect scream, Miss Sally Sue," I told her.

"Shhh," she quieted me and pretended to be listening again. I knew she was doing no such thing. "No," she said, "it is not they," giving up her pose. "And now will you tell me, Missie, why your face is completely devoid of any color—nature's or the rouge pot's—or are you wearing that new ghoulish white stuff on your mouth? You look like you fell in the flour barrel. Or are you going to try show Maybelle just how white a white person can get it? No tricks, my girl, I want this golden humming bird to be happy, happy as a bee."

"If you'll just excuse me, I'll go put my face back on," I said in a trembling voice.

"Well, I should think so," she retorted stoutly. "How did you get it off? Did the Haynes' big collie dog jump up and kiss you?"

"No, I carry my own spot removers all built in," I replied. "Tear ducts."

"Who made you cry, child?" she asked, her bantering tone put aside for the first time.

I told her how ever since the day in the city I had found this miraculous secret of crying over everything from the fact that we had chocolate pie for dessert to my having needlessly let the air out of my car tire. Be it ever so humble, no subject was too insignificant for little old me.

"Why I think that's wonderful!" she exclaimed. "Maybe you can teach me. I love to cry."

"You're laughing at me," I sobbed.

"And you're crying at me! Isn't that remarkable? And pretty soon we'll change off and you'll know how to laugh and I'll know how to cry, and then we can go on the stage as living theatre masks. And while we're practising and waiting for *la Belle d'Or* let's have a little liquid refreshment."

"What is it?" I blinked down at the glass she handed me.

"Champagne, the golden river of life!" she cried, and toasted the white plaster cherubs and curlicues on her front parlor ceiling. I realized then, with open fascination, that she must have been quite drunk even before I arrived. I had never seen a truly drunk woman before—just a few girls at dances, the not-nice girls. I tried to summon my moral code to cover this form of indecency, but I discovered I didn't have one, and I felt buoyant on surprise. I sipped the champagne. Then I went to make up my face.

"You know," I said, upon returning, "Daddy doesn't like to drink and Mommie has no head, so I've never tasted champagne before. Not even at weddings. But I'll bet you I could make almost the same thing out of apple juice and sparkling water."

"Shame on you!" she said, stopping short in her prancing around—which showed signs of having been very abandoned while I was out of the room, for her hair was untidy and she had kicked off, or taken off, her shoes. "*You're* the one who has no head, saying such a thing. Shame, shame!" she cried, reactivated again. "Here's to every whiskey in the world, to every bourbon, every rye! With or without a W!" And she did a perfectly amazing thing, a feat of performance for me unequalled, and kicked her foot up as high as her head, though it's true she cheated a little and ducked down toward her knee, as dirty a trick in ballet as cheating at Solitaire in cards. But this woman was eighty years old!

"Miss Sally Sue!" I gasped and ran over to support her, for I was sure she was going to fall, but she shook me off.

"Apple juice, phew!" she said. "Sparkling Wa-ah-ter!" and went into an impassioned if discordant rendition of a song obviously entitled "Sparkling Water," since these were the only words, to the tune of *Water Boy*. Like the mime I realized she was, she sang most of it in proper concert-singer style, her hands placed between stomach and chest, one over the other, throat and face up, diaphragm in proper use. While singing, if one could call it that, she had even sauntered over to the closed baby grand piano, as if an accompanist awaited her there. Her stage presence so carried me along that I might have sat there for hours if I had not heard—who knows when?—the knocking at the back door, the rattling of the knob, and, finally, the turning of the key, and said, "Miss Sally Sue, she's here!"

And that was enough to restore Miss Sally Sue, who broke off in the middle of a note, as if she'd never heard it before, and returned to the center of the room, away from the shuttered alcove where the piano stood, and went forward to meet her guest who emerged from the kitchen, where Jimmy had left her. The meeting took place in the dark dining room, and from the sounds of it was warm and unstressed.

Maybelle, radiant as a tulip in her smart yellow coat and cashmere dress, entered, Miss Sally Sue tripping after, and said, "Hello, there," to me as she took off her coat, revealing her golden skin around her dress, which appeared as perfect, as esthetically right as if it had been painted there.

"Sit down, Maybelle," Miss Sally Sue urged heartily, once our hellos were over, and she had carefully folded up Maybelle's coat on a chair, "and I'll get you a little glass of something. We're drinking champah-gne," she said, exaggerating a syllable that my French teacher had warned me against. And I felt very ill at ease, sipping my unaccustomed nectar, wondering what Maybelle would say.

"Champah-gne's my drink," she answered at once, "if that's what both of you head-starters are having." And she turned her corruscating smile on me, exactly as if she had been my intimate friend for life, like Ridey, for example, and I gave her back a smile in kind, an unconscious one, the I've-known-you-all-my-life variety. I don't know what would have happened if I'd had to account for that smile in that moment, but I didn't. Miss Sally Sue took it from me.

She strode up to Maybelle and said, "Golden child," and took her hand. "Look at our two hands together." They looked, clasping hands, and Miss Sally Sue said, "Like two flowers. One a lotus, painted gold, and the other an old withered fritillary, a wild spotted lily." And then she let Maybelle's hand go and gazed at her own. "How proud Papa was of this hand!" she said. "He valued it because it was small and soft. I wonder if he would like it now?" And she held the wizened, liver-spotted hand at arm's length, as if it were a glove without a mate and gazed at it with distaste. It was Maybelle, not I, who stopped her.

"Are you drunk, Miss Sally Sue?" she asked her—a question I would never have dared to ask.

And Miss Sally Sue, obviously as drunk as a lord, (or lady) answered: "I'm a fritillary, withered and dry. And you are golden. Please let me by," and staggered over to the fireplace where she collapsed on one of the loveseats, unconscious of verse-making, unconscious period.

"Now what?" Maybelle said to me. I shrugged. We stood there a few minutes staring at our inert hostess, not knowing what else to do. "Maybe we ought to go," Maybelle murmured. "Jimmy told me where I could reach him in case something happened—" she gave a short laugh to herself. "Now I know why he did."

I didn't know what to say, or even what to think. Was this the end of my enchanted evening? I felt cheated. Nothing had happened, simply nothing. No conspiracy, no mystery, no particular delight. Just an old woman, sodden with drink, cutting up in front of two girls. It was exactly the same as if Ridey Marshall or Dot had been along instead of Maybelle.

Then at that moment Miss Sally Sue rallied, as if some inner reveille had been sounded, popping upright like a jack in the box and said, "Why don't you two young things sit down? We're having such a nice time," then she drifted off again, receding into that private chamber of fantasy which she had politely left long enough to re-greet her guests, murmuring as the light died from her eyes, "time, time, mother time and daughter time." She heaved a large sigh, "—But we go on forever."

Maybelle and I exchanged looks of inquiry. But we were wrong, it wasn't sundown. Miss Sally Sue had just had an eclipse, for she said, more to Maybelle than to me, looking out from hooded lids, "Don't mind an addled and pickled old woman." Then she suddenly drew herself erect, got up and walked over to us. "Missie," she addressed me sharply, "Tell your sweet mama for me—your sweet hot mama—that I'm leaving her the receipt for champagne pickles. She'll find it under Bequest Number 69 in my will, all writ out for her, tried and true," and then the stream of consciousness nonsense began to seep back inside Miss Sally Sue, disappearing as if down the dark cavern of her mouth, which she left ajar, into an underground river. Eyes shut, and with a gait like Frankenstein's monster, she staggered to the love seat she had occupied before, curled up, looking curiously like a collapsible cigar store Indian, minus a war bonnet, and had a little nap.

Maybelle looked at a little circlet of silver on her arm of gold, and said, "Do you think she's gone for the night?"

"I don't know," I replied. "I know her only a little better than you do."

"Well," Maybelle sighed. "I told Granny I'd be home by twelve. Jimmy's coming back for me about a quarter of. That leaves us three hours more or less to kill. What do you think we should do?"

"Sit it out," I said. "There's lots of champagne." I took another sip and added, "I like it, do you?"

"Love it," Maybelle declared. "This is the first I've had since I've been down here going to school. I never go anywhere much, you know. And I have such pretty clothes—they just hang in the closet."

"You certainly do have pretty clothes," I assured her. "I used to always notice what you had on when you were in our creative writing class. Why did you drop out?"

Maybelle gave a soft little private laugh, showing her beautiful teeth. "I didn't drop out, I was dropped out. Since it wasn't a required course, Dr. Macon wasn't obliged to let me take it."

"Oh," I said sadly. "I see."

"No, it wasn't *that*," she corrected my impression swiftly. "If it had been my color he never would have let me sign up in the first place."

"What was it then?" I asked, perplexed. "You wrote some very good things, I thought. We all thought so. Dr. Macon certainly did." I didn't add that it had made a lot of other students mad, Dr. Macon's praise for her work. Around campus for a while there, some wag started a rumor that Dr. Macon was writing a novel called *Pride* in *Prejudice,* but it quickly died as it was not only obscure (Macon was Pride, the Nigra was Prejudice—get it?) but as light and airy, once grasped, as a lead balloon.

"Well, I never thought I'd have anybody to tell it to," she said with a sigh, looking at me carefully, "and maybe I shouldn't, but here goes. He wanted to go to bed with me."

I was glad the lights were so dim in there, for I blushed to the roots of my hair—over the shock, yes, but mostly over my own naiveté. "I should have guessed," I murmured.

"Why? I never expected it. But what really hurt was that he offered me money, in the same breath."

"What an awful, awful thing to do," I murmured in deep shame.

"I didn't tell Granny even," Maybelle went on. "I was afraid she'd try to make me quit school. And I don't want to. Among other things, staying is a personal challenge. If I don't stick it out—or hold out, if it comes to that—I might just as well say, 'Okay, Dr. Macon. Where's your money?' "

"Maybelle!" I exclaimed.

"It's the truth."

"You mean you've actually thought about becoming a—streetwalker?"

"Never," she said with a laugh. "I was simply trying to illustrate how much winning this—this freedom—means to me."

"Why?" I asked. "What's this little old dinky university?"

"It's where my grandmother is. It's in her hometown. If I get through, then maybe she'll believe in me—and the rest of us, what we're trying to do. You *know*," she gave an easy shrug. "I talked enough about it the other night. Tell me about you. I see you driving around in your car with your friends. And I think of you sometimes—even before I ever talked to you, I did—and I think, maybe someday there goes me." She interrupted herself with a laugh. "And it helps me, Hallie. Every day is another inch. But the world is big and wide. Lots of ground to cover."

I yearned to say something to her, but all I could think of to say sounded pinched and petty when I tried the words in my mind; mean compromises. "I wish you weren't so damned lonely!" I blurted out feelingly. "Don't you know *anybody* you like you can go out with?"

"Well, that poses a big problem: the caste system again. If there were any interesting young Negroes here in town on Granny's high social level, first of all, they'd leave soon enough, and, second, if they didn't leave they would be simply 'interested' rather than interesting; interested in settling down with a good-looking young colored gal like me—oh, I'm quite a prize even though I'm nearly twenty—and I'm not interested in settling down to live in a Negro ghetto, no matter how much money he might make for me to spend elsewhere. I don't want any more second-class life."

"Well, how about people in the city then? Your grandmother must know lots of people there."

Again the soft laugh, the dazzling smile. "Yes, but Granny's just a second-hand clothes dealer to them, so that makes me nothing. She's a well-to-do woman for her race here, but in the city, no. They've got *real* money. It's like I told you the other night; it's the same, white or colored. Oh, I suppose if I lowered my sights and really worked at it, I could land one of those big fish in that middling city pool. But why should I? Anyway, honey, don't look so worried. I *do* go out once in a while, and I still have some boarding school friends I'll visit eventually. And I did go to Philadelphia for Christmas—but that, that was a dark horse and a loser called 'Nostalgia' out of 'Mistake.' I can't make it there any more. People feel too sorry for me. And that's never any good. So don't you go feeling sorry for me, hear?"

I flashed her a bright smile and sat up straight, minding her request as if she were a photographer taking my picture. "But what about after school?" I asked.

"Europe, if I can manage it, or New York if I can't. I'd like to get as much education as I can stuff into myself as fast as I can stuff it. Then I'll sort it all out and apply it where it does me and everybody the most good. When I talk like this, Granny just shakes her head—all wrong, she says, all wrong. But I think she buys the Europe idea. However, you know what she'd really like me to do?" Her eyes curled up in lovely amusement. "She won't quite say it, but I think she'd like me to cross the color line. Just so she could proudly say that one of hers made it. Do you think I'm light enough to cross the color line? Be honest now."

I looked at her good and hard. "There was a South American here visiting at Christmas, and yes, I think you are lighter than she was, and with those blue eyes of yours—" I stopped, and my mouth hung open. "Why, they *aren't* blue, they're brown. What made me so sure they were blue?"

And she laughed that melodious laugh of hers. "Because sometimes they are. And sometimes they're green. I've got two pairs of contact lenses, and since I started school wearing the blue ones, I thought it was politic to continue. Also, the idea of a blue-eyed *'nigger'*—"she spat the word out"—is hard for white people to fathom. These are my real eyes I'm wearing tonight. My very own."

"But how can you see?"

"How can I see? Perfectly. 20-20 vision. Sweetheart—doll—haven't you heard of contact lenses without correction? They've been *the* thing for a long time."

CHAPTER SEVENTEEN

I N THE COURSE of time Maybelle learned, and I learned from Maybelle, that there were all kinds of things I hadn't heard of, and it was strange how oddly her sophistication meshed with my naivete. The things about which I felt myself to be wholly naive, she seemed to me to be wholly sophisticated. Then in the middle was middle ground, a lot of it. Even that first night at Miss S.'s, Maybelle, at some point just before Miss Sally Sue snapped to, said, "You know, we compliment each other in a curious way. Look," she held her arm against mine for contrast.

We both looked, and then we laughed. It was so funny to see the two arms side by side. Almost the same size, they looked like a pair, except mine appeared to have been overbleached in the wash. It was the first time I'd ever been critical of my beautiful skin, so white that it looks like matt finish. Then we looked at each other in Miss Sally Sue's pier mirror. Again, much the same size, much the same figures. "Why, Hallie, we even sort of look alike!" Maybelle exclaimed.

"Yes, identical twins with different markings," commented Miss Sally Sue's voice behind us. "Ought to tie your tails together, as the saying goes, and throw them over the garden wall. Come over here, you two, and let me get a look at you. No, over here in the light," she directed us. "Um hm," she grunted while carefully looking us over, as if we were prize stock. "Yep, you two ought to team up. I've even got names for you—Haley and Mayley, white as the moon and gold as the sun—"

"Oh, now Miss Sally Sue, stop," I protested with an embarrassed laugh.

"You wouldn't like that, huh? You don't want to team up with no colored gal. Well, see here, Missie, you're an uncolored gal if I ever saw one. Maybelle, Hallie came in here tonight looking like a walking bar of Ivory soap with a dress on. Wept her makeup plumb off'n her face. Now come on, both of you, and tell me how you're going to team up."

Maybelle had drawn back slightly, her dislike of Miss Sally Sue's affectedly rude jargon quite apparent—and not because she was too dainty either; she was personally offended.

Miss Sally Sue was quick to see this. "Oh, ho, ho," she coddled her, drawing Maybelle's rigid figure to her with her huge arm. Fixed around her waist, this grappling hook of flesh and blood brought Maybelle's one hundred and ten pounds forward as easily as moving a dressmaker's dummy. Then Maybelle began to laugh at her own helplessness, and one of her shoes came off. She collapsed in a heap of cackles at Miss Sally Sue's feet. "Is that your true risibility?" Miss Sally asked, bending over to inspect her. "If it is, remind me never to make *you* laugh again." Maybelle let out another squawk, and Miss S. S. threw up her hands. "Saints preserve us!" she said in a thick Irish brogue. "I've found me own teammate! Golden child, don't you know no better than to laugh like that? Don't you know dat what help land me in de pokey?"

Maybelle's mirth died an instant death. "If you're going to make fun of the speech of my people, I can't stay," she said coldly as she got up, brushing her dress off.

"Now, listen here, you little ole pickaninny—" Miss Sally Sue began again, thinking to jolly her out of it.

"Sorry," Maybelle said crisply. "I just can't listen to it."

"Moughty techy, ain'tchee?" Miss S. S. launched into still another dialect, then sharply returned to her normal speech which was clear, refined, really quite beautiful. "If you have no sense of humor at your age, you're not likely to get one—for love or money!"

"I might say the same thing to you! Just because you've got a glib tongue and a good ear, you don't have to perform all the time. What kind of woman are you anyway?"

I saw Miss Sally Sue Sutherland—the last of the Sutherlands—go white under her powder, and her mouth creased into a long flat scar across her face. "I beg your pardon, Maybelle. You're absolutely right. I find myself amusing, and apparently Hallie does too, or else she grins out of politeness, which is a quality I admire in strangers but not in friends—" she paused and her mouth relaxed a little as the stiff anger left her. "I prefer honesty in friends, and I thank you for being my friend and for being honest."

"You shouldn't tease crippled people about being crippled," Maybelle said in a low small voice.

"We're all cripples, you fine young fool!" Miss Sally Sue roared. "Haven't you found that out by this time? We've all got to laugh at each other—to keep from crying. The Irish, the Jews, the Negroes, the Mexicans—"

"Yeah. God bless America. Home of the free," Maybelle said in sullen sarcasm.

"If you don't believe that—the spirit of it, at least—then go where that pot of gold lies!" she yelled, and to my already shattered eardrums came this amazing crescendo, "Uncolored gal, bring us some more champagne!" and immediately she dove back into the fiery furnace of her argument. "Yes, go, you idealistic bitter colored child, and bring me a gold piece from the pot! I'll *give* you a pot of gold to go find your variety!" Then she yelled at me again, quite in a rage. "Champagne! Fetch the champagne, I say!"

I jumped like a lackey; this was the mystical rite, all right. A human upside-down cake. I'd never seen anything like this before, and maybe I never would again. A Negro standing up to a white Southern lady! Absorbed in the spectacular, I moved over toward the wine cooler to get the champagne as requested, but not wanting to miss a word, a gesture. "Stop!" Miss Sally Sue's command rang out. She was looking at me with great loathing. "You see, Maybelle? I've just given you a sample of what goes on all over this earth of ours. I've just demonstrated how a people are enslaved—I've put your words into action. In two more minutes this gentle child, white in her heart as she is on her head, would have virtually been my slave for life. If she had touched that champagne, we could have never been friends again, for she would have feared me and there can be no fear among friends! Do you follow me, Maybelle? Do you, child? This is a lesson I want neither of you to forget all of your lives. He who yells and intimidates best commands best; he who flinches first serves first. The law of the master and the slave. You and your fine theories," she sneered at Maybelle. "It's practice that makes perfect, my girl! We learn from actual experience, and theories remain theories until tried. That's why I say, yes! America is the home of the freer, if not the free. Here at least it's possible, elsewhere it is not!" For a moment she had gotten a little calmer, but she was right on top of her anger again, looking pitchforks and brimstone at Maybelle.

"Your reasoning's a little faulty, but I take your meaning," Maybelle said, rather bored.

"Want another demonstration? Want me to take you unawares and yell at you?"

"Just you try it," Maybelle warned her between clenched teeth.

"I wouldn't dare," Miss Sally Sue assured her heartily. "Think I want to be murdered, or that I want you to murder me? A hurt animal kills; it needs to kill or be killed—and its odds are bad both ways. That's why I wish you'd lose a little of your starch. You're not a wounded tiger cat; your wounds are all psychosomatic."

Maybelle made a nasty little face at her, and continued her sulky silence.

I cleared my throat. "I want to say something, Miss Sally Sue, if I may—"

"For God sake's don't be so meek and polite! Have I scared the wits out of you, tell me! If I have I have crippled *you* for life!" she roared, then she rolled her eyes to the ceiling and said, "Oh, saints presarve us!" then added under her breath, "That's right, I mustn't say that."

"This is your house, say what you please!" Maybelle's nostrils were dilated.

Miss Sally Sue ignored her. "What did you want to say, Hallie?" she asked in a voice that was beginning to sound its age.

"I'm afraid I've lost my moment—I can yell, but I don't get an awful lot of practice.—" Miss S.S. curled her lip in slight amusement at this. "Mostly I whine, to get my way, but I'm young and strong and willing to work—"

"Come on, get to the point, child," Miss Sally Sue snapped her fingers tiredly.

I opened my mouth to go on, but no words came. Then I said to Maybelle, "Want me to walk you home? Miss S.—as in snake, Python Snake—is incorrigible—"

"Oh, for Lord's sake, Hallie. I beg your pardon—seems all I do is apologize in my own house. Now, please go on. You were saying?"

"That I was fixing to bring you champagne because you are my friend, not because you hypnotized me with your battle yell. If I had thought you meant to command me, I would have instantly walked out of your house, mortally offended. It was simply that I was absorbed in what you two were doing to each other—making history, at least for me—and since I'm on to your gruff ways, I never thought—"

"Yes, yes, child, I know. But you seem to have missed the point."

"I don't think she did at all," Maybelle spoke up. "I think *you* did—if that was *your* demonstration of *my* theory. It was not only highhanded, presumptuous, but in error—"

"Let's all love each other," Miss S. S. broke in, almost histrionically quavering. "Please. Please. And one of you, will you please pour some more champagne, and let's not fight anymore, hmm? But getting back to you, Hallie, you forget that generations and generations of fine breeding have gone into you. Like a fine race horse, breeding's the whole thing. It's a simple matter to hitch a racehorse to a plow, but you break his spirit and he dies. You don't know how easy it is to break a fine spirit—"

"Well, *I* do!" Maybelle shouted. "Generations of breeding! Fine spirit! What do you think those slaves from Africa were made of?"

"Cast iron, apparently," Miss Sally Sue skillfully jumped in to say, "if you're any sign. Can't put *you* down, no siree bob!"

Tears stood in two glistening globes in each of Maybelle's eyes. "Some of those slaves were royalty! They had *thousands* of years behind them, not mere generations!"

"Yes, and the royalty died out, and the boys and girls you have left have thousands of years in front of 'em!"

"I thought you said, 'Let's be friends,' " I said, my voice flowing into the heat like cool water into a hot parched throat. In other words, it created steam and gagging.

"For God's sake, don't misquote me!" Miss Sally Sue fumed like a very old person.

"Oh, good night!" Maybelle stormed, furiously trying to ram her arms into her coat. "No, Hallie. I'm going. She's completely impossible. I knew eventually she'd worm her way around to color. I swore before I came out that I wouldn't let her provoke me, but I could see it coming even the other night—baiting me, patronizing me. Don't you interrupt me, you evil old woman!" She roared, and Miss Sally quietly closed her mouth.

Maybelle, coat on, but collar twisted half in, half out, stood there panting. There was complete quiet except for sounds she made getting back her breath. "I suppose I should thank you for something. Like Hallie, you've made history for me, given me something I never thought to find in the South—an old line Aristocrat fighting like a dirty nigger with a dirty nigger, but fighting fair, I must say, not once trying to pull rank on me. Yes, I thank you for that. If I thought white people could be noble, I'd think you were noble. But I don't."

"That's prejudice, Maybelle," I said. "By your own definition."

"Prejudice?" she turned on me. "Why you're *twice* as prejudiced as she! Don't think I didn't see you flinch when I took your arm and put it next to mine. Talk about prejudice!"

"Yes, I will. In the first place if I'm only twice as prejudiced as Miss Sally Sue, then real progress has been made since she's nearly four times older than either of us. And as for flinching, didn't you too do a little flinching? Didn't you make yourself pick up that white arm of mine to see if you could bear to touch it?"

"You forget I let you hang onto my hand the other day!" she blasted back, meaning the lunch-counter episode.

"Okay, so you did!" I returned. "But I was the one who reached for it! The white hand reached out to the black, not the other way around."

"Colored, if you don't mind. My skin is colored. I am not a black."

"Bravo! First step forward. She knows she's not a black! Does she also know that's prejudice?" Miss Sally Sue cackled out recklessly.

"Black, colored, it's all the same—" Maybelle turned on her in a fury.

"Black, colored, *white,* it's all the same then!" Miss Sally Sue cried triumphantly.

"Oh, shut up, do!" Maybelle stamped her foot in exasperation, then qualified the degree of her defeat by breaking into loud and curious bellows. Her expression of grief was on a cacophonic par with her laughter.

"Guess we better not let her cry either," Miss Sally Sue observed. Then she turned to me. "Lovie, do be a dear and pour me a mite of that bubbly," she said happily, trotting out her Cockney accent now. It was safe once more; all the bombs had been dropped.

She knew she'd won.

CHAPTER EIGHTEEN

B UT NOBODY EVER really wins; the balance constantly changes. But what the three of us had learned together, as if we had painfully pored over a Rosetta Stone, was that each of us could decipher a little, and that together we might eventually decipher it all—a thing none of us could accomplish alone.

After Maybelle had given up her scene, Miss Sally Sue announced that now was the time for her surprise. She looked exhausted, so we both demurred, saying wait until next time, but she insisted. She left the room, and no sooner was she gone than Maybelle said to me, "About that hand-holding business, and your saying I flinched when whites touched me, you forget something—"

"I know," I put in, smirking at her wisely, for not only was I on to her about *that*—she was going to remind me that her family had had white servants—but it kind of tickled me to see how she held on; she had to have the last word on a subject.

"You *don't* know," she informed me quickly. "If you're thinking about the fact that we had white servants, that's got nothing to do with it as you perfectly well should know yourself. In that case, there would be no racial prejudice here in the South where kids are still practically suckled by Negro nurses—"

"Okay, you win," I said, but still amused. "What point were you going to make?"

"You forget, as I did momentarily, that I have spent the better part of three years in white colleges—"

"Then you should have flinched less than I did, not more."

"I didn't flinch more," she said stonily.

"All right," I said. "You didn't. But tell me this: did you have many white friends on campus at that college in Pennsylvania?"

"Not many, no."

"Any?"

"The same number I have here," she replied, smiling sheepishly.

"One?"

She nodded.

"And are you still friends?"

She shook her head uncertainly, then said, "No, I wouldn't say she was my friend."

"Why not?"

"Ready girls!" Miss Sally Sue called out airily from the hall. "Close your eyes until I get everything fixed."

We dutifully closed our eyes. We could hear Miss S. S. vigorously shifting furniture. "Tell me, were you playing Truth or Consequences when my back was turned?" she asked once when she had evidently paused to rest. "I love that game, you naughty things. Trust you to—play—behind—my—back," breathing heavily, she painfully got out these words. Then we heard a mighty shove and a thousand thinklings of glass like needles in your ears. "Oh, damn!" she said, not much concerned. "Great Grandmother's crystal candelabra. Perfect prisms too. Oh, well. You can look now, girls. No! No! Just a minute now! I forgot something. Now!"

There in an improvised Gypsy tent, quite cleverly done, sat an incredibly hideous old crone, complete with warts on her face. She leered at us, exposing several gnarled old fangs, brown as wood. No other teeth in sight. She sat among the wreckage of Great Grandmother Sutherland's crystal candelabra, but there were no Sutherlands discernible. In the dim light of a Gypsy lantern she beckoned us to the tent to have our fortunes read, and as we came forward Gypsy music rose to weave its spell.

"Come, come," the old crone lured us, slowly turning her ban-danaed head to the music, her long golden earrings catching the light. Under her breath she said to us in Miss Sally Sue's voice, "I did this at the Woman's Club carnival one year and scared those nursing mothers so bad that they curdled the little bas-tards' milk—blessed little tykes, they were; some grown to full-size idiots now—"

I looked at Maybelle and she was grinning in amusement too.

"—No sir, they'll never forget me," she cackled, the Gypsy again. "Be-utiful young ladies, come see the future!" Before her she was spreading a deck of very strange cards. "Tarot tells all!" she whispered in a voice of doom.

"Who goes first?" I asked.

"Both together. You're teammates. You don't think I really intend to tell these dam' fool cards, do you?"

I had been rather hoping she would. Wonderingly, we sat down in the two straight chairs placed in front of her table, our wide eyes watching her as she went through the motions of arranging the cards. "I really can read these things, you know," she whispered, "and sometimes they're uncanny."

We said nothing, our eyes glued to her in fascination.

"Make a wish, make a wish," the Gypsy spoke again, her voice dreamy as if she were going into a trance.

"Oh, Miss Sally Sue," Maybelle complained, breaking my spell as well as her own.

Miss S. S. looked at her sharply. "Make a wish, dammit!"

"What kind?" Maybelle inquired irritably.

"A real one," Miss Sally Sue urged.

"All right, it's made."

"You made yours yet, Missie?" she asked of me, Miss Gypsy Sue.

"Yes'm."

She took a deep breath and moved the cards around. "I see money," she intoned. "Lots of money, but not lots of money."

"What does that mean?" Maybelle whispered in a mockery of our Gypsy's tone.

"Shhh," said the Gypsy. "No bother fortune-telling lady. She get mad big heap, no tell Tarot cards."

"That's no Gypsy, that's an Indian."

"Me part Indian," said Miss Sally Sue, and as she said it, I wondered if it wasn't absolutely true.

"Me also part Indian," Maybelle said with a grin. "It true."

All three of us were grinning now, and Miss Sally Sue had her old alert look under the gypsy makeup. "Are you spoofing us, little ole gal? You talk pretty good Indian though."

"Me make accents good as Miss Sally Sue when me want," Maybelle managed to gulp out before she went into her machine-gun volley of laughter.

"Oh, Lord! Look what I started," Miss Sally Sue cried, hopping up from her Gypsy role. "Now, hush, Maybelle, and let me get on with my work. You're interrupting!"

"Can't help it," Maybelle said chokingly, shaking her head. But she did subside, then said, in her normal voice, "I really am part Indian, coincidentally enough. Granny told me not long ago."

"What kind?" Miss Sally Sue queried, scrutinizing her.

"Crow. About an eighth."

"Crow? No wonder you're so mean!" crowed Miss Sally. "I'm part Crow too. But *you* couldn't be an eighth because that's what I am, and I'm generations older than you are, child. Icie must have meant *she* was an eighth, that would be plausible."

"No, here's how she explained it," Maybelle began, and then those two blood sisters went into their entire genealogies, so it seemed to me, for their discussion occupied the whole of the next hour.

When they had finished, I had no further need to wonder how much Negro, how much white, how much Indian, how much any kind of blood Maybelle had in her veins, for she had told me—or rather Miss Sally Sue, and neither of them had a word to say to Indian-bloodless me the whole time. Maybelle was about three-fourths white, as it worked out, and probably would have looked absolutely white if it had not been for her Indian blood, oddly enough.

"Then why in the hell are you going around calling yourself a colored?" Miss Sally Sue wanted to know when the whole tedious lineage bit was over. "Can't you cross the color line and work just as well for the Negro people from our side?"

"You can't mean that seriously," Maybelle rebuked her.

"No," Miss Sally Sue admitted regretfully, "I guess I can't. But it does seem a pity. Especially in view of what I've decided to do. Here, I might as well out with it," she said, swooping back into the Gypsy tent and bending over. She picked up a couple of large envelopes from the floor and handed one to each of us. "I was going to request that you not open these until after I die, but I don't know as I trust either one of you to carry out an old dead woman's crackbrained wishes, but do spare me the humiliation of opening the envelopes in my presence—wait until you get home. Anyway, I'll tell you what's in 'em, and why." She turned to me. "Now, you, Hallie, I know you don't really need the money—I know your grandma left you all pretty well fixed and that she left you a little something all to yourself that you'll get when you're twenty-one—yes, child, there's money in your envelope, cash money—but when I got this idea, I was going over in my mind trying and trying to think how we might best help Maybelle out, and how I might do something worthwhile with all the Sutherland means before those fourth cousins of mine out in Texas—that's what *they* call themselves, I'm satisfied to call them what they are, turkey buzzards, or vultures in good plain language—before they get to it. And I thought and I thought, as

I say. So then I began thinking about what I was telling you girls the other night, about my life—about my years at Wellesley and later on in Europe, getting myself all smartened up fit to kill, to the point of no recall, and then I thought of what Maybelle had said about young Negro boys not minding that so much in their women. And *then* I thought, well maybe *everybody's* changed, or is changing, black and white, and maybe the day's almost here when a gal will *need* brains, will need to train herself to use 'em, and then I thought, pshaw! even if I'm right, and the whole world agrees with me, nobody in this hick town will, not for another generation of two with our talent for being first in the cultural lag, and po' little ole Hallie will never get a chance to go out in the world and be a scientist or something, even if she's got the wits to do it, because her mama would balk and say it was unladylike—am I right?—and her papa would stand by her mama, just as he always has, the damned fool, and by the time little Hallie got through and her granny's money was there for her to spend as she liked, they would have worn her down to the point where all she wanted to do was use her money to supplement her natural charms and beauty and entice some grand rich fellow into marrying her. Then I said to myself, so what? And maybe that's what she wants and it's none of my business. But then I thought, well, I'll take a chance and give it to her anyway, but on the condition that she uses it like I say, or doesn't use it at all, and this is where you come in, Maybelle." She patted my hand, then turned and gazed at Maybelle fondly.

"With you, my plans were already cut out for me—I *knew* what I could do for you the instant I knew I was serious—which came after I had reviewed my own life and I'd decided that the world was changing, and how. Because you had already told me two things, two important things: that you didn't have any money and that you wanted to educate yourself. So I thought, well, let her, and give her the money to do it! And that's that. But it wasn't, because I began thinking over all you had said, all that talk about prejudice and how to get rid of it, and I said to myself, why, Sal, that little ole colored gal's just as prejudiced as she can be, that's why she was talking like that, trying to persuade herself by her own arguments that she's the most broadminded thing that ever came down the pike! And she's not! If she were, she wouldn't be a joiner, and she's a joiner if there ever was one. Probably a field secretary of CORE. And while I like the cause, I reckon, I don't like for my little ole Maybelle to be a white-hater as she may be the rest of her life, even if I do give her the money to make something out of herself. She'll be grateful to me, maybe, and like *me*, but I'll be, at best, just one among few whites she'll ever accept, and those she accepts she will have to black-wash first anyway. So then I thought, I'll just fix that little so-and-so. I'll fix *two* little so-and-so's, because I know another just as bad off in the prejudice department as Maybelle.

"Anyway, when you gals get home and open up them fat envelopes—and no sir, I'm not going to tell you how much is inside 'em—you'll read what I'm now going to tell you. Putting you both on your honor, naturally, since my original plan was to ask that you not open up your letters until I'm dead, I told you, Maybelle, to use your money to go to my old alma mater, Wellesley, provided you had not by that time already graduated, and if you had then to proceed to step two: go to Europe and go to any university of your choice. Now that doesn't sound particularly hard to do, does it? But there was a stipulation—maybe a hard one, maybe an easy one for the future, who knows? but certainly a sentimental one, and one I still believe in with all my heart: that you embark on this educational venture with Hallie as your sidekick—or some other white gal of your choice, if you two had fallen out by then—and that you room together at Wellesley for a period of not less than a year, or take a flat together in London or wherever for a year, if you were at stage two. A year, it seems to me, would teach both of you a whole lot not only about each other as people, but about your respective races. You might end up loathing each other personally, or even racially, but at least you'd know why. I see you all are looking at each other shame-faced, and like you think I'm crazy. Well, crazy I may be, but I think I've got the right idea even if you two have already made up your own minds that you aren't the right team, and if that's the case you both know you can do about it. And further, to finish off this little matter, I might as well tell you what I requested in case neither of you could bring herself to spend a whole year closeted with a member of an alien and hostile race. And remember I was leaving the thing entirely up to your honor. Both of you I requested to forfeit your money—you, Hallie, were to donate it to the NAACP, and you, Maybelle, were to hand it over to the Ku Klux Klan.

"And now I think I'll go bring out our refreshments for it's nearly time for Jimmy to come."

CHAPTER NINETEEN

T HE REFRESHMENTS WERE chicken sandwiches, watercress sandwiches, cucumber sandwiches, and tomatoes stuffed with cottage cheese—bridge party food, in other words. Very dainty and ladylike, so I had had an evening out with the girls after all, and excluding the surprising climax, nothing more.

At the back door, for Jimmy was to drop me off too, we both tried to thank her, and she said, "Don't thank me yet, either of you. You may live to hate me for it, and I may even live to hate myself for imposing my will on others—I don't always trust my judgement myself, so I could be just dead wrong about this thing. But one thing I know—and this is why I want you to open those envelopes tonight and start thinking about it—If I am wrong I want to live to suffer for my mistake along with you girls, and if I'm right, why I want to get some pleasure out of it too. You'll have all the rest of this school year to make up your minds—and I mean that two ways because Wellesley has high scholarship and stiff requirements—and then in June if you've both decided to go through with it, then I'll write off and enroll you. If they're full up, we'll choose another place. Remember too, not to be tempted to give up the idea too soon if by summertime you've decided you detest each other; they're lots more white gals and lots more colored gals—"

"Miss Sally Sue, whether you like it or not, I'm going to thank you," I broke in impulsively.

"No, I'm not going to let you—not for this. I'll take what's coming to me after the test, if I live to see it, provided you make it. But if you want to thank me for the evening, I'll let you do that—though no, on second thought, I can't accept that either. No matter what's to come, you two gals have given me some very happy and stimulating hours—just the first of many, I hope—and you've made me feel not so much young again, as old ladies are fond of saying when they've been allowed to horn in on the younger set, but like a human being, myself, instead of the freak this town expects me to be."

"And I," said Maybelle, "humbly thank you for exactly the same thing."

Miss Sally Sue patted her on the head—she was that much taller, and said, yes, she understood, and that together we three would help each other.

We waved good-bye and started off for Jimmy's car where he was waiting, the engine idling, but Miss Sally Sue called us back. "One thing more: Hallie, even if you are all for this scheme all the way, as far as you're concerned, I can foresee a battle with your conscience over what you would say to your parents, and I want to say right now, say nothing, ever. If you decide to go to Wellesley next year, I'll take care of them. I'll go to them and tell them I want to take over your education, and I'll be so charming—oh, you'll see—that they won't be able to resist giving into an old lady's whim, one that will make her supremely happy. Naturally, I won't mention that my purpose is what Harriet would consider ulterior, and Henry might. We'll just leave Maybelle out of it. And if I'm dead by June, I think you'll be able to handle it yourself, for I'll leave a letter with my will—I'll write it tonight—addressed to you, to be opened by you only, and then you can put the money with it and show that to your parents, as if that was the way it was received. I'll make it a good strong letter too, so that Harriet even would be hesitant to try to persuade you to divert the money to other uses rather than use it for Wellesley and Europe, as I shall request."

Maybelle was looking as if she felt left out of things, and Miss Sally Sue noticed this. "Child," she said, "this goes for you too if that Icie Belle Brown should take it into her head to try to stop you from going, or inquire too closely about where you got the means to go. If I'm alive, I'll come talk to her myself and tell her I want to put you through school, and if I'm not—"

"I'm not worried about that, Miss Sally Sue," Maybelle said rather coldly, "but it did occur to me while you were talking that it seems funny to me that you used cash instead of a check. Are you ashamed that somebody might find out you were helping the enemy?"

"Oh, you haughty, prissy, ignorant super-sensitive thing! Don't you *know* that you can't cash a check on a dead person's bank account, and that even if you could, the bank, my relatives, everybody in town would do everything they could to stop you? Why I wouldn't even trust Billy Stickney, my lawyer, and I've known him all his life, and trusted with everything just short of my life, to handle a thing like this. He may think he wouldn't be too prejudiced, but I know better. There's not just *some* money in that envelope, my girl, there's a lot of money! Just you feel again how fat it is! And every bill in there is good too. I sent off to Washington for 'em myself, told those fellows up there just what I wanted 'em for tool And they just got here this morning, air-mail special delivery registered, as requested. I'd about given up thinking they'd get here in time, if they got here at all. Guess those Yankee boys in that Federal Reserve Bank think I'm as crazy as people in this town do. But I thought to myself, where can I get bills of a size like that without attracting too much attention? Even going to the city for 'em would have been risky, even if the banks there carry bills like that. So I hit upon this solution—and they may have even had to print them up special for you gals, for all I know!"

Then Jimmy, who had been waiting an inconscionable length of time, got out of the car and walked up to the back porch. "Miss Sally Sue? You know what time it is?"

"Certainly, I do, Jimmy!" she told him in reproval. "It's past midnight, time I got to bed, and time you got yourself back in that car and drove these guests of mine home."

He grinned at her and shook his head. "You sho is a caution tonight, Miss Sal," and he went off toward the car, as did we moments later.

When I got home, turned off the porch light and the lamp they had left burning for me in the living room, for Mommie, for all her threats, had not waited up, I suddenly sat down on the sofa in the dark because I knew I didn't want to face the contents of that envelope. As long as I didn't open it, I wasn't committed, was I? And I could go, first thing in the morning, and simply hand it back to her sight unseen. Yes, I could do that, and I wouldn't be hurting anybody. I'd just say I'd thought it over and I couldn't allow her to make me such a large present—how large? I wondered, but I knew I'd better keep off *this* line of thought or I'd find myself opening it whether I wanted to accept it or not, just out of curiosity. Did I want to accept it? I dared not think. For once I opened the envelope I would have accepted it, for myself and Maybelle, or for the NAACP—a startling thought! But how much more startling for Maybelle to have to choose between me, or a surrogate me, and the despised Ku Klux Klan! Was it a fair opposite organization to the NAACP? No, I decided, it was not and tried to think of one which might be, but I didn't know enough about Negro organizations—or even about pro-white racial groups—to get very far. But I did know, was sure, that the Klan was about the worst thing *I* could think of and wondered why Miss Sally Sue had deliberately loaded the dice. Then it came to me, and I could have jumped for joy! Miss Sally Sue had deemed Maybelle to be more prejudiced than I—what a marvelous compliment! Why else would she have made Maybelle's penalty, in case she wanted to forfeit, such a heavy one?

And on this note I quickly ran upstairs to open my envelope, or to get ready to, that is, for I'm sort of compulsive, have to turn around in my nest three times, so to speak, before I can do anything. So I hung up my coat in the closet, after I'd turned on the lamps I use when I'm going to stay up for awhile and putter around, then seeing that sweet old Aunt Stell had laid a fire in my fireplace for me, I got it started, pulled up my easy chair and sat down, and stared at the envelope in my lap. Then I decided to take off my shoes and stockings and my dress and get into a robe. Then I'd be really ready.

At this stage, I began to kind of hurry, as I was pretty excited and didn't want to wait much longer. And then the wind died down and my sails went slack, for glancing at that envelope—waiting for me now on my dresser—from time to time as I undressed, an explanation for Maybelle's super-prejudice, (or one I had adjudged in a sudden insight to be greater than mine,) came to me as clearly as if it were written there, just below my name: my relatively slighter prejudice was not the product of me and my intelligence, but of my time, my place, and the color of my skin. I could afford to be tolerant, Maybelle couldn't, and for exactly the same reasons that I could! The minority always has more to resent than the majority, if they are truly at odds. So what it came down to was numbers, size, or more factually, the matter of power. I belonged to the master race, and she to the slave. I was up among the elephants and she was among the fleas. No wonder Miss Sally Sue had loaded the dice! She *had* to make it harder for Maybelle than for me, for if I was tempted to take back my envelope unopened—. I stopped. Wouldn't it be funny if Maybelle had beaten me to the draw, if she had had Jimmy turn her around and head back so she could hand over the envelope tonight, unable to wait for morning? I persuaded myself that this was exactly what she had done, or what she would like to do right this minute if, like me, she had postponed considering the matter until she actually reached home. Wonder who will get to Miss Sally Sue first in the morning? I asked myself as I went back to undressing, now getting ready for bed. I set my alarm clock for eight—it would be indecent to put in an appearance on a Sunday morning before nine—propped my envelope against my clock so I'd be sure to see it first thing, in case my sleepy mind needed an explanation when the alarm rang for the necessity of getting up, turned off the light as soon as I got in bed, and turned over on my side to go to sleep. But I couldn't.

I kept thinking about everything, trying to remember if I'd noticed the expression on Maybelle's face when Miss Sally Sue was talking to us, but I knew I had not. I'd been listening too intensely, watching Miss Sally Sue too intensely, to have been aware of anything else. And I tried to remember what Maybelle had said after she had been given her explanation for the envelope, but I couldn't. I couldn't remember a damned thing that might help me. How I wished I had the nerve to pick up the phone and call her and ask her candid opinion about all this! But I lacked that too. I lacked guts, that's what I lacked. There were no two ways about it. I was just plain wishy-washy on top and truly gutless underneath. Otherwise, why had I so speedily rejected the challenge of even opening the envelope, let alone the challenge inside. And for the first time it occurred to me to wonder if I was being entirely fair, for maybe taking the envelope back untouched was tantamount to forfeiting the contents—she might even make me send the money off myself. Then I had a really horrible thought: suppose, because I refused to play the game, she called the whole thing off and made Maybelle send off her money to the Klan, or anyway to give it back. But she couldn't *do* such a thing. It wouldn't be fair to Maybelle. Her purpose in all this was to help Maybelle, not to punish her for somebody else's mistake—no, not mistake, but lack of courage, error through default. No, she'd let Maybelle keep her share and play the game alone—decide whether or not she wanted to go to college or Europe with a white roommate for a year, or whether it was a fate so much worse than death that she preferred giving the money to the hateful Ku Klux Klan. I wondered which she would choose. Then I wondered if my decision to decline the gambit wouldn't have some influence on her choice. Her first white friend she seemed to think had let her down, and now wasn't her second planning to do the same thing? Would I ever be able to make her see why I had given Miss Sally Sue the unopened envelope although I still valued our friendship? Of course not, because it wouldn't be so. If I turned back that gift untouched I would be admitting that I had never been serious about wanting to know and like Maybelle, that it was the idea of the thing which had appealed to me, not the reality itself. And was this the case? At that stage, I honestly didn't know.

Then it came to me that I was wrong in thinking Miss Sally Sue was doing all this just to help Maybelle—maybe Maybelle was her primary concern because as she had explained, Maybelle's need was greater. But wasn't she trying to help me too by giving me a chance to grow, to strengthen a little? For no matter what my decision after I opened the envelope, wouldn't I have changed through the process of having to weigh both sides to the question? I would, certainly I would, and if I didn't—this minute—open the fool thing up, I'd be lost forever as a decent human being, drowned in the milk of my own milk-toastness.

I turned on the light, tore open the envelope and twenty one thousand dollar bills fell out.

CHAPTER TWENTY

AVING TWENTY THOUSAND DOLLARS in your hand—even if you are holding it for yourself in escrow, so to speak—adds an extension to you as palpably real as another leg or arm, and in our particular case, mine and Maybelle's, the leg or arm image is right, for while extra things like that may be useful, who wants three arms? It isn't chic; in fact, if the word got around that you had been the recipient of such a questionable blessing, you'd be in physical disgrace and pronounced a monster, something to be set apart from the whole of mankind. Therefore, we both would have been fools not to consider excision, or, specifically, simply backing out of the whole thing and refusing to take the money or give it away, except back to its rightful owner, Miss Sally Sue. But, as if she had been the master mind of all times, even this total negativity added up to a positive, for it brought me and Maybelle closer together.

We never saw each other to speak except at Miss Sally Sue's on Saturday or Sunday nights, but we did talk on the telephone, quite openly, and quite often—I calling her M.—which my family thought stood for Em somebody or other I'd met at school—and she addressing me as Beanie, a diminutive(?) of my middle name which is Bean, a girl she told her grandmother she had met in the colored beauty parlor in town. And since I don't sound particularly "white," having a rather thick Southern accent—though it is, of course, a "nice-people" accent, easily distinguishable from the trash variety—I felt perfectly at ease calling up and having Icie answer the phone. "This is Beanie," I'd say quite fearlessly, even if I knew Mommie and Daddy and even Bill were straining their ears in the living room. And Icie, who thought she knew all about her granddaughter's friend Beanie, would call M. to the phone, as Beanie chose to call Maybelle. Naturally, Icie had asked Maybelle what was wrong what the name Maybelle, and had received the previously prepared answer that it was too long for breezy Beanie, and besides it was kind of tacky. Icie didn't like that, of course, and especially didn't like it because the Belle part had been put there originally in honor of her, so she left off asking Maybelle to bring Beanie home so she could meet her, a side effect we had both hoped for.

As for my family, since I do have a great many friends and I'm always hanging on the phone with somebody or other, "keeping my telephonitis in shape," as Bill says, they couldn't have cared less who this Em person was. For Maybelle's voice sounds no more specifically "colored" than mine does white. Her inclination toward a Southern accent has increased, whether she'll own up to it or not, since I first heard her speak in creative writing class, so my parents and even ole sharp-eared Bill never once took her for a Yankee. It was my brother, however, who asked what Em or whoever she is called me that silly name for, and when I told him it was because she was a silly girl, he was perfectly satisfied.

And so things went, but as the saying goes, "Give 'em an inch and they'll take a mile," so also things went—as applied to the three of us. But I think Miss Sally Sue was the one who felt the most constraint, the most need to "take a mile." She badly wanted to broaden our field of activity. Maybe if we'd been able to meet at my house or Maybelle's occasionally things wouldn't have seemed so cramped to her, but, as she so often pouted, "Why, there's just *no* place we can go, except maybe for a drive with Maybelle scrooched down in a corner until we get outside the city limits, and who wants to just drive? I'd like to take you kids out to dinner occasionally, go to the city and take in a show, have a little fun, but umm, umm, all we can do is sit cooped up in this house with the shades drawn, and I get good and sick of this house I can tell you, after eighty—almost, no don't you ask me again either one of you how old I really am, and don't start guessing either, you can do that behind my back. Yes," she would fume, "after eighty years, I've got a right to get bored with this place all the live-long day *and* the livelong night."

"Now, Miss Sally Sue, you know that's not so," I'd say half teasing, though she didn't tease easily—as a matter of fact, she was the hardest person to provoke I ever saw—but meaning it too. And I'd go on and say, "You know you love this house. If you didn't you wouldn't live here—not that you do nearly as much as you're trying to let on. You're always out terrifying the country-side in that car of yours, or up town or somewhere—instead of staying at home. I know you're never in when I call you—"

"Maybe I just don't feel like talking to you," she'd tell me with a malicious grin and then wink at Maybelle.

"Then I'll save my breath and my money next week," I'd tell her. "But all the same, I don't care what you say, this house isn't what's eating you—you could sell it and live anywhere you liked. The thing you don't like is the fact that we *have* to stay here—and we don't like the idea of that any better than you do. But it just makes you mad because you can't have things your own way."

"That's right, Missie," she would agree quite cheerfully. "You've got me pegged. And right now, if we could persuade this stubborn gal here, I'm wild enough to do most anything—flaunt society's face off—have me a great big ole tea, ask Lutie Pickard, Sukey Stephens, Mrs. Dr. Henry Hamilton—every 'leader' of society in town, every durn one of those arch snobs—and have Maybelle right beside me in the receiving line. My, how I'd love that!" Her black eyes sparkled so that you could almost hear a crackling sound and smell the burning flesh of her victims.

"I offered to go out to dinner sometime with you in the city," Maybelle reminded her, putting on a roguish face which somehow didn't quite distract attention from the note of reproval in what she was saying. "But you refused. And yet you were the one who told me how easy I'd find crossing the color line."

"I've told you a dozen times, child," Miss Sally Sue would speak up in a loud voice, "that it's not that I don't think we *could,* but that I don't think we *should.* We're not the only people in this town who can afford to go to the city on a spree. Suppose someone recognized us? No, if we're going to do something, let's not do anything else *sneaky,* let's go the whole hog and have a big elegant tea—"

And here at this bend in the road would come the impasse, and for the next half hour or so they would busily hurl themselves against it, or try to leap it, or circumvent it somehow. I would retire to the edge and just stand by. I knew I'd never be able to do any better at it than they did. And then, rather tired from all the verbal exercise, Maybelle would confine herself to a vigorous-looking if somewhat mechanical shaking of her head, a continuous response, to Miss Sally Sue's every word, whether a reply was appropriate or not, and would keep this up until Miss Sally Sue moved on to her next proposed solution, which Maybelle called "Cloud Ten."

Cloud ten was where Miss Sally Sue stored her absolute belief that the three of us could at Easter vacation, which was late this year and just around the corner, somehow manage to hop a plane and go off to New York and "have a ball," as Maybelle, intending it sarcastically, had taught her to call it. This plan was not without feasibility—Miss Sally Sue had worked it out that we wouldn't take the same plane and therefore would not be under suspicion by any natives who happened to be malingering about the airport—but it interfered with my plans. Easter vacation I had already promised to spend in Louisville with Peter love, visiting his family.

"You and your love life!" Miss Sally Sue had absolutely exploded when I told her.

But I was firm. Easter with Pete meant everything to me and I refused to give it up.

"How about if I made it Europe instead of New York?" that beady-eyed old horse trader tried to trap me, and of course, my crest fallen, I had to admit that for Europe I would give it up, so she dashed to the phone and began making calls furiously to find out schedules, and all that sort of thing. But then when we sat down to work it all out, feeling high as kites on anticipation, we sadly concluded that the trip, even by jet, would give us something just over a day in Paris—the place we had all picked. So Maybelle and I—not Miss Sally Sue—backed out. Who wanted one day in Europe? And think of the expense—it would be downright immoral. And why couldn't we all do it this summer, surely we could wait until then? But not Miss Sally Sue. So she dangled first Bermuda, then Nassau in front of me. But I wasn't having any. Neither of them was so appealing as Paris. Then she tried the Virgin Islands and San Francisco, and currently it was Alaska—though I had said often enough how much I loathed the cold—and I knew the next one would be Hawaii, our fiftieth state, and I was only hoping that connections there would prove to be as difficult as those to Europe so I could turn that down too, for I really did want to visit Pete. And anyway, there was something else.

I had never told my family that my walking nights out on the weekends were being spent at Miss Sally Sue's, and if I suddenly announced that she was taking me off to Europe, California, the Caribbean, Hawaii with her—where didn't matter—would they even let me go? Suppose, for instance, it was true that Miss Sally Sue had once upon a time before she got too old for it been a lesbian, and that this was common grown-up knowledge, still out of bounds for my tender ears? Why the family would pack me in dry ice with a pack of psychiatrists keeping a twenty-four hour watch. How did I know? I couldn't conceivably ask her, and I didn't want to ask anybody else; not really; why put ideas into people's heads? Of course I knew I could ask Daddy; it was just his sort of question, and I was momentarily tempted, for it would be a good way to let him back in—he was still desperately trying to curry favor with me as he had been since the night of his Big Defection, the night of the sit-in strike thing, and had been having as much success with it as Aunt Stell has with hollandaise sauce.

But I wasn't ready to let him back in, and I wasn't ready to hear anything bad about Miss Sally Sue; I doubted that I would ever be.

So this brotherhood of man idyll continued. People got accustomed to my refusing Saturday night dates, and though they wondered what I was up to—Dot Paranoia Carter particularly, who was certain I was seeing Leroy since she no longer was—I got quite glib at fibbing. Perhaps if, at this point, Maybelle, Miss Sally Sue and I had been able to conduct our friendship openly our enthusiasm for it would have died down. But the forbidden, when secretly indulged, has amazing regenerative powers, and I can think of only one evening when the three of us were so bored and yawny that we had to resort to television. That evening was just before Easter vacation when my mind was clearly elsewhere and Miss Sally Sue's was glum because Cloud Ten was, after all, going to be full of rain. And Maybelle was in a moody mood; nobody could get through to her.

A little before twelve, Jimmy knocked on the back door, coming to collect Maybelle and take her home. She gave Miss Sally Sue her usual brush kiss on the cheek, and with a vague wave in my direction, she was off. I thought this was kind of peculiar, even at the time—and the time was at the end of an especially absorbing movie on TV—because I knew there would be no chance to actually see each other until I got back after the holidays.

A few minutes later, the show being over, Miss Sally Sue switched off the TV and I stood up to go. I yawned and stretched a little, feeling quite happy and rather sleepy, and gave Miss Sally Sue a big smile by way of apology for the latter condition. Then I realized that it should have been for the former instead.

"You must not lord it over Maybelle that you are white and privileged, Hallie," she said severely. "The poor thing went out of here tonight absolutely crushed. Don't you ever think how she must feel when you're chattering away like a magpie about your dates and fun? I don't ask you over here to share these evenings just so you can hurt her. And I just plain won't have it!"

I couldn't believe my ears—I, the heart and soul of consideration—and began a mild sort of defense of myself which soon, of necessity, became a wild and stormy one. The chips flew, mostly in the beginning from Miss Sally Sue's shoulder, but I had a few of my own. It was a genuine fight, and I don't think a single recrimination was left unturned. I accused her of 1) being a spoiled old woman 2) a jealous one because her life was nearly over 3) angry at me for frustrating her Easter plans 4) hopelessly partial to Maybelle. And she found me wanting in 1) breeding— said I was irrevocably middle class, for which I promised never to forgive her—2) brains (toad brains, she called them) 3) beauty (just empty China-doll prettiness as I lacked both style and character) 3) generosity.

Voices raised on high, we both declared we never wanted to see each other again, and then, of course, we kissed and made up. It was Miss Sally Sue, with her sly sense of humor, who remarked even as she wiped the tears from her eyes, "Our first quarrel." But we did part on the theme that had been the cause of it: the need for exercising tact and discretion to safeguard Maybelle's feelings.

At the door Miss Sally Sue said, "You know Maybelle has friends in Louisville, part of that fancy rich set she likes to talk about, poor child, and though she didn't come right out and say so, I believe she had hopes of being invited up there for Easter too. I don't know what happened, if anything, or even how it came up when we were talking just before you got here. But she looked mighty blue all night. And you, you little rascal, and all your talk about Pete and the dinner dance and the Easter parade and the this and the that—" She gave me a little playful tap by way of punishment which made me say my good-byes in a hurry before she got started up again.

But she had succeeded in making me feel guilty and wide awake to my responsibilities: it was one thing to conduct my ordinary friendships in a lazy, self-indulgent manner, but quite another to perform the same way with Maybelle. Maintaining a friendship with a colored girl living in the South called for more than liking and loyalty and limited companionship—exactly what I did not know, though my intuition told me that the obligations might prove to be bitterly hard. Whatever they were, I determined to find out, and to do something about them.

CHAPTER TWENTY-ONE

WHEN I GOT OFF the plane at the Louisville airport, I stepped into Pete's bear hug and a whirlwind. I had never been to so many parties, met so many charming people, or been so admired by so many charming people before in my life. Each day was faultless, and the memory of that visit is simply dazzling; it had all the beauty, fire and brilliance of a great crystal chandelier, and all the lavish elegance. Pete's parents—Miss Miriam and Mr. Fred—couldn't have been more wonderful. They made my own seem dowdy and lacklustre by comparison. They were so exciting, such vibrant people, so unlike the parents of my other friends. And toward the end of my last evening Pete asked me to marry him. So I returned home laden down with spoils—nonnegotiable, it's true—but I wore all the signs of my triumph. My eyes sparkled, my complexion was as clear as the sky, and I bloomed.

The next weekend Pete came to visit me, and the one after that I went back to visit him. My mother and Miss Miriam were exchanging polite little notes through the mail about "our boy and girl," and my parents were exchanging looks of huge satisfaction because I was copping a prize. There was nothing official, of course, no formal announcement as yet, and there wouldn't be, all agreed, "right away." My mother had married young, before she was out of college, and she now firmly declared that this sort of thing was a mistake—somewhat to Daddy's unflattered surprise—so I knew this not "right away" jazz that she was giving us, and fast selling to his parents as well, meant that she expected me and Pete to wait a year at least before getting married.

In the first rosy flush of the dawn of happiness, time, like practically everything else, meant nothing. We simply didn't talk about it; we were too busy smooching or looking for a place to go off and smooch to consider time or any of those other earth-bound cares that beset earthbound spirits. So the sun was well up, smiling benignly on our relationship, before it came home to me what a thing like a year's waiting period could do. Waiting for what? We both asked ourselves, for so far we had waited for noth-ing. I had gone to bed with him the second night I met him, so that was certainly not the issue. And as far as going on to college went, Pete had no objection if he had an educated wife. I could go to the University of Louisville, either part time or full time, whatever I wanted to do. But Mommie, when we tried to pin her down, wouldn't pin; not even when we refuted her arguments with hard, cold facts, a number of which actually made her blush, such as having to persuade her that we knew enough not to have babies (these she said would interfere with my continuing college as a married woman) or why else would I have gone out and had myself fitted for a diaphragm? She was shocked, she told me later, to think her little Hallie was that hard sex-wise kind of a girl. I did not remind her of the rumble-seat sex she had described as existing in her day, or that I knew all about my brother Bill hav-ing been a "short term" baby.

So my mother's adamant stand was the first drawstring that pulled us down toward the harsh cruel world again, but of course it was not the last, nor did we expect it to be. We readied our united front for what was to come.

I guess it was on that second visit I made to Louisville—a somewhat quieter time—when I knew the moment had come when I couldn't put off telling him about Maybelle any longer. It all came about one afternoon when we were at the picture show. We were sitting there, holding hands, looking at the newsreel which they showed before the picture began. I hate newsreels, consider them just about obsolete since we get the same sort of thing daily on TV, and wasn't paying much attention until they showed this sit-in strike somewhere or other, maybe Atlanta. Where was not important, but the thing was I saw Maybelle. Right there, on the screen. Just one flash. Then the camera concentrated on all the Wilfred types milling around, and I suppose it really was very funny for they were carrying atomizers and spraying something in the air just over the strikers heads—perfume, suffocating gas, or something—I missed whatever the commentator said because I was so busy watching for another glimpse of Maybelle, and anyway Pete was laughing as was half of the audience, so maybe I wouldn't have been able to hear anyway. Then just before the news moved on to something else, I got another good look at her. It was Maybelle, all right. This time I knew I couldn't be mistaken, and you know what immediately came to my mind? The sneaky cheat! Yes, that was what I thought of her, and I whispered at once to Pete to ask him if he knew how old the newsreel was. He didn't know either, so all the way through the movie I stewed, trying to fix the date when the strike had taken place by comparing it to the rest of the news which had been covered. But I hadn't been paying strict enough attention to the newsreel or to the newspapers either to get much of anywhere.

However, I was pretty sure that it was within the last month. Could it have happened during the Easter holidays? Was it before? Or was it maybe even more recent. Naturally, I didn't want that to be the case, for I had been virtually out of touch with my secret pals ever since my first visit to Louisville. My thoughts of them had been scarce, fleeting and guilty, and it occurred to me that maybe my own guilt accounted somewhat for the ready resentment I had felt when when I saw Maybelle in the newsreel. But I swept that to one side. Why hadn't she told me she was a real pro at this nasty business, that she traveled around the country sitting in places where she wasn't wanted, stirring up trouble?

Did Miss Sally Sue know she did things like this? Innocent sweet Maybelle indeed! No money, hah! She probably had an expense account as long as your arm. She was just a colored counterpart of Wilfred, that's what she was. And to think I'd felt sorry for her because she was lonely; that her mock pathetic air had caused that fierce attack Miss Sally Sue had made on me! And all the time she was privately leading this full dedicated life, going off and taking part in all kinds of things without saying a word to anybody. Or maybe she was saying plenty of words to Miss Sally Sue behind my back. Maybe that accounted for why she had arrived before I did all those evenings. After all, Miss Sally Sue might be classified as a sympathizer, if not something stronger. She admitted she gave money to the NAACP. And it was then for the first time in weeks that I remembered those twenty thousand dollars hidden away upstairs in my stocking drawer. Twenty thousand dollars that I myself would soon be giving to the NAACP. I was so horrified that I felt sick. But not sick at the thought of giving away all that money, or at the place it was going to, but sick with shame. How thin was the veneer of my tolerance, how easily wiped away! It was in actuality no more than a film.

Deeply troubled, unable to follow the picture in front of me at all, I tried to think what to do. It was then that my resolution to be truly Maybelle's friend came back to me as I had formulated it that night after the quarrel. How quickly I had discarded that—I hadn't even seen her since, nor had I tried to. One telephone call, one lousy telephone call to each of them just after Easter was all I had done. Or hadn't it been Maybelle who called me? Yes, I was afraid it had been, though I knew that I was right in thinking I'd called Miss Sally Sue. But this excused nothing. Not only had I been remiss in my behavior, but to Maybelle I had been hatefully, utterly faithless. In deed and thought.

After we got out of the movies, we went to this cocktail lounge, and on the way there I made up my mind that I wasn't going to just sit on this thing and be "strangely quiet;" the right moment and the right person had come along together, and it was time to break my silence.

When I say that Pete was the right person, don't get me wrong. I had no notion of what reaction he would have, or what he would think of me after I told him my tale, and I didn't even consider it in those terms. It was simply that I had a very complicated problem which I couldn't handle myself and what better person to ask for help than someone you're in love with, to whom you've told all sorts of intimate and maybe even boring things already? But after we sat down in that twilight zone of the cocktail lounge, I realized I was going to have trouble picking out a place to begin. While he ordered our drinks, I shuffled through the pack of possibilities, looking for the key card, the trump I needed. Then I knew that wasn't the right way to handle it at all. The right way was to simply put my cards on the table, one by one as they turned up. So that's what I did.

"Listen, Pete," I began, "do you remember about the time I first met you everybody at home was talking about this Negro girl who was enrolled at school and . . . ."

It took almost two hours for me to tell it, talking almost steadily without interruption, except for an occasional question he would put to me to clarify some detail or other. His expression throughout was sober and for the most part detached. I felt like a client of the law firm where he's a junior partner, telling my troubles to him so we could work up my case. If it hadn't been for his squeezing my hand at two or three points this illusion would have been complete.

When it was over and he saw that I had not paused but had actually finished, he said, "Sweetheart, I love you," and his voice was husky with admiration.

So that was a perfect weekend too.

But on the practical level of what to do to help Maybelle, he had a quite simple but obvious solution: introduce her to some people.

"At home?" I said with a frown.

He laughed at me. "No, I mean here. Or rather people from here. I know quite a number of guys who have crossed the color line in the opposite direction."

"Socially?"

"More or less, though everybody's pretty quiet about it. As a matter of fact, I even know a colored fellow she might like—though we couldn't take him down there. He's not light enough to pass. But you say she has friends here, so she may even know him."

"Could be," I said with a shrug. "As I frankly told you, I don't really know the first thing about her as it turns out."

"Well, honey, she's just not sure she can trust you—or anybody down in enemy territory—yet. She will. You wait and see. By the way, do you think she'd take offense at being introduced to friends of mine?"

"She hasn't even met you yet," I reminded him with a giggle.

"That's right. First things first," he said signaling the waiter for the check. "And we'll remedy that situation next weekend. And by the way," he said looking at me in that mock serious way he has when he's about to say something really funny, "should I be looking around for something suitable in Miss Sally Sue's age group too?"

CHAPTER TWENTY-TWO

"H E'S JUST THE HANDSOMEST, dearest, nicest young man I pretty nearly ever saw!" was how Miss Sally Sue ecstatically described my Pete back to me, as if I'd never met him, on the phone the day after his inclusion at our Saturday night meeting. "And after you all left, I even got Maybelle to admit that she liked him. She thinks he's just right for you."

"And what do *you* think?" I asked, and at the same time took Pete's hand which was reaching for mine as he joined me in the hallway by the telephone.

"Oh, pshaw, Hallie, you were sure to pick a winner."

"Well, I like that," I said airly. "What makes you think he didn't pick me?"

She laughed and she laughed, rewarding this quip far more than it deserved, but she was in excellent spirits. Then we cut the conversation short for Mother had come into the living room.

Later that afternoon when we were out driving, it was all I could do to keep Pete from dropping by Icie Brown's for a little impromptu visit with Maybelle. "You've got to shock her," he kept saying. "She needs a shock. The mountain's got to go to Mohammed."

"Not that kind of shock. It's no good if it humiliates her, as dropping in on her would do. I thought you were the one who was supposed to have the cool, logical, legal brain."

"It's just that I feel so for her. Tell me, is she always so timid? Or was it just me?"

"She's timid at first," I said remembering the first part of that ride back from the city. "Though you wouldn't know it to look at her in class or something. And she didn't act timid in class either, just sort of dignified."

"Boy, she's certainly that. I don't know many gals her age with such presence. She's a real thoroughbred."

As gratified as I was over the impression she had made, I didn't particularly want him to be too overwhelmed, and when he asked me for the fourth time why I had kept this little cache of exciting treasure for so long to my selfish little self, I said, "For heavens' sake, stop treating me like a fraternity brother or something! I'm supposed to be your girl!" And he stopped the car right in the middle of the road and bit me on the ear.

After I saw him off on the plane that night, I called Maybelle from the airport. I wanted a long talk with her, without any Ems or Beanies, at least on my side. I don't know why I expected her to be reticent about him, but she wasn't. She said she really liked him, thought he was very intelligent, nice-looking, witty, and that he seemed to be one of the fairest persons she'd ever talked to about the integration problem. I asked her why she had been so quiet with him then, and she said because she was listening; she wanted to hear what he had to say. I couldn't quarrel with that.

"And what did he think of me?" she asked.

"The world," I said.

Then I asked her if she'd like to meet some of his friends. "I'd have to think about that," she answered. "I don't know how I'd feel about dating white boys."

I don't know why, but this made me feel quite cheerful. Then I told her about the colored friend he had in Louisville he had thought of for her, and asked if she knew him.

"No, I don't know him as far as I know," she said, and asked eagerly, "Did you meet him?"

I had to admit that I had not. Then she asked me what Pete's parents were like, if they shared his views.

"Gosh, I don't know," I had to tell her, for it had never occurred to me to think they might. They were originally from Memphis after all, and very social and all of that. Only I didn't say this to Maybelle.

Then Maybelle got around to telling me how glad she was for me about Pete, and how she did hope too that Mother would relent and let us go on and get married soon. "The only thing is," she said wistfully, "now I know if I decide like Miss Sally Sue wants me to, I'll have to start all over again."

I was very touched. "But just think of all that nice money the NAACP will get from me," I said lightly, but her voice when she spoke again was filled with gloom.

"No matter what she did to me, I don't think I could ever bring myself to give my money to the Ku Klux Klan."

"Well, there's no need to!" I cried, jolly as all get out.

But it did no good, for when she answered me, she didn't, and the gloom had turned pitch black. "I've got to get back to my Spanish." So we said good-bye, and I hung up, feeling, as I walked away, as if I'd left more in that telephone booth than a coin.

The next weekend the weather was so bad that all planes were grounded, so I stayed put and so did Pete. I went to Miss Sally Sue's, but Maybelle did not. She was in bed with a virus. So we played cribbage for an hour or so and I went home. Daddy was there by himself, back in his den grading test papers. Having such large classes, as he's a very popular teacher, among other things, he's partial to the true-false test. Anybody can grade them, since all you need is the key, and I've been helping him out ever since I can remember. So I offered to take over a batch.

As we graded, we chatted along, and he asked me about Dot and if I knew of any reason why she was doing so badly in school this semester—she was failing half of her courses, it seems—and I told him about her break-up with Leroy, and he listened and was sympathetic, as he always is, and gave me some good advice to pass along to her at the proper moment. Then he said some nice things about Pete and indicated that he thought Mommie would give in in a month or two. And I began to sort of to relax, and get back into that old, warm, comfortable daddy-love mood. And I guess I was the one this time who spoiled it all.

He was talking about something or other, and I was listening, thinking what a smart man my daddy was, how terribly much he had stored away in that head of his, when I suddenly blurted, "Oh, say, Daddy. There's something I've been meaning to ask you for ages, ever since that time I got fed into that sit-in strike: what's CORE.

He told me, and told me a little about it too. CORE stands for Congress of Racial Equality and already has over twenty thousand members. He went on to say that it was an interracial group with branches all over, and that its chief function was staging sit-in strikes and that was why the judge and the policeman who arrested me had questioned me about it so closely. Then, bingo! it had happened and we were right back where we had been for the last few months.

I don't know whether he said, "By the way," or whether the introductory phrase really was, "While we're on the subject," as I think it was. In any event, this phrase, or another, was the preamble for this:

"I think I ought to tell you that I know that you've been getting pretty friendly with Miss Sutherland. You were there tonight, weren't you, Hallie? All right. You don't have to tell me if you don't want to. I would be the first to agree that it isn't my business to tell you what to do—not any more. You're a grown young lady now and it won't be too long before you'll be living in a home of your own, and in no way accountable to your mother and me for your actions. But just be careful, that's all I want to say, and I think you understand perfectly what I mean . . . ."

The speech trailed off into the wide berth I'd given it from its beginning, and I felt his eyes search my face. There was nothing on that impassive mask that could be of the slightest satisfaction to him, I'd seen to that.

He gave a heavy sigh. "I've displeased you again I see, and I'm sorry for that. I'm sorry if I seem to malign your friend; that is not my intention. I am a staunch admirer of Miss Sutherland's in many ways, but for an intelligent woman, she's the most reckless I can think of, and recklessness, Hallie, is contagious, and habit-forming. Its powers are insidious, stronger than any drug, and it strikes down the strong and the weak alike ... ."

I don't know whether he had really finished or not, but I took advantage of this new pause and stood up. "Good night, Daddy," I said in a perfunctory but not unpleasant way and walked out on him. Let *him* figure that one out; he was the psychologist, not I.

And I wondered as I brushed my teeth just what all that reckless talk about recklessness really was about. I had a hunch he didn't know a damned thing, except whatever he may have learned from eavesdropping on my phone conversations. If he had stooped to that, then I'd have to be more careful about calling Miss Sally Sue when he was lurking about. For if that was his source of information—and why look further since that one was right at hand—it wouldn't have taxed a mind a fraction the size of Daddy's to put two and two together: if I talked a lot on the phone to Miss Sally Sue, it logically followed that I'd also see a lot of her, since that's what friends do. And as for warning me against her recklessness, what else? If he and Mother saw a lot of her, I might feel like warning *them*. Only why, since it was the most obvious thing about her, the one personality trait she was famous for, did he think he needed to point it out to me? No, I could only conclude that he was trying to bait me, get me to tell him something; I couldn't imagine what he could possibly think I might know that he needed to know. Oh, well.

But Daddy was right about recklessness being a virulent disease. However, I must say the worst case of it I ever caught was not from Typhoid Mary Sutherland, but from my very own semi-fiance. And we had a very, very narrow escape.

It all happened the following weekend when Pete came back to town. He had decided to drive, even though it meant a very long trip and less time to spend with me than usual, and it simply baffled me until it became all too clear.

He arrived late Friday night, too late to do more than drive out to the Lucky Horseshoe for a beer, and Mommie even objected to that on the grounds that Pete was really too tired. She never believes in letting people speak for themselves if she can speak for them. Anyway, Pete was all for it, and as I went upstairs to get my things so we could go, I heard Pete say to Bill, "How about coming along with us, fella?" and I was quite surprised.

In the initial days of our going out together, Pete had, I thought, discovered one person at least who was totally impervious to his charms and that was my sweet little brother, who is just about impervious, period. And when I say little, I mean little, for he isn't more than three inches taller than I am which puts him at about five five. He's quite handsome and all, is as blond as I am, but he's the smallest man in our entire family and has never forgiven anybody for it. Even Mommie, for instance, is taller than he is, which may be one of the reasons she pets him so—by way of apology, sort of—because both of us are said to inherit our blondness and our extreme shortness from the Craddock side, Mother's immediate family. But to get back to Pete, not only did Bill fail to respond to Pete's blandishments in the beginning, he went further and took a real aversion for him—possibly because Pete is so tall and has this marvelous physique. My brother is pretty childish. And, as usual, Bill had made no effort to hide his antipathy. It was so strong that he was downright rude to Pete, and even Mommie got after him about it when he'd do such things as leave the room when Pete walked in, or if he stayed not speak, etc., even to say hello, much less answer any remark Pete addressed to him. So naturally I thought Pete had long since written him off.

But the miracle of miracles was to hear my brother say in response to Pete's invitation, "Yeah, I think I will." So I rushed upstairs and rushed down again, because all this was pretty exciting. Bill just *never* went anywhere with me or any of my friends. He says we're all wet behind the ears. He goes around with a crowd quite a bit older than himself; a sort of rough crowd. "People who have no standing," to use Mommie's grieved words.

When I came back in the room, Pete and Bill both stood up. (Pete because he's a gentleman, Bill because we were leaving anyway.) "Good night, Miss Harriet," Pete told Mommie affectionately. "We won't be long." Then, "Good night, sir," to my father, extending his hand. And we were off.

Pete has a new black Lincoln Continental convertible, "as smart as a nineteenth century French funeral display," as Bill critically remarked; he hates high style and all that jazz. But other than this crack, everything went fine. The top was down— the day had been that pretty, and the night was no less so. I felt happy, very chic, and quite keyed up sitting between those two beautiful people, rather as if we were posed for an ad in *The New Yorker* for something madly elegant to fit the tastes of those "who know and can afford the very best."

And while the Lucky Horseshoe may have all the rustic simplicity of a sharecropper cabin and no charm whatsoever, it is still, alas, "the very best," for it's the only thing of its kind around that the mothers will even remotely approve of. I'll never forget the surprised look on Pete's face the first night he was taken there. "This *roadhouse?*" he said. "*This* is the local nightspot?"

So we pulled up in all our contrasting grandeur and went inside. Everybody was there. Fay Nesbitt and her date made a point of getting us to join them in their booth just so she could tell me, I gathered, that Tom was pinned to a divine Chi Omega heiress from Texas. "He always was an oily type," Bill said and jumped up before anybody could fail to laugh and went over to speak to some funny-looking divorcee type laughing her head off near the jukebox. But I appreciated what he had tried to do all the same. Then Pete asked me to dance.

"Where does Bill find them?" he asked, indicating this about 29-year-old woman Bill was now holding rather lazily around the waist.

I shrugged.

"Why don't you introduce him to some non-beasts?"

"Who did you have in mind?" I asked suspiciously, already sensing what was coming.

"Like Maybelle." He grinned winningly. "He talks to her on the phone all the time anyway—as Em. I bet you could get away with it."

"It's impossible," I told him seriously, adding, "—And so are you."

"Not at all," he assured me and then outlined his little plan, and I now understood why he'd brought the car. I could have kicked myself for ever having mentioned that Mommie and Daddy were going away over Saturday and Sunday—it was the annual hiking-field trip of this kooky bird watching bird loving society they both are so fond of.

"You go too far," I told him before he had gone what he considered far at all into the intricacies of his plan. "Anyway, don't you realize that Aunt Sophie's coming to spend Saturday night to chaperon us?"

His face took a good hard, well-deserved tumble. "In that case," he admitted, "it might be difficult."

"Besides which," I rubbed it in, "how do you know Maybelle would be willing to cooperate in this fiendish sport? Or did you have some idea of disguising Bill, having him go in black-face and white tie?" For Pete had brought his dinner clothes, so sure he was that he could pull off this brilliant little scheme.

"You told me yourself that Maybelle had asked you several times what the Iris Club was like, and that you felt sorry for her because she'd probably never get to go," he persisted doggedly.

I felt really annoyed with him and frightened at the mere thought. The Iris Club was *the* exclusive place to go in the city when you really didn't care what you spent for dinner so long as it was a lot. They had a real French chef, French wine and everything, and a menu out to here. I'd been there all of twice in my life and considered myself lucky, for Maybelle was by no means the only one of my friends who had never set foot in that sanctified luxury and probably never would. Rather sourly, I mentioned this, and also reminded him that Maybelle had not as yet expressly agreed to date any white friends he might provide.

"But it would be so good for both of them," he said persuasively. "There's old Bill, so prejudiced against desegregation that I'm downright embarassed over what he thinks, let alone what he says. And then there's Maybelle who isn't sure she wants to know white men except at a distance. And we'd bring them together and bang!"

"Yeah," I said, " 'bang!' why don't you go to Oak Ridge and separate atoms? I think you'll find it easier work than trying to put those two together."

"Well, it was a beautiful thought," he said, "and they'd make a handsome couple."

"Do you seriously think Bill wouldn't know in an instant who Maybelle actually was? After all, how many girls do we have around here who are that good-looking and with that particular kind of coloring? How do I know he hasn't had her pointed out to him on the street or somewhere? And how, for that matter, do you know he's even free tomorrow night, or that he'd consent to double-date with us, the Iris Club notwithstanding? I think he'd just say plain no, regardless of who his blind date was, Ethel Waters or M.M. He usually goes out on Saturday nights, number one, he's *never* been out with us, number two, and number three, Bill is stingy and proud at the same time. You'd never be able to convince him that the food there is really a bargain, and he, on the other hand, would be offended if you didn't accept his half of the check. No, Pete, just no."

But he had brightened. "If I undertake myself to fix it up with both of them will you go along with it?"

"No," I said flatly. "I won't. It's the kind of thing that would have simply monstrous repercussions. Don't you see that? First of all, suppose Bill is willing to go out with us and my friend Em and finds out later that she's Maybelle, and of course he would—I just can't describe the row there would be. Not just with the parents, but all over town. And who would be blamed? I would, and ultimately Miss Sally Sue might even get dragged in. Don't you see? You, *you* can afford to live dangerously—you don't live here. You can light the firecracker and run. But I can't. And if you did take the blame, my parents might think you were too crazy—*and* reckless—to be trusted to take care of their little daughter in the staid reliable way that her future husband should, and they'd break us up."

"I guess it was sort of a far-out idea," he admitted. "But boy! it was a beauty. And I still say it would work—you're even half persuaded it would yourself. I can tell by the way you're arguing."

"I can see I've been wasting my breath," I told him, weary and worried. "I'm surprised at you, Pete. Do you *know* the trouble I'd been in if you even approached Bill?"

"None, if I proposed introducing him to your pal Em."

"All right. Maybe not then. But it might make it dangerous for me to continue talking on the phone with her. How do I know how much he knows now even? And if he ever mentioned to her, in case he answered the phone when she called—"

"If, if," said Pete. "Why don't you just take a chance and let me handle it my own way and see? I promise to bring all of my legal genius to bear so that it won't involve you in any way."

I didn't relent, but I did say, "Maybelle is the first person to be considered, Pete. You *can't* even let yourself think about anything like this without considering her reaction."

"She might think it would be a lark, going out with your all-white brother under false pretenses. Might agree that it would be a good thing."

"Why can't you just wait until she gives you the go-ahead and then bring somebody down from Louisville for the weekend? Wouldn't we all have more fun—I know *I* would. Why does it have to be Bill? I'd die of nervous exhaustion before the night was out."

We batted the subject back and forth for the next two hours, or until we left. He brought it up the instant we'd hit the dance floor to dance, and would revive it every time the others left us alone for a second in the booth. The general comment was that we seemed so absorbed in each other, and wasn't love grand?

At this point, I had my doubts about the latter, but I certainly couldn't deny that we had a lot to say to each other. In one of my saying periods I tried to tell him what would happen if he tried to level with Bill, as this insane integrator was now proposing that he do, and was rewarded by having Pete casually ask Bill as he rejoined us if he was busy Saturday night. I thought I was going to come down with the ague.

"He's thinking about Aunt Sophie," I quickly explained. "And who will be there to have dinner with her."

I gave Pete's hand that I was holding under the table an awful pinch in case he ventured anything further. But he didn't just then, not when I pointed out that Bill would consider Pete's proposal good for both ten rounds and ten days in the public pillory. What greater insult could he offer to a disliked brother-in-law candidate, rife with prejudice, than an evening out with a colored gal, who, it turns out, is secretly his Nigra-loving sister's pal? "If he ever had scores to settle with me, real or imaginary, even Bill would think himself in my debt after that!" I blew up at him.

"All right, all right," he said. But he didn't sound as if he meant it, and he didn't.

So *that* night ended in nervous exhaustion. On the way home, happily we were alone, and temptation was out of the way—Temptation (brother Bill) having decided to stay on for awhile and hitch a ride with one of his buddies. "Why do you want to do this thing?" I asked Pete curiously, not satisfied with his original reason.

But he just repeated it. "I think it would be good for Maybelle and it would stir Bill up, might change his thinking."

"No," I said emphatically. "It would stir Maybelle up and change Bill's thinking—into something probably violent and active."

"You might be right. You know them both, really, and I don't," he conceded. "But I won't settle without a compromise."

"Let's have it," I said, hoping it would be something fey like kissing me on the neck, or typically crazy like driving out to the frog pond and going swimming in the middle of the night. But here's what it was:

That I help him coax Miss Sally Sue, until victory was ours, into joining us and Maybelle for dinner at the Iris Club tomorrow night.

"And who is going to coax Maybelle?" I asked darkly.

"I'll take care of that," he said looking irresistibly wicked, "with a little help from you and the Devil."

CHAPTER TWENTY-THREE

WHEN I TOLD PETE that compromises were odious, he said, "No, sweetheart, you're misquoting. It's comparisons you're thinking of."

"Not I," I denied. "It's definitely compromises."

Then we were home, and there was no more time for talking of it, for instead of the darkened house, the living room was as bright as when we had left it. I hated to go in if they were up; when they burned the midnight oil more often than not it meant trouble. But Pete had already hopped out, alacrity being spurred by the realization that my parents were on to the fact that he hadn't kept his word about not staying out late since it was obvious that they were still up and about. I could almost hear the prepared unguent blandishments and amends chiming sweetly as he rang them through his head. Being married to a charmer was going to have its drawbacks. Already I was beginning to feel like the wardrobe mistress waiting in the wings, ready with the velvet cape for the next scene's magic.

Naturally, we got through that one all right, and even without Pete it would not have come to much. Sometimes one forgets that one's parents have lives of their own. They had stayed up, they declared, looking rather youthfully bright-eyed and at the same time apologetic, first to watch the old Noel Coward movie, "Brief Encounter," one of the mementoes of their romantic past together, and then had just gotten carried away with reminiscing and hadn't noticed the time.

"You make it sound like an old fan and a dance card," I said fliply, then a look at my mother's face told me I had been unkind.

I kissed her gently and said good night to get out of it. And as I made my not so graceful but slick exit up the stairs, I could hear Pete placating them, or showing off; talking about vanity and the cruelties of youth as if he were their contemporary and hung up on the subject. I could almost see the fascinated and grateful looks on their faces, and hear the ensuing ardor and candor. It would be one of those periods of confession and narrative auto-biography which I found so dull, so embarrassingly depressing. And tomorrow he would snicker behind their backs, passing on something juicy and hitherto private to me about their personal lives. Couldn't they see that in letting down their hair with a member of the younger generation they were revealing all their bald spots? I knew he wasn't really a friendly audience, that he was too much of a snob and a sophisticate to really like them as well as he pretended. Even Mommie sensed this, for while she admiringly called him a "smooth operator," I knew this could easily turn into damning praise without changing a word. The three of them would be up all night, I decided; the parents giving out and Pete soaking it in. Well, he wanted to become a politi-cian, and this was better practice than kissing babies.

What, I wondered, was this Pete of mine really all about? He kept me on my toes all of the time, and it was good to be stimulated, but he was something of a rascal, too devilish for his own good. But, I told myself firmly, he is not a scoundrel; his heart is fine and fair. Like me, he was just young; maturity could wait. But it worried me. This Maybelle-Bill folly was no impish prank, and he would have gone through with it too. Now that I re-thought it, I couldn't devise a more Machiavellian plot; but why? Who was this dirty trick supposed to have been on, and why? Nobody had hurt Pete; not even brusque, rigid Bill.

The next day Mommie and Daddy, looking rather foolish in their hiking clothes and knapsacks, enjoined the younger set to be moderate, sober, and as well comported as if they were there. And as if to tacitly remind us that God's eye never closes, Mother even made Pete promise that we would go to church on Sunday. Daddy gave me a wink that was sly, a smile that was dry, and a grin that was shy; he didn't hold much with Mommie's unpredicted gusts of old-time religion that sprang up always unwanted and unseasonable five or six times a year. Easter was a day for hats, Christmas was a time for trees and trophies, and general too-much-too-soon in Mommie's lights; she was about as Christian about these obvious times for worship and mediation as a Druid, and this had always been true of her. But just let the thought of family Bible readings, regular church attendance and the beneficence of daily prayer go out of everybody else's head, and it was back to the Baptist Church for the lot of us. I could tell how foolish and rather plebian Pete thought she was from the surprise on his face as in agile cooperation he solemnly gave his word, even rather rashly throwing in on the handy spur the moment made, his intention to drag Bill along to church with us. He hit the target as squarely as if he had been playing horseshoes, for Mommie just beamed, and went off in perfect confidence.

If she but only knew, I thought dolefully.

And no sooner was she out of the house, and Bill out of earshot, than he was on the phone softening up Miss Sally Sue.

Yes, the evening came off. Miss Sally Sue listened to his line of reasoning and with very little hesitation agreed: the chances were next to nil that we would be recognized since people from here prefer, in the main, less elaborate, homier and cheaper nights on the town, and if some of her high-living city friends recognized her, so what? If we succeeded in crashing Maybelle through the color barrier at all, as we kept confidently telling each other we certainly could, then why should she think their eye would be more expert than the management's? She reckoned she didn't, and yes, we'd all have the exuberant time of our lives.

Maybelle agreed with the speed of light, so fast, in fact, that it took my breath away and made me wonder a little if advance warning could have been given. Then I decided that this was simply the opportunity she had been waiting for for so long, remembering that more than once she had hinted to Miss Sally Sue that she would be willing to risk such an experiment. I idly wondered why, then, Miss Sally Sue had never thought of the Iris Club as the perfect place it was for staging it, and then recollected that it hadn't crossed my mind either. For despite all of her money and position, her (to my mind) dash and flair, she was still essentially provincial, as was I. The patina of worldliness acquired in her youth had dimmed with age and usage. In actuality, she was really quite countrified—a thing that struck me in toto when we got to the Iris Club and she saw fit to exaggerate her yokelism in a self-conscious effort to cover it up. And I realized for the first time what Miss Sally Sue and I would have looked like, what droll spectacles we would have been, had the three of us attained Cloud Ten and decorated the courts of Europe and New York.

But if Miss Sally Sue and I would have been tacky festoons, Maybelle would have been as right, as quietly rich, as effortlessly perfect as that elaborate, incomparable dinner we were served. Miss Sally Sue almost ruined it for me because she kept craning around, gushing, giggling, conjecturing, commenting, making asides, running the whole scale from ostentatious dog-collar dowager hauteur with the waiters to picking her teeth with her little finger, saying she was a country bumpkin so could be excused for it. Also, she didn't add to my happiness any by setting herself up as sort of guide on tour of the palace. She kept telling me to notice how the effect of simplicity had been achieved when, had it been lacking in taste, it could have been showy; and to notice what the young ladies at the next table wore—that was the way to dress.

Until then, I had thought myself almost as well turned out as Maybelle, and a great deal better so than Miss Sally Sue. But she made me ashamed of my Dior copy, and I knew that it wasn't that it was so wrong—how could it be?—but that I had hoarded it too long. It was clearly last season's. And conscious of this now, I was in an agony at what must have been said when I had worn it at Eastertime in Lousiville, and I looked fearfully at Pete. But he, like Maybelle, was perfectly self-possessed, was clearly having a good time, not in the least bothered by Miss Sally Sue's antics, but quite amused, and looked just lovely. Gazing at them together, him and Maybelle, I couldn't help but think that speaking of beautiful couples, they were certainly one. But it was clear that they did not think of themselves in tandem, and I could not complain of any slight in Pete's behavior to me. He was solicitous, tender, light, engaging, deft, witty, with all three, as the need arose, always discreetly favoring me, as was right and fitting. The perfect host. He reminded me as he skillfully played and beguiled his way through his evening not so much of a writer, producer, director, actor performing in his own creation, as a humming bird whose presence and purpose may seem purely decorative and delightful, but who really has only one object in mind: to gather honey. Food. Serious work. And with this observation came a drop of icy misgiving. Why? He was courting all three of us, as his position indicated he should, but why had he aspired to such a position? From his flashing smile, I could not tell, from his darting flirtatious manner with Miss Sally Sue I could not tell, from his open admiration and flattery of Maybelle (delivered, I noticed, only when he was touching my arm or making some such intimate gesture) I could not tell, and as for his manner toward me, he looked as if he had never found me more excitingly desirable and desirably exciting.

All evening he took turns dancing us around the small floor, leading off, of course, with Miss Sally Sue, her age giving her precedence, not seeming at all aware of the curious looks she was given as they set sail. She had on a get-up that couldn't have been less than forty years old, and she had reeked of mothballs all the way from home to the city as we drove in Pete's car, the top up, the windows closed, in deference to her magnificent headdress topped off by a bird of paradise yet.

Her dress wasn't too terrible, except that it was a little grand for the occasion (she told us she had once worn it to an inaugural ball, though she didn't mention which president's) and, aside from that thing in her hair, she would have looked as okay as any other elderly lady in the place if she hadn't gained about ninety pounds in the stomach since the dress was purchased. I knew how she felt about girdles, but I doubted, even had she worn one, if she could have avoided the appearance of mother-to-be at the age of eighty. It was clear she was giving her spectators quite a turn and much food for thought.

But when Maybelle and Pete got up to dance the effect, if much different, was magically so. She was like a golden moth in her chiffon dress, and even the music they got for her turn seemed played on purpose—dreamy, filmy, heartbreakingly fragile. I actually felt a catch in my throat, and Miss Sally Sue murmured something about how fleeting, how ephemeral was youth and loveliness, how tragic was time.

So with much dancing, much champagne, Maybelle's white debut and Miss Sally Sue's come-back went on. She was, I noticed quite drunk, but had apparently worn herself out earlier, before she became so, in her hearty efforts to make a parody of her own attributes and shortcomings. Now she murmured an occasional passage from her interior stream of consciousness monologue that probably flowed at all times anyway, but these murmurings were very subdued. Probably she fancied that she was home, passing out on a loveseat in her own parlor and was just talking to herself.

Maybelle, on the other hand, looked vibrant, though she was not too talkative when she was sitting down. She smiled a lot and listened a lot then, her eyes very bright. However, I noticed that when she and Pete were dancing, she kept up her end of the conversation, in what looked to my watchful eyes as an agreeable and lively fashion. No, there was nothing in anyone's after-dinner manner of which to complain. And, I, too, felt more relaxed and satisfied. Perhaps the whole thing had been a good idea after all, and my heart went out to Pete in an expansive surge of gratitude for being so good, so kind, and so clever. This party was just the thing.

We got back to Miss Sally Sue's, where we dropped off Maybelle too for her cover-up drive home with Jimmy, at three o'clock. Pete was all for accepting Miss Sally Sue's sleepy invitation to come in for "an after-the-ball breakfast," but I declined, and she admitted that she really was falling apart. Then impetuously he suggested that he and Maybelle and I drive out to the diner on the outskirts of town for something to eat and pretended that it was a joke when Maybelle and I both sharply rejected that. His old mischief-making apparatus had been so dormant for hours that I guess I had thought it was dead.

On the way to my house, I chided him about it again, and he said quite coldly, "Now I know what it's like to be married," but softened this a few moments later by reaching over for my hand.

That was Pete.

The next day we went to church, which was awful, and came home to family dinner, also awful. Aunt Sophie, who had accompanied us to church (as Bill had not; he played tennis instead), seemed to have picked up a germ from the sermon, and she treated us to its full flowering—i.e., that there was no psychotherapy like the belief in God. I knew she wouldn't have had the nerve to sound off if Daddy had been there, but he wasn't, and all of us were poor stand-ins. Bill was too bored, I was too embarrassed, and Pete was too removed by disdain. Only Aunt Stell seemed to enjoy it, and they kept up a running conversation, not only while Aunt Stell served, but even while she was in the kitchen, having made this possible by propping open the door of the serving pantry so they could holler back and forth. I thought this was pretty nervy of both of them, and I knew Mother would not have approved of such informality, but it didn't seem to be my place to do anything. I listened to the endless nonsense as long as I could, then asked Aunt Sophie if Pete and I could be excused. Bill had left the table sometime before without bothering to ask her permission, and, indeed, she hadn't noticed.

Upon escaping I suggested that we pick up Dot and go for a drive, but Pete said he'd get enough driving later on and that he thought he'd like a nap. I was disappointed; left at loose ends. When he woke up, I was still reading the Sunday papers so he read too. Looking at him over the top of the page, I wondered what he was thinking; if he was tired; if he was bored; if he had something on his mind, or were we just prematurely settling into a married state, for all the world at this moment like Mommie and Daddy? If Maybelle were here, I couldn't help deciding, he'd sit up and take notice. I sadly concluded that I guessed the new had worn off me.

He left not long after that, and I kissed him long and sadly, getting the feeling that parting this time, even if it was just for a week, wasn't going to have the meaning and importance it had always had for him before.

"You've been so silent since last night, Pete," I whispered to him, my arms still around his neck. "Did something happen?"

"I love you," he said, and gave me a grin and a kiss on the tip of my nose. Then he was gone.

He telephoned on Tuesday night in huge excitement to tell me he had landed his first major case, and that as time was of the essence they were trying to rush it to court right away. He would be working day and night, he said, for at least the next two weeks. I suggested that maybe I'd better not come up for the week end then, and he complimented me on my understanding and promised me a rain check large enough to cover a monsoon.

Consequently, I called Miss Sally Sue during the week and told her I would be available on Saturday after all. "Good, honey," she declared. "It'll be fun to have our old three-way stretch again. We'll have a lot of things to talk about. And we've got to help

Maybelle make her plans for next year, you know. Can't let her get discouraged and back out after she's come this far just because life's going to work out differently for you."

I agreed that we could not, and then, impulsively, I said, "Miss Sally Sue, seems I haven't gotten a chance to talk to you for ages, but tell me something—something I've been wanting to ask. Did Maybelle ever mention anything about Atlanta to you?"

"Atlanta?" she repeated.

"I think it was Atlanta. You see, I saw her picture in this newsreel of a sit-in strike somewhere—"

"Oh," said Miss Sally Sue. "That. If you come early we'll talk about that on Saturday. I told Maybelle she ought to warn you, or you'd catch her on the silver screen, but she seems to think you don't much approve of sit-in strikes through you may appreciate what they're trying to accomplish. She's still a little afraid of you, Hallie, where's she's not of me, because you see, well, I'm an old person and you know as well as the next fellow that young people are sharper critics of each other, less inclined to take the long range view—"

"I wish she'd told me herself," I said coldly.

"Now, Hallie, don't you go getting yourself worked up! That girl thinks the world of you. There's just nothing about you that she doesn't admire. She's just afraid she's not good enough for you, that you think she's better than she is, that's all. If you knew how anxious she always is for your approval—"

I listened to some more, assuaged somewhat, but still smarting in spots, and promised to come early.

Saturday evening around six, Miss Sally Sue called, sounding very low, and said she was in bed with a temperature and Dr. Spears told her she mustn't have any company.

"What a shame!" I exclaimed, thoroughly disappointed, and found it taxing to go through the motions of solicitude for her health, inquiring about symptoms, etc., and listening to her answers. I longed for her old person's voice to stop droning so I could hang up and start making calls to drum up something else to do with my time. Promising to call and see how she felt tomorrow, I was just about to hang up when I said, "I'll call Maybelle for you right away," remembering that the phone communications between them could work only one way.

"Oh, no need," she said. "Maybelle couldn't have been with us anyway. She got an invitation on Thursday to go visit those friends of hers in Louisville, at long last. I was so pleased for the girl. But I thought you knew that, honey. Last thing she told me was that she was going to call you because I told her maybe you'd change your mind and go up for the weekend too. You're sure she didn't try to call? Maybe that brother of yours took the message and then forgot to—"

"Certainly, I'm sure she didn't call," I replied very irritably although I wasn't sure at all; I had been out a lot.

So when I got off the phone, I went in search of Bill and found him in his room putting on his tie. He, at least, was going out. I stood in his doorway for quite some moments, and then I knew he was deliberately ignoring me. He hadn't been even his usual unpleasant self with me for some time. "Did you forget to give me any phone messages yesterday or the day before?" I asked finally.

"No, I didn't forget to give you any phone messages yesterday or the day before," he mimicked, nasty as could be. "Why? Who were you expecting to call? Louisville Luke, or whatever that simpering bastard's name is?"

"No, I thought maybe my friend Em," I answered feeling too intimidated by his manner to express the anger I felt.

"*Em!*" he spat at me with acid hatred. "You and your Em!" And he vacated his room as if I had polluted it with my presence so that it was no longer fit for his use.

I was puzzled by his manner, but then I always was. So I wandered off in the direction of my own sanctuary to do some telephoning and to think.

CHAPTER TWENTY-FOUR

NATURALLY, BY THIS TIME everybody I called was already busy. Even Ridey had a date. And I felt so depressed that I hardly touched my dinner. But in all honesty, it did not occur to me why I was really depressed until about eight o'clock whem Mommie, having suggested a game of Russia Bank, since Daddy had had to go out and the two of us were alone, said, thinking to cheer me up, "If people didn't know you were going steady, dear, you'd be just as popular as you were before. And I'll bet Pete is feeling just as blue as you are tonight, sitting at home working on his case. He'll probably call later, don't you think?"

I mumbled that I supposed so and let it go at that, but I couldn't wait for the game of Russian Bank to end, so anxious was I to get upstairs on my private telephone and put through a call to Louisville, just to make certain . . . .

It was nine when I finally got through. Their maid answered the phone and said, no, that Mr. Lockridge, Jr. was out for the evening and could she take a message? "No!" I shouted into all listening ears and hung up, hornet mad. Then two minutes later decided that hadn't been so smart, placed the call again and this time had the operator leave word for him to call as soon as he came in, even if it was after twelve. This instruction was in strict disobedience of my parents' house rules, and I didn't care, I didn't care!

As I lay there on the bed, waiting, waiting, waiting, I saw it all so clearly. No wonder he had seemed distant last Sunday after our Iris Club party Saturday night. His conscience, of course. And that clever little ruse he had cooked up to put me off, to prevent my coming. And Maybelle, silent as the grave all week. Oh, that one! What a devious deceitful thing she was. Well she wouldn't get by with it so easily. I was on to her now, and had actually had my eye on her almost from the first, beginning with that business about the contact lenses. Pretending to have blue eyes, and yet, at the same time, pretending not to want to appear white! Ugh! It made me sick. Totally dishonest, depraved. Well, she wouldn't get very far with all this, she'd see. I'd fix her little red wagon. A sneaky cheat, that's all she was. Rushing around with her filthy Nigra business, sitting-in striking right and left. She was quite right, I didn't approve. As a matter of fact, I thought the whole thing was awful. Ugly. Black.

How long I lay entertaining these green passions, I don't know, because Mommie came in at one point feeling lonesome too and wanting to talk. So I had to talk with her. It wasn't any good though because she immediately got off on Bill, asking me wistfully what I reckoned had made him the way he was, and how she wished he had nice girls, like some of my friends, and why wasn't I nicer to him, why didn't I encourage him to become a part of our group. I finally yelled at her that it was her fault for spoiling him and that everybody hated him including me.

My heart was still carrying on as a result of this when the phone at ten thirty gave one sharp half ring. The reason it stopped was that I lunged at it like a panther, viciously said hello, and it was Pete.

"Sweetheart?" he said in concern. "Is something wrong?"

"No," I said, then asked roughly, "where were you? I thought you weren't going out."

"I didn't go out," he said in surprise. "I was at the office up until fifteen minutes ago. I just got in and found your message and called you right up. I was afraid something was wrong. Why aren't you at Miss Sally Sue's?"

"She's sick," I said. "At least she said she was. Did you know that Maybelle's in Louisville?"

"No. Was I supposed to?"

"Not specifically," I hedged, catching on now to what I must have been sounding like.

"Well, that's great," he said. "Maybe I can meet her for a drink somewhere or something tomorrow. Is she staying with the Hunts or whatever she said were the names of those colored friends of hers?"

"Yes," I said bright with relief since the danger had passed, and cooperatively told him that I thought Gordon was the first name, that he'd probably find it listed in the telephone book.

"Seems a darned shame I didn't know before," he said as if apologizing to me, "but I've been so busy, sweetie, that I don't think I could have tried to take her out and introduce her around anyway. Maybe next time. Maybe you can both come up on the same weekend and we'll fling a ding."

I waited to see if he was going to be more specific about when such a weekend, or any, would be, but he wasn't; and after telling me how relieved he was to hear that there was nothing wrong, how much he loved hearing my voice even though it reminded him of how lonesome he was for me, we exchanged parting endearments and broke the connection.

But I was again only partially satisfied. I decided on Monday that my jealousy had been as totally unreal while I had indulged it as had been my grounds for having it; that it was just sort of a sickness that had come on me because of restlessness and disappointment over being separated from Pete; that I liked Maybelle fine, always had, but I just wasn't very happy. My malcontent was all due to frustration and nothing would really be right again, thought I, until Pete's damn case was tried and won. I even dismissed from my mind the serious consequences that might have resulted from the phone call with Pete if I had been one hair's breadth slower in changing my angry tune to a more detached one. And then, hardly consolate, but in the mood to talk to somebody, I called Maybelle to ask her all about her visit and to see if she and Pete had been able to touch hands at some point.

Icie Brown informed Beanie that M. would not be back until Wednesday.

This was quite a shock, and before Wednesday, long before, that old black magic of the green-eyed dragon had me thoroughly entangled in its spell. I was afraid I was going out of my head, and I kept longing to talk to somebody about it, but who was there to talk to? Only Miss Sally Sue, and I was afraid to talk to her, because if I was going out of my mind, if all of it were just sick, sick, sick I didn't want her to see it. It would just get her back up and put her even higher up in Maybelle's grandstand. I didn't think I'd be able to bear one of her tongue lashings about how I looked for evil where there was only good, how much Maybelle thought of me, how Maybelle would never in her life think such dark thoughts about me, and what made me think a friend like that would betray me... on and on. Yes, an imaginary conversation with Miss Sally Sue was enough to make me know I could expect no succor from that source, so as a result I twisted and turned and suffered and then it was Wednesday.

I called Maybelle. Yes, she had had a very good time, thanks. Well? said I. What all did she do? and she spread out her itinerary for me, and it was as flat and lifeless as a collection of picture postcards. I wasn't getting through to her, and she was being remote, preoccupied with me—or was it the reserve of pity, smugness, guilt? Why couldn't she just tell me she'd seen Pete, laugh it off lightly. What was she waiting for. Well? I said again, and she ended, laughing her furry little laugh that was now as maddening to me as it had once been soothing, literally like a garment of fur in the red hot summertime, and said, "Well, I'll see you on Saturday, I suppose."

I almost called her back to demand what right she had "to suppose"—if suppose it was—that I'd be free to come. Or did she already know that my beloved was not expected here or expecting me there? Or did she know something more than I, that I was no longer his beloved? That I was banished forever and she had usurped my place? Oh, Daddy, Daddy, I cried to myself. Daddy, help me!

And that's when I decided for once and for all that mental telepathy did not work, for otherwise Daddy would have heard me inside my cage pleading with him to come help me, help me to fly again. But he never once gave a sign, never once felt the fluttering of my broken wing. Instead, on the surface, everything was as usual. Same schedule, same food, same banal family exchange, same air, same water, same bathtub, same shampoo.

My breaking point came on Saturday night while I was getting ready to go to Miss Sally Sue's. I *had* to talk to Daddy, I had to tell him everything, yes everything. He would protect me and guide me, he would combat them for me, he would tell me what to do. Half dressed, I rushed frantically down the stairs calling to him, but he was nowhere and Mommie had disappeared too. Then I tried the bathroom off the hall, and, sure enough, the door was locked, which meant somebody was inside. I pounded on it, and pretty soon Bill in a bored voice, but a loud one, hollered for me to shove off.

Okay, I thought, I will, but if you know where my daddy is you're going to tell me, so I stationed myself, sitting in my slip, on the living room couch. He came out at last, and steadying my voice—he was the last human on earth to whom I would expose my distress—I asked, "Where are the people?"

"What do you care?" he snarled. "Do you ever bother to ask them anything? Or tell them anything?"

"About as much as you do," I countered, outsnarling him by far. He didn't know he'd stepped on the tail of a wounded tiger.

"Well, at least *I* knew it was their wedding anniversary," he boasted.

"Oh, really, did you now?" I said, employing one of Miss Sally Sue's most infuriating devices.

"Yes, really, I did now," he mimicked me. He was at the front door and on his way out at that point, saying nothing more, including good night, and I knew I'd have to humble myself, ask where they were, how I could get in touch with Daddy.

"Try praying," he advised. "Maybe God will tell you, I won't!"

"Oh, Bill!" I beseeched him, but my piteous appeal had no appeal for him. I might as well have been a kitten entreating a cat hater to help, for he had gone; deaf to the cries of baby sister. Why, oh, why, I thought as I miserably dragged myself back up the stairs, did they ever have to have us those dangerous three years apart?

CHAPTER TWENTY-FIVE

I DON'T KNOW what ever made me do it, maybe telepathy works after all, but I gave into my fanteague and natural laziness that night and took my car instead of walking. I guess I thought since all the family was out when I left that all risk was gone. However, I did take the precaution of driving down Hatch Hill so I could enter by the back driveway, as Jimmy always did, and park my car in the rear where it wouldn't be readily seen. I was a little late, but I didn't want to be too late. I knew my nerves wouldn't stand it if Miss Sally Sue turned grumpy and reminded me that she was a very, very old lady who did not care to be kept waiting by youth and all that jazz. Inconsiderate, imperious tyrant that she was.

So of course entering the back way I didn't see the cars in front—even needing, as much as I did, the questionable solace of the evening, I still would never have committed the folly of turning up at Miss Sally Sue's when I knew she had company. And, not having seen these cars, when I knocked at the back door, I thought, I hope she hears me for it was possible that Jimmy had come and gone and she and Maybelle would be listening for the front, not the back. So I pounded good and hard.

I was still pummeling the door when it opened and there stood an almost unrecognizable Miss Sally Sue peering out at me in tremendous fright. "Thank God, it's only you!" she said in a voice trembling with age and terror, more like one of Miss Sally Sue's parodies than anything else.

I stared at her in shocked disbelief. "What is it? What's happened?" I cried. She looked as if she were going to disintegrate.

Gone was the tall stately independent Miss Sally Sue who looked and acted about twenty years younger than her actual age, and in her place was this stooped-over trembling old lady.

She quivered her head around and stared over a hunched up shoulder into the darkness of the back hall; a palsied hand quietly shut the door. Then, drawing me into the shadows of the back porch, she whispered, "I told 'em it was my cook at the door, but they probably don't believe that either, so you better skedaddle, fast as your legs can carry you or they'll be after you too."

"Who?" I cried frantically. "What are you talking about?"

"I'm in deep trouble, child. Bad trouble." She put a shaking hand on my arm. "So just go on back home. I'll call you when it's all over. They'll leave pretty soon now."

"What about Maybelle? Do they—whoever they are—have her too?"

"Oh, my!" she said in the tone very old people use when talking to themselves. "Yes, you better wait down by the road and stop 'em when Jimmy brings her. Can't have her turning up at a time like this. That's all they need."

"But who is 'they?' " I demanded to know. "I won't leave you unless you tell me."

"Shhh," she cautioned me, then sounding like herself for the first time, a faint whiff of humor in her voice, she whispered, "I'm being paid a formal call by the White Citizens' Council."

I groaned and she shushed me again and hurried me on my way.

I stealthily crept off the porch and got back in my car, (which she hadn't noticed, thank heavens; it would only have added to her distress,) terribly conscious of every sound I had made. Then I told my failing wits I was being foolish. If I were supposed to be Miss Sally Sue's departing cook, I might be expected to make some sound since cooks are generally flesh and blood. I started up my car, and was just leaving the driveway for the street when Jimmy's car turned the corner.

In a matter of seconds he was turned around and on his way to get Mr. Stickney and Maybelle was in my car, sitting beside me.

"I'm not sure that this is the best idea," she said, sounding very unsure indeed.

"What else is there to do?" I asked her. "*You* think of something. You agree, I hope, that it's more important to get Mr. Stickney right over there to her than what happens to us?"

"Yes, but I don't like the idea of us going to your folks' place and waiting even if they aren't home. What happens if they suddenly come back?"

"They won't, I assure you," I said flatly, wondering indeed just what would happen if they came back, but I had to talk to Maybelle face to face. I had to.

"I still don't like it," Maybelle said slowly, shaking her head. "I think it would be better if I just got out now and walked home. That way there wouldn't be any risk and you could call me as soon as you hear from Miss Sally Sue."

"But there *isn't* any risk," I insisted. "And she said she expected them to leave soon so then we can maybe go back." If she thought she could get away from me before question and answer period in re Pete, she was crazy.

"How do you know that this anniversary party of your parents is going to last 'all night,' as you put it? I thought you said they always retired early."

"Well, by 'early' I didn't exactly mean sundown," I told her sarcastically. "Anyway, what are you afraid for? I'll simply introduce you to Mother as my friend Em, if they should come in. Scared you couldn't pass the test?"

"Thanks," she said, her sarcasm far more acidulous than mine. Then added, "And what about your father? Do you think he's going to go along with this deception, or do you think he'll fail to recognize me? Which?"

"They won't be there," I said stonily, "so all this is purely academic."

"Stop the car," said Maybelle. "I'm getting out."

"That's right," I told her, stopping. "Cut out. Desert ship."

Maybelle hesitated, her hand on the door handle. "All right," she said finally, "but if anything happens you'll be the one to be sorry, the one to be blamed."

"I know that," I replied, and drove on toward my house with my prisoner.

I'll admit I felt very scared about what I was doing, but once I had started it I couldn't quit. Everything Maybelle had said was right—from suggesting that maybe Miss Sally Sue didn't want Mr. Stickney dropping in sort of accidentally-on-purpose to her misgivings about my family's return. There was no sane reason for me to insist that she come to my house except that I wanted her to—yes, I really did. In addition to the information I was determined to have from her own lips, that poor little scrap of friendship I had left for her had flagged at me, and I remembered how much I had previously wished for the natural pleasure of having Maybelle see our house, see my room, all my treasures, get to know me on the basis that other friends knew me. Is this so wrong? I asked myself, and whatever sensible decent part of my consciousness still remained said yes, in these circumstances it is, because you're lying. Then the feeble battery flickered out and we were there.

With relief I noticed that there was still just the one lamp on which I had left in the living room which meant the coast was clear.

Going ahead, I threw open the front door and she walked in. I followed and went around switching on more lights. Maybelle remained near the door, gazing around. "This is very nice," she said.

"Nothing very grand," I replied, my heart pounding my ribs like a pile driver.

"And your room is upstairs?"

I nodded. "Would you like to see it?"

She said that she would, but even as she said it I knew my nerves wouldn't stand the strain unless I stole a few minutes to be alone and collect myself, so I said I'd go get a couple of Cokes to take upstairs with us.

In the kitchen my apprehension flew up around me like a flock of birds. Somehow, some way, I *had* to get her out of the house, but fast! I must have been out of my mind bringing her here like this. But I couldn't think, I couldn't think. What excuse could I invent? What about saying I found a note from Mommie in the kitchen saying they'd be back about ten—for they would, I felt certain of that now. What time was it getting to be anyway? I looked frenziedly at the kitchen clock, but somebody had unplugged it again for the electric can opener. That lazy bum of a brother of mine. Why could he never put anything back? Why was it there were never enough sockets for the appliances in this house? I grabbed up the Cokes and went back, knowing that my excuse to get her out would not do.

"Look," Maybelle said when I got back in the living room. "I think I'll leave now. I don't feel right being here and I can tell you're uncomfortable."

The look of relief I gave her must have told her that it was all true, but what happened? All my stubbornness, all my fanatic determination to get her to admit the truth about what she had done in Louisville came right back. "No. You just got here," I said. "Here, drink your Coke."

She shook her head. "I'm going, Hallie. You know that's the right thing—" she was saying, and then the phone rang.

Nervously I dashed to it.

"Hey, Hallie, what on earth are you doing home on Saturday night?" Dot asked.

"Nothing special," I muttered and glanced into the living room to see what Maybelle was doing. She was standing thoughtfully by the desk, then she moved, so she was out of my sight, and the phone cord wouldn't stretch any further.

"Our bridge game just broke up, so I thought I'd run over for a minute," she said further.

"Oh, no!" I expostulated.

"What?" Dot asked in surprise.

Then I recovered myself. "Nothing," I said. "Psyche just did something wicked." I looked around what I could see of the living room for the poor innocent thing, but she wasn't in sight either. "Look, Dot," I said. "I'm already in bed."

"You sick or something?"

I could tell she didn't believe me, but I couldn't have cared less. "Yeah," I said.

"You don't sound it."

"Well, I am."

She hung up good and mad.

When I went back into the living room, Maybelle was stationed at the front door. "I tried to slip out as soon as I realized it wasn't Miss Sally Sue calling," she said. "But I couldn't get the door open."

"It sticks," I said. "Sit down." The fact of the matter was that so great was my consternation over having brought her here that I had, without knowing what I was doing, double locked it.

I sat down myself and stared at her vacantly, thinking what a close shave *that* was! and feeling chilly all over because Dot only lives a few houses down the street. Suppose she should take a notion into her head to come over anyway? Holy sweet Jesus! I closed my eyes for a minute and inwardly shuddered.

When I opened them back up Maybelle was still standing at the door, looking at me doubtfully. "What are you trying to prove, Hallie?" she asked. "You know you really want me to go, and I want to go—"

"Oh, no, no!" I hopped to my feet. "You can't go yet."

"Why?" she asked curiously.

"Because you must—because that was somebody on the phone who lives practically next door—" I couldn't blurt out that she had to confess about Pete before I would free her.

"I heard your conversation," she said coolly. "You were talking to Dot Carter and she wanted to come over. I think you'd better let her because I'm going."

"No!" I said, and took the silly precaution of barring the way; I'd forgotten she couldn't get the door open.

"Hallie, you're not making any sense," she told me.

"Maybe not," I said, "but stay just a few more minutes."

"I get it," she replied after a moment. "You're afraid Dot Carter will see me leave." She laughed quite goodnaturedly it seemed to me and went over and sat on the couch. Then the phone rang again.

It was Miss Sally Sue. "Hallie?" she said, her voice still not right. "Well, they've gone. Gone but not forgotten."

"Well, thank the Lord," I replied, sounding like Mother.

"But, child," she went on, "I don't think you better try to come back tonight. I'm just done in. Billy's here with me, thank you for having sent Jimmy after him. I was so upset I didn't think to call him. He made them leave me alone."

"What were they trying to do to you, Miss Sally Sue?"

"Just threatening me. Talking ugly. Pigeons come home to roost, you know. It was that Wilfred Lumpkin started it, I'm pretty sure, though they wouldn't say. But who else could have told them I paid off all those Negroes' bails?"

There were any number of possibilities, but I didn't bring this up. "Were they anybody you knew, the committee I mean?" I asked instead.

Then she told me who all had been there; of the three names only one sounded vaguely familiar, but she seemed to know them all. Two, she said, were men from out in the county and the other one was Joe Tarbell who ran a grocery store down on West Main, just off the Square. "And he has a big colored trade, too," she said.

"I just don't understand it. Seems to me it would ruin his business for him to get mixed up in an organization like that. Do you know if Maybelle got home all right?"

"She didn't go. I brought her home with me," I said, impulsiveness and a touch of triumph making me speak the truth.

There was a lengthy pause. "Hallie, was that wise?"

"The family's all out," I answered, lowering my voice. Just to be on the safe side, I eased the hall door to. "She'll be leaving pretty soon," I added.

"Even so," said Miss Sally Sue in great doubt.

"Well, hon, I'm glad you're all okay and that nothing happened," I said hurriedly. "Can I stop by tomorrow?"

"Not in the daytime," she answered. "They'll be watching my every step from now on, and while I don't think they'd try anything, there's no sense in them connecting you with me more than they do already."

"You mean they do?" I cried.

"Uh huh," she said. "Your name was mentioned, Maybelle's too. We aren't as slick as we think."

"You mean they know we see each other?"

"They implied it, but I don't think they really know anything—just feeling me out. But, Hallie, I think you better have a talk with your father the first chance you get."

"Why?" I asked, getting more shocked by the moment.

"Because I think maybe he's been approached."

"But Daddy would have told me!"

"Not necessarily. Maybe he didn't want to worry you, and as far as he knows anyway whatever they said wasn't so. Hallie, are you there?"

"Yes, I'm still here. I was just thinking."

"You mean you did tell your daddy something?"

"No, ma'am, I did not." I wasn't lying, but I was remembering he had told me *something*, or tried to.

"Well, Missie, I'll say good night and ta ta," said Miss Sally Sue in her old lively manner. "And just don't you worry."

"And just don't you," I told her. "Sleep well." And after one more "good night" each, we hung up.

I opened the hall door and went back into the living room and found Maybelle gone. She had been able to get the door open after all.

CHAPTER TWENTY-SIX

WHEN BILL CAME IN not three minutes later, I knew I was in for it. He didn't say a word, but his eyes, which can pierce and blaze and hurt like Daddy's, were trained on me like acetylene torches. I said nothing. Obviously he had seen her, but if he wanted to make no comment other than this infantile visual one, it was more than all right with me. Anyway, I had my story down pat, and it would stand. What did he know? Let him do me one. So confident was I of success that I continued to sit on the living room couch while he strode straight through to the kitchen, in search of food or drink, or both, cutting his eyes away from the opened but untouched Coca-Cola Maybelle had abandoned.

When he came back I had finished drinking mine and was vaguely making a search for Psyche again. I had not seen her all day.

"Was that your so-called 'Em' who was slinking away from here when I came home?" he asked, his contempt sounding as if it came from an infected wound.

"Yes, if you must know, it was," I sneered at him, showing off my derision like fangs. "And I'm sure she wasn't 'slinking,' as you so prettily put it."

"I don't know why not," he returned. "If I was a nigger coming away from visiting a decent white family's house when everybody was gone but their trashy nigger-loving daughter, I'd shore as hell slink!"

I got up and slapped him across the mouth with all my might, and he promptly knocked me down. But from my ignominious position on the floor, I was heartened to see that my heavy high school class ring had cut his mouth, and he hadn't hurt me at all. I got up, smoothing my skirts, disdaining him, and he pushed me very hard so that I landed on the couch. I tried to scratch him, but he caught my hands. "You see I'm on to you, you little— aaagh!" he released me as if my foul corruption stung him. "I don't know why I bother. Why don't you and your nigger-living boyfriend get married, so you'll stop stinking up this place? You thought I didn't know, didn't you? Thought you and that nigger and that crazy old witch were being so smart! But you weren't. I've been watching you ever since that night you and that stuck-up prick carried me out to the roadhouse with you, planning to trick me into going out with you and him and that piece of poontang to that ritzy city place. Your own brother! You'd do a thing like that to him!" To my utter fascination I saw that tears were running down his cheeks. "Next time," he sobbed, trying to regain hold of his anger again, "next time when you're doping out your plans, look who's standing right behind you. I ought to kill you, that's what I ought to do, but you're not worth it. But I've fixed her—Miss High and Mighty, and that nigger'll get run out of town for sure—tarred and feathered if I had my way about it."

So that's how it was, I found a faraway voice beneath the frozen wastes of my no longer senate being say. It wasn't Wilfred Lumpkin at all, Miss Sally Sue, it was just my brother Bill. "Are you a member of the White Citizens' Council?" I heard a voice, not unlike the one I used to have, ask him.

"You're durn right I am!" he blazed. "And when they got through with her there wasn't much left."

I wet my parched lips. "Did you come home early to trap me?"

"I was going to beat the shit out of both of you," he promised me beneath clenched teeth.

"Why don't you get in the car and go run her down then?" I asked him contemplatively. "That would give Daddy something to really be proud of you for. And I, personally, would love to see you in the electric chair—"

I broke off, seeing a startled look on his face, turned around and there was Daddy in the door. "Go to your room, son," he said, but he was staring at me.

Bill, ducked his head slightly and, without a word, withdrew. Daddy motioned me to get up and follow him back into the study.

He closed the door and we both sat down. I could see he was highly agitated and so distrait that he didn't even think to seek the soothing, restorative powers of his all-faithful friend, his pipe. "Hallie, Brother called me at Percy's and asked me to come home right away, he said he wanted to show me something." He broke off and shook his head. "Hallie, Hallie," the sigh he uttered was so full of his anguish that I thought he, too, was going to cry. Then he forced himself, remaining dry-eyed, to go on. "Your mother and I were enjoying ourselves, so I told Bill that we couldn't leave just yet, and asked him what he wanted to show me. He didn't want to tell me over the phone, but I insisted. Then he told me." He paused again for quite a long time. "And I agreed to leave Mother there and meet him and come home with him and confront you and poor Maybelle. I thought it best. I know my boy, and I was afraid for all of you. Then on the way, he told me what he had done to Miss Sutherland, how he had sent those men around to 'teach her a lesson.' Hallie, Hallie, what folly, what recklessness have you two done?"

I still made no response; I couldn't. I didn't even know where to start. I looked at his thick white hair as the lamplight glowed from his bowed head. Long hair. Didn't Mommie know he needed a haircut? It was much too long, and not silky the way it usually looked. Sometimes his hair looked exactly like Psyche's. "Where's my kitty cat, where's my Psyche?" I blurted.

"Dead," he said tonelessly, not raising his head. "Someone poisoned her. Your mother and I didn't want to tell you. We found her this morning and I buried her in a little white satin box your mother found, out in the garden by the—"

I heard the screams, but I didn't know they were mine. They came through even way down under the frozen wastes and I thought, someone must be in awful pain. And then my cheeks were smarting and I knew Daddy had had to slap me because I had gone hysterical, out of control. He was chafing my wrists, kneeling beside me on the floor. And I thought, that's all right, Daddy, you don't have to look so worried because I understand what you're doing. Don't you remember? You told me what to do when people get hysterical. They can go into shock. You have to keep them from it, even if you have to hurt them a little....

I came back to myself two days later. I was in bed and there were lots of flowers in the room and the birds were singing outside. And later on that afternoon when Daddy saw that I wasn't just saying it, but really was strong enough to talk a little about it, he told me the rest. That night when he and Bill came up the walk they saw Maybelle leaving; she wasn't ten yards away. And Daddy had acted on instant decision and simply dropped back, not letting Bill know he wasn't following him until Maybelle was well down the block. Then he got back in Bill's car and went to intercept her. Which he did, and Daddy told her what had happened and what to do as he drove her home. She promised to do as he said, to wait until the next morning before she made a move, to wait until she had a call from him.

"Wasn't she scared?" I asked.

"No, Maybelle is a very brave person, hon," he told me sincerely. "If she hadn't been she would never have come here in the first place, or continued to work as she has. She was very quiet about it all. If she showed any signs of concern, it was about you. And she said, 'I told you, Dr. Hamilton, after the ride back with Hallie and Miss Sally Sue that night that I couldn't trust myself to stay uninvolved. I needed friendship too badly, and worse, I needed to talk to people who were alive and stimulating, outside the circle of people I work with. After all, all we can talk about is color and from only one point of view though we try to be broad-minded and measure the effects of what we're doing.' "

"Where is she?" I asked.

"She's gone, hon."

"But she so wanted to stay in school, to finish out the year!" I cried.

"We've all agreed to give her full credit for her courses," he said. "She was an excellent student, so it wasn't too difficult to arrange it. And in view of what followed it seemed the only wise way—" he paused and gave me a searching look. "You're sure you feel strong enough, for I have another shock for you?"

I sat up quickly, using my elbow. "Pete?" I cried.

He shook his head. "No, hon. Not Pete. Miss Sally. I under-stand she told you a few weeks ago that she had a cold or a touch of virus, or something like that. But she just didn't want to worry you, Hallie. Dr. Spears told me that actually she'd had a stroke. Not a severe one, and perhaps if Bill had not acted so rashly. Well, but I mustn't blame my own boy, and when people get to be Miss Sutherland's age.... Anyway, hon, Miss Sally Sue died day before yesterday. The funeral's today, and your mother sent the bier— and signed it in your name."

He finished with tears standing in his eyes. I could hardly see them from the blur in mine.

He stood up and patted my hand. "Why don't you see if you can't get a little more sleep?" he said.

I closed my eyes, feeling the tears squeeze out and down along my cheeks. "Yes, that's a good idea," I said.

So by and large that's what happened. When I was up and all right again Mommie and Daddy had some trouble convincing me that I should go back to school and take my exams. I was too afraid of what all my friends would say, oh, not directly maybe, but indirectly, for no matter what Daddy said about the whole thing having been very hushed—the White Citizens' thing were even most cooperative in this as they were terrified if it all came out they might be held largely responsible for Miss Sally Sue's second stroke and her death, and she was after all, a most leading citizen and you don't just go around killing leading citizens on suspicion, even though that's exactly what they did—all the same, I felt that Dot and Ridey and all of them *knew*, and they'd let me see it in their faces. But the family finally got me into gear, however and you know how? It was Mommie. "If you don't show them that you can be brave, that you can take troubles in your stride and just go on, you'll be giving Miss Sally Sue an awful letdown. But worse, dear, you'll be letting down Maybelle. Daddy's told me all about her you see, dear. And I think any girl anywhere should be proud of having such a remarkable, fine person for a friend. And I went to Icie Brown and told her so. It wasn't easy, but I just felt I had to do it. We owed it to her."

"Mommie," I murmured, catching one of her hands. "You didn't." And we both just boohooed on each other's shoulders.

Somehow, in all of this, I decided that next to Maybelle, Mommie was really the best. She had the most to swallow and in the shortest time and she did it with gallantry, intelligence and courage. She did everything she had to do, even to accepting the fact that Bill ought to go away for awhile. Naturally, Bill being the eye-apple that he is around this house, the "going away for a little while" was going wherever he wanted to go, and he chose Alaska for the summer, of all the ironical places; said he thought he'd like to try his hand as a lumberjack, for even if he is small, he's got a wiry strong body. And the last letter we've had from him sounded very happy. He even sent me his regards—something for him.

But I know that in spite of his acknowledging how wrong he was, he still secretly thinks he was right and would probably do it the next chance he got. Because Bill, even though he's got a good mind, just doesn't understand. I'm not saying he never will; Daddy says it's wrong to think people don't change, he says it indicates rigidity on the part of the person who says it, but I say seeing is believing. Anyway, I'm just as glad he's gone.

Pete called me about a week after Miss Sally Sue's funeral to say how sorry he was about everything, and he did sound so terribly contrite. He said we'd talk all about it when I go up there the day after school is out; we'll have a whole week. And by that time he expects his damn case to be over, and won, thank the Lord.

CHAPTER TWENTY-SEVEN

I T SEEMS ALL the way through this season of my life I was either yakking on the phone, dashing off in my car, riding in airplanes or meeting them. I guess, with all that talk and action, the whole thing could be summed up under the heading: Communication and Transportation. And stripping it down to its bones, that's exactly what that turbulent period was: communication and transportation. I will probably never again communicate so well or be so transported as a result. I know that season carried me far, and I know, too, that I balked a good part of the way, and made things awfully hard on others sometimes. But Experience is the best teacher—and she's *my* pet whether I'm a favorite of hers or not—and I have every intention of going right on with my schooling. But these are all hindsights—a good title for the story of my life.

Other people have foresight and make accurate predictions, such as Mommie's and Daddy's that I would reenter the old playpen of my life with the crowd as easily as if I'd just been returned by my nurse after my afternoon nap. They couldn't have been sweeter, and those of them who had heard about the Maybelle affair all ended up saying, once their curiosities were satisfied, "You know, I wanted terribly to get to know her, but I didn't know how, and I didn't have the nerve," and I always answered, "Neither did I." So you see I was quite the opposite of shunned; I was treated as if I had been a real live participant in a myth, for that was what Maybelle's memory on campus had become. A myth as wonderous and as golden as something from glorious

Greece. But I was sanguine enough at this point to realize that myths only became glorious when that's all they are—just stories about nonexistent or vanished people—and there were only a few who confidingly whispered that they wouldn't mind at all if the gods would again come; if more Negroes enrolled in our little university, thus offering them a chance to beat my record, or at least even the score. And I heartily concurred in this hope. There was nothing I would have liked better.

It was Daddy who warned me not to become a Negrophile on the basis of Maybelle alone. "Fine a girl as she was, hon, she was as human as the rest of us, and I'd hate to see you over-idealize her. It will make you set your sights too high for the future, for one thing, and anyway, how do you know your paths won't cross again?" Not a chance, I thought, but I was Daddy's girl again, and I didn't want to let him see that I sometimes found his wisdom too mellow; in other words, like cheese—it stank.

Therefore, when I arrived in Louisville to take up again with Pete where we'd left off—the day after school was out, and my birthday, too, by the way—I was about as prepared to see Maybelle Brown grinning at me from the front seat of his convertible as I was to see a human-size bumble bee. And I stood back, stung, as Pete happily cried, "Surprise, surprise!" And I know I looked at her as if I were thinking (which I was), Is *she* my happy birthday present?

With as good grace as I could obtain, I got in the car—she insisted on scooting over so I could sit between them, next to Pete—and using the noise as an excuse, created by us as we rushed down the wind, I hatefully and privately thought my thoughts: Had Daddy known that Maybelle and Pete were together? Why had they—any of them—let me come? Were they so advanced, or declined, that they believed in polygamy along with integration? Because Daddy had confessed to me, in *camera* (almost *obscura*) that he, too, was a NAACP member, had been for years, an American Civil Liberties Unionite, ditto, and was now also doing what he could for CORE—and no, he was not a communist; did he look like one?

I was glad now I hadn't answered that question. At the time, had I answered, I would have said, I've never seen a communist. Now I was beginning to wonder. Having once heard that a very rich and famous owner of a world-renowned American department store was a communist, I was no longer so naive as to think that they had to dress in blue jeans or rags. So, could be. I looked at my bumble-bee friend, Maybelle on my right and Pete, the yacht club idol, on my left. And I must admit, communists or not, I admired their disguise. Maybelle was wearing a yellow linen dress with a black scarf or something at the throat, and if I had been more charitable, I would have thought of wild canaries, seeing her there in Pete's top-down beautiful sleek black convertible, rather than bees. But—and I knew I was right in thinking this—the least he could have done was tell me. Maybelle was a cruel surprise, and seeing them together, how well they looked together—I studied his profile as if it were a statue's in a museum—I felt like the odd figurine on the mantel. Somehow I didn't fit.

In consequence, I was rather surprised when Pete pulled over to the curb, right in the middle of the business section, in heavy traffic, and Maybelle got out, saying, " 'Bye, sweetie, see you later," touching my hand.

"Isn't she terrific?" Pete, dazzling me with his smile, wanted to know.

"Absolutely," I murmured tonelessly, but driving was as much as Pete could cope with just then for we nearly got smacked by a truck.

After we moved on to quieter streets, Pete put out an arm and pulled me over. "What's the matter?" he teased. "You a virgin all over again? It hasn't been *that* long." And though I had thought myself as immovable as cement, the deposit of anger having weighted me down, I was under his arm as light as a feather. I even squealed, and then he did what he so often does: stopped in the middle of the street and kissed me. What a frail thing it is to be a woman! How scant, how flimsy. No wonder men think of us as bits of froth.

Certainly, I had no great conceit about my solidity or depth when we got to his parents' house. I felt so inconsequential that I hoped they weren't home. But they were, on the tennis court, playing doubles with a couple I didn't know, the man half of which was like a caricature of an Indian rajah wearing a turban. I'm glad I didn't snicker and observe this out loud, for that's what he turned out to be, only an ex-one, rather.

"Hi!" Miss Miriam called gaily, looking just smashing in a pair of white tennis shorts, her very long tanned legs as good as anybody's I ever saw. But it was her serve, so she didn't come over from the court, but hollered at us to sit down and have a drink and she'd be with us in a minute. Mr. Fred grinned and waved at us with his racket, then watched his partner; he took his game seriously.

Pete suggested we go into the house first and get me stowed away. He carried my things up to my room himself and watched me hang them up and unpack them into drawers, chattering from the chaise longue, where he lolled, about the Derby, which, of course, I had missed (though *he* hadn't, I noticed spitefully; busy, huh?) and about their house guests who had been here since and seemed to be staying on. The woman, with whom the rajah was having a mad affair, having pursued her on three continents, was a once famous fashion model, and still a great beauty; hadn't I noticed? He mentioned her name, curling his tongue around it possessively, full of vicarious pride, and when I said I'd never heard of her the little pause that followed seemed to me a silent rebuke for my ignorance. Then he jumped up energetically and telling me to change into something light and cool, he went off to change clothes himself, and to get us a couple of "martins;" he hadn't had a drink all day.

And I, I thought after he had gone, haven't had a drink all month—had it been just a month? had it been a whole month since the Iris Club? Waiting for him to come back, dressed in a light blue batiste Southern-belle style dress, full skirted and awfully fussy, I knew, in contrast to tennis shorts and halters, I stood by the window which overlooked their two acres of rolling lawn, and felt sluggish as I watched the players sprinting about the tennis court. Sluggish, if not out of the race altogether, because everything seemed out of whack, as Daddy might have described it. And today was my birthday, and coming here I had felt very nineteen. But that was before I had seen Maybelle peremptorily installed in Pete's car, ostensibly for the sheer joy of my arrival; that was before we had come "out home" where I found I wasn't the guest of honor at all—the feted birthday girl—but simply one of Pete's friends who was staying over. Not that I had expected them to fuss over me; no. But—what was it? Yes, I felt as I had at ten or eleven when I'd gone to somebody's house to spend the night and found that her parents had a large dinner party in progress and that we were to eat supper in the kitchen with the cook, then do whatever we pleased as long as we kept our giggling, wriggling distracting selves out of sight. And who had minded? It had been a treat; we had been handed the privacy we would have sought anyway. But there the similarity between my house-guest visits at ten and now at nineteen ended, for Dot, or Micheline—I hadn't thought of her in years—or whoever had been as pleased as I was over our freedom, had sopped up every moment of it, wantonly flinging ourselves away from adult sports and pleasures—if such boring pursuits could be so termed—with the vigorous abandon of dancers on Walpurgis night. And now, I could tell, Pete was pointed in the other direction, as if his parents and their fascinating friends were magnets; did he expect me to follow, or was he trying to run away? I don't know.

But I do know he had forgotten it was my birthday, and I was deeply hurt. I kept waiting for something, some sign. At dinner,

I told myself. Then two other couples arrived for dinner—friends of Miss Miriam's and Mr. Fred's, so I knew no surprise birthday cake was going to turn up with dessert, for as eagerly as Pete dove and swam into the adult conversation, and was suffered to do so, and indeed was rather admired, it was still their party, and we were mere juniors. After dinner his parents went off with their guests to a theater party, and Pete looked rather longingly after—they couldn't take us, Miss Miriam apologetically, winningly drew me aside to explain; I did understand, didn't I?—and I wondered if, perhaps, Pete had a crush on their previous house guest, the model. Because I was sure now he was avoiding me, as best as one can avoid a person sitting next to him. And when, after they had gone and left us alone together (still no birthday present in sight) he enthusiastically suggested we jump in the car and go to this great place to listen to some jazz, I accepted defeat without a murmur, resigned to an evening of human silence with the roar and blare of instrumental noise in my ears.

And that's the way it was. We sat at a small table for two right in the heart of the storm, since Pete has "influence," and with the smoke swirling around us, blinding as snow, we silently witnessed this glorious display, this stampede of trumpeting rhythmic sound, thumping and rocking and bellowing, Pete's eyes never leaving the bandstand, his foot never stopping its tapping, his hand gripping the table, pulsing with the mechanical accuracy and faith of a metronome, except twice when he interrupted himself to signal the waiter and reorder bottles of beer. On the way home he seemed tired, and for good reason, and the hand that he reached over for mine was as limp as a dead animal.

And there did I marvel my birthday away, to misquote Dylan Thomas.

The next day, Pete's cousin Paula Lockridge, a stuck-up bitch who had made her debut at Christmas, gave a luncheon for me whichwas so chintzy and the people invited so tacky that I knew it hadn't been her idea. Were Pete and his parents really trying to get rid of me, I wondered? If so, there were easier ways. And why had I been allowed to come in the first place?

The remainder of the afternoon gave me no clue; Pete and Paula and some other girl, some toothy fright whose name I've forgotten, (one of the luncheon guests,) and I drove down to the Yacht Club to see what was doing, then out to Cherokee Park for a drink with some of Paula's friends. It was all indolent, uninspired, and the talk, what there was of it, was all about Louisville things—things to happen in the future, after I'd gone, or things that had already happened, before I got here. When, I thought, was Pete planning for us to have that long, long talk he'd mentioned on the telephone when he had sounded so contrite? Not one mention had he made of Miss Sally Sue's upsetting and quite tragic death, my illness, or Maybelle's enormously puzzling presence. I wanted to think this was accidental, but I knew it wasn't. And so I waited.

On the way home, after we'd left the fright and my luncheon hostess, I casually remarked, fingering my already withering corsage of roses (acquired through the auspices of Paula since I was luncheon honoree), "Are we going to have a chance to see something of each other tonight?"

"Honey, that's all we've done," Pete told me, his smile as disarming as ever, but didn't I detect a note of impatience in his voice?

I tried to control my expression, not to let it look hurt or shocked, but I guess I didn't make it, for he added hastily, "You'll love tonight. Wait and see," and gave me a pull toward him, which somehow felt half-hearted and dutiful since I knew so well the real spontaneous thing. I hovered in the crook of his arm like poor Psyche used to do when strangers fondled her, stiff, ready to jump away at the moment of release. "Relax, gal," he pretended to scold me. And with a breaking heart I recognized that cheerfulness had replaced ardor, that obligation had replaced desire, and that he would never call me sweetheart and mean it ever again.

The party we were going to was a progressive dinner party, "a great big fancy informally formal thing," so he described it. And as I dressed I baked myself in the heat of resentment to harden myself, so that I might become inured to whatever bitter surprises might rise up to spear me.

The first of these was the shocking knowledge that cocktails, stage one of the party, were being given at the home of the Negro.

Oh, there was nothing wrong with the home, or the Negro either. On our way out there I kept looking at the huge houses we passed, magnificent estates, great undulating lawns of grass so green it seemed to be specially dyed, and at last when we turned into a massive iron gate, beside which a small discreet marker in black and white read, "The Hunts," I hardly noticed. We swept up the drive, smart and grand ourselves, and then with an electric shock of recognition, the name Hunt fitted into the slot and registered. First name Gordon. Gordon and Nina Hunt... "Nina laughed all the time, even when she didn't feel like it...." Maybelle's friends. Maybelle's black Nina from boarding school. Maybelle was here.

I kept my eyes straight ahead as we drove, not daring a look at Pete's face, not wanting what I might find there—smugness, pleasure, anticipation, or the set jaw of the trapped man, grimly determined to do his duty, get it over with.

Then we were there, in front of a great Georgian mansion of white stone. He touched my hand lightly, "Ready?"

A good question. Was I? Then impulsively I turned around and faced him, my eyes reading his. "It's Maybelle, isn't it?" I asked in a whisper.

He looked at me pleadingly, as if it were in my power to withdraw my knowledge if I just would. Then he gave up. "Yes, it's Maybelle, Hallie. I'm sorry, but there it is. I thought if I saw you again, gave our thing another chance—"

But I wasn't listening any more. I had jumped out of the car, slammed the door, and was hurrying up the drive.

CHAPTER TWENTY-EIGHT

NSIDE WHAT IS KNOWN as a brilliant party was in progress. If I told you some of the famous people who were there, black and white, you wouldn't believe it. I hardly believed it myself. But all the glamor, all the glitter could not shine in this hour of my own inner darkness, and my only thoughts were for getting to Maybelle and tearing her apart.

This wasn't easy. First of all, there was Pete, who had sped in right behind me, his nervous hand anxiously at my elbow, ready to restrain me from making a scene, and then there was the matter of manners itself. How far was I prepared to go in my witch hunt, defying graciousness and politesse, in this brilliant assemblage, gathered for the purpose of entertainment and enjoyment, not carnage. And skillful Pete saw to it that I was guided into coves of social obligation where I would be rendered harmless, for I could not altogether put aside my breeding, my poise, my instinct to appear at my best. First, I met my hostess, a Negress almost as light-skinned as Maybelle herself, but by no means so pretty. Then her tall, rather distinguished looking husband, graying at the temples. It was he who got me a drink. Then someone whose name was so famous in contrast to his quiet appearance and humble face that my mouth dropped ajar. And then I moved into a circle of women, all light Negresses, all brilliantly turned out, so that I felt I had moved into a strong sunlight where danced a string of golden butterflies. Then more men, more women, some white, some black, some gray, some tan, some raven blue-black, some mud-colored, some red. It was amazing, but nowhere did I see Maybelle and now Pete, too, had disappeared.

Then someone at my side said we were moving on to the next house for the first course, and someone said, "Come on!" and tugged at my hand, laughing, and we were out on the drive, crunching along the gravel, and then we piled into a big Cadillac and roared off. I was in the back, sitting beside a white man and two Negro girls. The white man was the one named Joe who had come up to me and said he had been wanting to see me again. Didn't I remember him from Easter? Then I recollected that he had been one of Pete's particular friends who had given me a mild rush at a dance.

This went on and on, from one house to the next—all big houses, whether on the grand scale of the Hunt's, or disguised as ranch houses, the many large comfortable rooms flowing end-lessly away at the back. For appetizers I had Joe; for the soup course I had a quite dark colored fellow named Marion Pitts, an atomic scientist, for the entree I at last had Pete, but lost him for the salad and the desert. I finally got him again for coffee.

Things were too hopelessly far gone for me to hiss in a pos-sessive whisper, where have you been? Besides, I knew.

All that I could say, I did say, "Pete, I'm going to leave tomor-row," and desperately saw him shake his head. Then some people came up and congratulated him on winning his case; they'd read all about it in the papers.

At last I slipped away, able to for the first time, and went outside the open door and stood on the terrace. The feel of the flagstones through my sandals was soothing, like a cool hand on my brow. Then her cool voice spoke, "Hallie," and, perhaps, knowing that I would not have turned around to face her myself, I felt myself being turned around by a light hand on my arm, and there we were, Hallie and Maybelle, gazing at each other.

"Good luck," I whispered at last, and tried to slip past her, but her hand was still on my arm.

"Good luck nothing," she said. "Bad luck. Bad luck to me for ever having let it get this far. I don't love him, Hallie."

I considered this, at first with a leaping sort of hope. Then it fell to the ground. The irony of it wore a hole in hope, the ferric acid of it still eating it away, even as it lay discarded. I couldn't use it whole or tattered. "What makes you think I do—now?" I asked bitterly.

She shook her head. "I don't know, I don't know."

"Why don't you marry him anyway?" I flared up. "He'd like that, I'm sure, even if his parents didn't—"

"His parents already know about me," she put in quietly.

"—Then fine!" I said, getting into the spirit of my fine false cheer. "And you and Pete can work for the cause together—you have so many friends—"

"I told you I didn't love him," she repeated doggedly. "I don't want to marry any man I don't love."

"And how long did it take you to find that out?" I jeered at her. "All this month while I've been bearing up at home, gilding your lily, making a shrine for you that I had come to believe in myself?"

"No, Hallie," she said in a monotone. "Not all this month. Yesterday was the third time I ever saw Pete out of your company."

"And I suppose he asked you to marry him on the first?"

"No, the second. The first was for a drink that weekend I came up here to visit Nina and Gordy—"

"And the second was the next night?" I ramrodded on. "Don't think I don't remember you were away not just for a weekend but clear through to Wednesday. Boy, how I counted and sweated those hours—I *knew* what you were up to, you see."

"Yes, I knew what you thought, but you were wrong. I didn't see him anymore that time. It wasn't until after I came back, to stay—and I didn't know, I didn't know," she said, sounding sick with despair. "I don't want something that doesn't belong to me, Hallie! Can't you believe that? Sure, I found Pete attractive—who wouldn't?—but he was yours. And you may not believe it, but moral principles with me have been known to kill all sorts of feelings—in fact in the past, all feelings. And as for my feelings for Pete, I just don't have any. They were killed before they ever got started. I cannot crave for, want, desire—I cannot *accept* what does not belong to me."

"How'd you get him then?" I demanded. "You admit you went out with him a second time—"

"Of course I did, Hallie! He was your friend. I was lonely, I was a nervous wreck with worry for you, for news of what had happened after I left. Of course I saw him! He was the obvious person to see, the only person to see."

"And then he just upped and fell madly in love with you?"

"That's about it—at least that's what he thinks happened. But it's not so, Hallie! He doesn't love me at all. If he really loved me I might even have fallen in love with him because then whether anybody liked it or not he would have been mine. But it's not so!"

"Well, he's not mine either, then!" I shouted at her. "So don't hand him back to me!"

"I don't," Maybelle said. "I'm not trying to give him back. I don't blame you for not wanting him. But don't reject me too!"

"Reject you too," I repeated acidly. "That's fine. You believe it's possible for me to reject you, do you? It never occurred to you that I never once more than superficially accepted you, that I was going along, having myself a new and daring experience—maybe like Pete's craving, only he has to call it love—"

Maybelle shook her head against my tirade, but her words stopped it. "You'd like to think that, maybe. Maybe you even believe it—always have. But it's not so—"

"Oh, isn't it?" I cried and quickly gave her a checklist of my betrayals of her, great and small, my suspicions of her, the character traits I found odious in her, and, yes, the downright comfort I took in being prejudiced against Negroes, the feeling of security I derived from being a privileged Southern white.

Maybelle looked grave but unimpressed. "The very fact that you can tell me all these things is proof you don't mean them—in effect you are confessing to me, trying to get all this guilt off your chest. All you have is, perhaps, the vestigial remains of prejudice, but this will go in time, and all of your guilt feelings are for doubting me, for you really like me, Hallie, whether you know it or not, you *really* like me better than all your Dots and June Bugs and Rideys or whatever, for outside Miss Sally Sue I'm your first *real* friend, the first person to give you an inkling of what it is like to be adult and to have thoughts and conversations, outside the schoolroom or family instruction, that had to do with the world not your wardrobe, your mind, not your wit, your heart, not your popularity. And you know it, Hallie! You know it!"

"Yes, I know it," I sobbed and added brokenly, "that's just it. That's what makes it all so terrible." And, as we had started, so we ended: me hanging onto Maybelle's hand for comfort while I cried myself out.

Well, it's not the happiest ending to a story, but it is not unhappy. I came back home the next day, and after that Pete just stayed away in droves. Daddy says I haven't seen the last of him, that he'll come around again when his ego is restored. For Daddy agrees with Maybelle—that Pete just had a sudden flash in the pan, that he fell in love with an irresistible image, not flesh and blood. But I don't know. I don't know whether I want him or whether I ever did or whether it's all gone. I *do* know, however, that there isn't anybody else, not even Tom Nesbitt who got himself unpinned from that Chi Omega oil heiress and has been following me around like Psyche used to do. And anyway, Mommie's right. I *am* too young to get married, and both she and Daddy agree that I'd be much better off going to Wellesley, like Miss Sally Sue wanted, and I'm waiting now to see if I can get in.

Maybelle's already been accepted and you know who she's going to room with? That white girl she knew at the college in

Pennsylvania, her one other white friend, the one she thought was no friend. And that's also just as well. The last letter I wrote her, I said so. Because it means we both will be branching out, truly integrating, and instead of one colored friend I will have, if I room with a colored girl as I've requested, maybe two. Then who knows? This sort of thing could go on and on. And that's what we hope.

But whatever happens—in case Pete should come back, and all the way—I have the consolation of knowing that Miss Sally Sue won, and she made me win. And maybe, who knows? the NAACP will profit by our winnings too. I'll be just as satisfied either way.

www.ingramcontent.com/pod-product-compliance
Lightning Source LLC
Chambersburg PA
CBHW031926060726
47496CB00007BA/2260